"I would be honored to have your escort," Elizabeth said softly, her blue gaze catching his and holding it.

Hal's chest expanded until he wasn't sure he'd be able to grab a breath. Of course, Elizabeth was merely grateful for his help. But the very thought of escorting her, of walking into some public place with her hand on his arm…

Elizabeth Lowery beside him in a carriage, her rose scent wrapping around his head. Her golden curls brushing his shoulder, the warmth of her body radiating toward him, her lips, the delicious curves of her body but inches away… The rush of images made him dizzy with anticipation and desire.

He tried to beat his thoughts back into order. She saw him not as a man but as someone safe and companionable. He mustn't make of it any more than that.

* * *

A Most Unconventional Match
Harlequin® Historical #905—July 2008

Praise for Julia Justiss

Rogue's Lady

"With characters you care about, clever banter, a roguish hero and a captivating heroine, Justiss has written a charming and sensual love story."
—*Romantic Times BOOKreviews*

"Readers will enjoy this superb historical romance... [a] captivating tale."
—Harriet Klausner

The Untamed Heiress

"Justiss rivals Georgette Heyer in the beloved *The Grand Sophy* (1972) by creating a riveting young woman of character and good humor...The horrific nature of Helena's childhood adds complexity and depth to this historical romance, and unexpected plot twists and layers also increase the reader's enjoyment."
—*Booklist*

The Courtesan

"With its intelligent, compelling characters, this is a very well-written, emotional and intensely charged read."
—*Romantic Times BOOKreviews,* Top Pick

My Lady's Honor

"Julia Justiss has a knack for conveying emotional intensity and longing."
—*All About Romance*

My Lady's Pleasure

"Another entertaining, uniquely plotted Regency-era novel... top-notch writing and a perfect ending make this one easy to recommend."
—*Romantic Times BOOKreviews*

My Lady's Trust

"With this exceptional Regency-era romance, Justiss adds another fine feather to her writing cap."
—*Publishers Weekly*

JULIA JUSTISS

A Most Unconventional Match

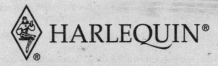

HARLEQUIN®

TORONTO • NEW YORK • LONDON
AMSTERDAM • PARIS • SYDNEY • HAMBURG
STOCKHOLM • ATHENS • TOKYO • MILAN • MADRID
PRAGUE • WARSAW • BUDAPEST • AUCKLAND

ISBN-13: 978-0-373-29505-0
ISBN-10:   0-373-29505-7

A MOST UNCONVENTIONAL MATCH

Prologue

London 1813

Leaning one broad shoulder against the wall, Hal Waterman exchanged an amused glance with Sir Edward Austen Greeves as they watched the bridegroom pacing in front of the hearth. 'Wearing out the carpet, Nicky,' Hal pointed out. 'Give the bride's family a distaste of you. Best get the ring on her finger first.'

Nicholas Stanhope, Marquess of Englemere and Hal's best friend since their Eton days, sent him an irritated look. 'I can't imagine what's taking so long. The priest arrived half an hour ago.' Halting before a side mirror, he straightened the white rose in his buttonhole and tugged on his cravat.

'Adjust that once more and you're going to ruin it,' Ned said. 'I expect the ladies will be here shortly. Patience, my man! Every bride wants to look beautiful on her wedding day, even if she's being married by special licence in a parlour instead of in church after a calling of the banns.'

Nicholas swung his gaze around to glare at Ned. 'Don't you dare imply there's anything havey-cavey about this! You both know—'

'We do,' Hal interrupted. 'Mortgage foreclosure and all that.

Had to rescue her. Great lady, Sarah. Good choice.' He nodded approvingly.

'Must be eagerness for the wedding night that makes you so testy,' Ned said. 'You know we fully support your marrying Sarah and understand the necessity to do so immediately. And her family's parlour might not be a church, but it's just as handsomely appointed.'

Ned gestured around the room, indicating the side tables covered with lace cloths surmounted by silver candelabra, the large vases filled with greenery and white roses set beside the rows of chairs facing the fireplace, the mantel where a cross flanked by candles and more rose sprays created an improvised altar. 'The ladies have outdone themselves.'

Though he'd resumed his nervous pacing, the tightness in Nicholas's face loosened. 'I want this day to be beautiful—for Sarah.'

'Great lady,' Hal repeated. 'Wouldn't mind marrying her m'self. If I wanted to marry. Don't,' he added.

'Your mama still after you with her latest heiress in tow?' Ned asked. 'As much as she disparages you, you'd think she wouldn't be so eager to try to drag you into the parson's mousetrap.'

'Wants to "improve" me,' Hal said glumly. 'Escaped her house, live in rooms, can't work on me. Thinks a wife could.'

Nicholas halted long enough to thump Hal on the shoulder. 'As if you needed improvement! You're already the most stalwart companion a man could want.'

'Hear, hear,' Ned seconded and then shook his head. *'Women.'*

Giving his loyal friends a grateful smile, Hal gazed up at the altar. If he were forced to marry, Nicky's soon-to-be bride would be almost his ideal choice, he thought. Lovely but not terrifyingly beautiful, competent, accomplished and kind, Sarah Wellingford never made him feel clumsy, tongue-tied and thick-witted the way the sharp-eyed, disdainful Diamonds of the *ton* his mother kept trying to foist on him did.

The way his beautiful, self-absorbed, society leader of a mother still did.

Since he had no intention, if and when he ever married, of wedding the sort of woman his mother preferred, he supposed he was fated to remain a disappointment to her. He shrugged off the dull ache produced by that old hurt.

'Ah, here they come at last!' Ned exclaimed as the parlour door opened.

The three men turned to watch as, led by the priest, the bridal party entered. First came the bride's sisters, all adorned in white gowns trimmed with gold ribbon and cream rosebuds.

Meredyth, Cecily, Emma, Faith—Hal silently counted them off as they proceeded, trying to match faces to the names Nicky had given him. He'd just caught a glimpse of Nicky's Sarah, resplendent in a gown of shimmering gold that made her silver-blonde hair glow, when the last sister in line turned toward him after easing the bride's long skirt through the door.

Elizabeth, Hal thought, before his breath whooshed out and his brain stuttered to a halt.

She was an angel come to earth. Nothing else could explain such perfection, the beauty radiating from her so intensely, as if she were lit from within, that Hal could feel the warmth of it all the way across the room.

His stunned senses took in the pure spun gold of her hair, the pale coral of her cheeks, the rose-petal-soft look of her skin, the pink bow of a mouth with its full lower lip. A slightly pointed chin imbued her face with character, saved it from a mere oval's bland symmetry.

And her eyes—blue as the summer waves of the lake on his country estate—impelled him to approach, as if he might discover the purpose of his life mirrored in the depths of those indigo pools.

An angel, his numbed wits repeated, or the reincarnation of the Botticelli Venus he'd seen in his well-travelled tutor's pastel sketches.

Without conscious volition he walked toward her. She turned to him and smiled. A shock raced along his nerves from the top of his head to the soles of his feet.

She was the loveliest thing he'd ever beheld. Flawless. More beautiful even than his mother. His senses clamoured to touch her, taste her.

The realisation halted him in mid-stride.

Beautiful. Like his mother.

Lord in heaven, what was he thinking?

'Hal, you escort Elizabeth,' Ned murmured at his shoulder.

Escort her? Panic filled him and a cold sweat broke out on his brow, dampened his fingers. 'Can't!' he replied in a strangled voice. Turning on his heel, he hurriedly paced to the furthest corner of the room.

Chapter One

Seven years later

Elizabeth Wellingford Lowery stood in her studio, brush in hand as she focused on the play of light across the flower in the vase on her worktable.

If she blocked out everything but the change of hues painted across the flower's surface by the ebb and flow of the clouds in the sky outside her window, she might be able to keep out of consciousness for a little longer the bitter awareness that her life had crumbled into pieces.

She should be able to concentrate. She always painted this time of the morning, while the northern light remained steady, often becoming so absorbed in her work she forgot to stop for nuncheon.

How often had Everitt had to knock at that door and come in to collect her? Her heart squeezed in another spasm of grief as she recalled how he'd approach her, a teasing smile on his careworn face as he coaxed her to put down her brush and join him and their son David for a light mid-day meal.

She needed sustenance lest she slip away, as ethereal as the angel she appeared to be, he'd tell her, giving a loving tug to whichever strand of golden hair had escaped from the careless chignon into which she always twisted it.

But he was the one who had slipped away unexpectedly, taking her secure world with him.

She didn't want to leave her studio, didn't want to emerge into the tangle of duties beyond that door where she would have to face how much everything had changed. Even after a month, it was still too much to deal with, losing the kindest man who'd ever lived, who'd cared for her as if she were a precious object too fine and delicate for life on earth. Amelia Lowery, his elderly cousin who'd run their household with great efficiency, had been so incapacitated by the shock of Everitt's death that, despite her own dismay and grief, Elizabeth had insisted the older woman give up her work and rest, and was therefore compelled to supervise tasks she'd never before had to oversee. To add to all of that, her entire family had gone on a long-delayed Grand Tour of the Continent barely a week before Everitt's untimely death.

Aside from Amelia, Everitt had no other close relations, so, with her own family out of reach, she'd had no one to turn to, no one to help her bear the agony and the crushing responsibility. The only thing that made life endurable was being able to escape for a few hours every morning into this haven where she might blank from her mind all but the task of capturing with her brush the shape and substance and hue of the subject on her worktable.

Leaving David confined upstairs with his nurse. Her chest tightened again with grief and guilt. He was suffering too, her precious son, missing the papa who had doted on him as lovingly as he had doted on her. How could she help him when she couldn't even help herself?

Tears welled in her eyes. Angrily she dashed them. Enough! She must pull herself out of this mire of grief and self-pity.

Some day soon she would do better, she promised herself. She'd wake to a new day without the constant, crushing weight of sadness on her chest. But for now, she would fix her mind only on the pure intensity of the hue in the flower before her.

A soft rap sounded at the door. For an instant, her spirits soared before the realisation settled like a rock in her gut. It couldn't be Everitt. It would never again be Everitt.

She took a deep breath as Sands, her butler, bowed himself in. 'Sorry to disturb you, madam, but…well, 'tis nearly a month since the beginning of the quarter and none of the staff have yet been paid. I've tried to stifle their grumbling, knowing how overset you've been, but it would be best if you would take care of compensating them.'

Elizabeth stared at Sands as if he'd been speaking in tongues. 'Compensating them?' she echoed blankly.

'Normally the staff are paid at the start of every quarter,' he explained patiently. 'From a cache of coins the master kept in the locked chest in the bookroom.'

Naturally the servants would be wanting their money. But she'd had no idea about quarter day, nor had she the faintest notion what amounts were owed to the various members of her household.

Where could she find such information?

'Madam?' Sands prompted, recalling her attention. 'I suppose I could go and ask Miss Amelia—'

'No, you were right to come to me,' Elizabeth interrupted. 'Miss Lowery must have absolute rest, the physician said, if she is to recover from her attack. Of course everyone must be paid. Thank you for bringing the matter to my attention.'

His task accomplished, the butler turned to leave. 'Oh, Sands!' she recalled him. 'Are there…any coins in the master's chest at present?'

'I have no idea, ma'am.'

'Very well. And…do you know where my husband kept the key?'

'I believe it is in the top-right drawer of his desk, Mrs Lowery.'

'The…the amount of each person's salary,' she continued, painfully embarrassed by her ignorance. 'Where might I find that?'

'I expect it would be recorded in one of the ledgers on the master's desk. Or his man of business might have a list. Would you like nuncheon served in an hour?'

Numbly she nodded. 'In an hour. Yes, that would be fine.'

Sympathy in his eyes, the butler bowed again and went out, softly closing the door behind him. Elizabeth put down the brush she was still holding and sank into a chair.

What if she could not find the right ledger? What if there was no more money in the chest? How was she to obtain more? Oh, she did not want to deal with this!

If only, after her marriage to Everitt, she had insisted upon taking over some of the housekeeping duties Miss Lowery performed so well, she wouldn't be this lost and unprepared. But one look at Amelia's anxious face as she curtsied to Elizabeth when the newly-wedded couple arrived in London, the elderly spinster's fingers twisting nervously in the fabric of her gown as she assured Elizabeth she quite understood the new bride would want to assume the management of her own household, and Elizabeth knew she could never wrest away from her husband's poor relation the task that gave her such satisfaction. Especially not after Everitt confided to her that, the Lowery family possessing few close kinsmen, Amelia Lowery really had nowhere else to go.

Which brought her back to her present problem. She drew a shuddering breath.

It was only a list of employees. It was only a supply of coin. She could manage this. She could.

She'd look in the bookroom later. After nuncheon. For now, it was still painting time. She would remain here in this tranquil space for just a little longer. Smoothing her dull black skirts with a trembling hand, she rose and walked to her easel.

Before she could pick her brush back up, there was another

knock at the door and Sands peeped in. 'Sir Gregory Holburn to see you, madam. Do you wish to receive him?'

Her immediate response was to refuse, but she bit it back. She'd not met her late husband's closest friend since the funeral more than a month ago, an event that, transpiring as it had in a blur of shock and misery, she scarcely remembered.

She hadn't stepped a foot outside the house after returning from the interment. And since Everitt had cared more for collecting his antiquities than for mingling with society and she had cared about mingling in society not at all, with her family out of England, she'd not had any callers.

Sir Gregory had always treated her kindly, almost like an avuncular uncle. He would worry if she refused to meet him.

With a sigh she stripped off the full-length apron she wore to save her gown from the worst of the paint spatters. 'Very well. Show him to the blue salon and tell him I'll join him shortly.'

She walked to the small mirror over her workbench, frowning as she scraped back the loose strands of hair and tucked them into the chignon. Her face was pale, her eyes dull. Everitt would say she looked like she was going into a decline.

And so I am, without you, my dear, she whispered softly. Gritting her teeth against another swell of useless grief, she forced a smile to her lips and headed for the blue salon.

Sir Gregory jumped to his feet as she entered. A tall, well-built man in his fortieth year, his light brown hair as yet showed no trace of grey, unlike the silver-tinted locks of Everitt, who'd been five years his senior. Friends from their youth, the two men had grown up in the same area of Oxfordshire and attended the same college.

His light brown eyes lighting with pleasure, Sir Gregory took the hand she offered and kissed it. 'How have you been getting on? I'm sorry not to have come sooner; estate business at Holburn Hall kept me tied up longer than I'd expected.'

'I hope everything is going well there,' Elizabeth said politely.

Absently she wondered how Everitt's neighbouring property, Lowery Manor, was faring. Since their marriage, they'd spent little time there, her husband preferring to reside in London where he might more easily acquire items for his collection.

'Some difficulties with the planting, but well enough.' Eyeing her more closely, he shook his head. 'You look tired and careworn. Is Miss Lowery still confined to her bed and unable to assist? My poor Lizbet, I knew I should have come back sooner to check on you!'

'How kind of you,' Elizabeth replied, acknowledging his concern. 'I'm afraid Miss Lowery is so far from recovered she must not even think of returning to her duties. I get on well enough, I suppose, though it is…difficult.' She attempted a smile. 'So many things to do! Reviewing menus, inspecting linens, checking silver, ordering coal—I had no idea how much was required to run a household. Did you know there are at least seventeen different recipes for preparing chicken?'

'Seventeen?' He chuckled. 'Who would have thought?'

'And where does one obtain the coin to pay one's servants?' She shook her head and sighed. 'Miss Lowery and Everitt spoiled me dreadfully, I'm discovering.'

Holburn took her hand and patted it. 'Dear lady, you are too young and lovely to trouble yourself with such trivialities! Now that I've returned to London, I do hope you'll allow me to lift some of those burdens from your shoulders.' Letting go of her fingers, he extracted a small purse from the pocket of his coat. 'How much coin do you need for the servants?'

Tempting as it was to transfer all her tiresome duties into his willing hands, Elizabeth hesitated. Husband's best friend notwithstanding, there was no link of kinship between them whatsoever. She could not but feel it went beyond the limits of what was proper to accept any of his kindly offered assistance. Without doubt, she knew she must not take money from him, even as a temporary loan.

'That won't be necessary, Sir Gregory, although I do thank you for offering. You must ignore my hen-hearted complaining! I shall learn to manage soon enough.'

'You are sure?' When she nodded, he continued, 'Very well, I shall do nothing—this time. But my offer stands. I should be honoured to assist you in any way, at any time.'

As the mantel clock chimed the hour, she rose. David would be waiting for her, anxious for his nuncheon. 'Should you like to join us for some light refreshment?'

'You will take it with your son?'

'Yes. By noon he's grown quite peckish.'

'I fear I must decline. Another time, perhaps?'

'Of course.' She escorted him from the parlour, secretly relieved he'd refused the invitation she'd felt obligated to offer. But Sir Gregory did not enjoy children—and David, perhaps sensing as children often do the attitude of the adults around them, most decidedly did not like Sir Gregory.

Some time this afternoon, she still must solve the riddle of paying her servants. Turning her visitor over to Sands, with a longing glance in the direction of her studio, Elizabeth walked upstairs to find her son.

In his bachelor quarters on the other side of Mayfair, Hal Waterman frowned at the notice printed in the newspaper. Having returned to London just last evening after spending two months monitoring a new canal project in the north, he was still sorting through the journals and correspondence that had accumulated in his absence.

Carrying the paper with him, Hal dropped into the chair by the fireplace where his valet Jeffers had left him a glass of wine, gratefully settling back against its wide, custom-designed cushions. Taller and more powerfully built than most of his countrymen, after his sojourn in assorted inns over the last weeks, he was thoroughly tired of trying to sleep in beds too short for his long legs and sit in wing chairs too narrow for his broad shoulders.

Scanning the notice again, he sighed. *Mr Everitt Lowery*, it read, *of Lowery Manor in Oxfordshire and Green Street in London, unexpectedly expired in this city on the seventh inst.*— almost six weeks ago now. *Surviving him are his widow, Elizabeth, née Wellingford, and one son, David.*

Elizabeth. Even now, seven years after his first glimpse of her at the wedding of his friend Nicholas to her sister Sarah, the whisper of her name reverberated through his mind, exciting a tingling in his nerves and a stirring in his loins.

Despite knowing Nicky's wedding service had been about to begin, he'd barely been able to keep himself from bolting from the room that long-ago day. As it was, drenched in panic, he'd had to station himself as far from the enchanting Elizabeth as the confines of the parlour allowed, remaining at the reception afterwards only until he deemed it was politely possible to excuse himself.

Until he had encountered Elizabeth Wellingford, armoured by a lifetime of scornful treatment at the elegant hands of his beautiful mother, he'd thought himself immune to those pinnacles of perfect female form who so easily enslaved the men around them. Which, for Hal, made Elizabeth Wellingford the most dangerous woman in England. Even knowing what she could and probably would do to him, he'd still been…mesmerised.

The only sensible response was to stay as far away from her as possible. Over the intervening years, keeping that resolve turned out to be easier than he'd first feared, given that her sister had married his best friend. A few months after Nicky's nuptials, shunning a Season, Elizabeth Wellingford had chosen to wed a family friend she'd known all her life, a gentleman more than twenty years her senior.

So, fortunately for his piece of mind, the bewitching Elizabeth had never joined the ranks of the hopefuls on the Marriage

Mart, that small section of *ton* society in which his mother took greatest interest. Each Season Mama had inspected the new arrivals, choosing those she deigned to honour with her friendship, whom she would then parade before her son in the hope, mercifully thus far unrealised, of enticing—or coercing—him into marrying some woman of fashion who might be trusted to try to remake her overly tall, totally unfashionable only child.

A hopeless task, if Mama would just cease stubbornly refusing to concede the fact. In a society that prized dark, whipcord-slender men like that lisping poet Lord Byron, Hal was too big, too fair-haired, and, from his years of fencing and riding, too firmly muscled to ever be considered one of the *ton*'s dashing young blades.

Prizing comfort and utility above all, he had no patience for coats that required a valet to wrestle him in and out of them, shirts with points so high and stiff they scratched his chin or fanciful cravats that threatened to choke him whenever he swallowed.

And though, with Nicky's help, he'd overcome the stuttering that had made his school years a misery, he would never be capable of uttering long flowing phrases full of the elegant compliments so beloved by ladies.

He sighed. He would always be an embarrassment to Mama and there was nothing to be done about it.

Shifting his gaze to the matter at hand, he looked back at the funeral notice he still held. So Elizabeth was now a widow. Too young and lovely a lady to be wearing black, he thought, a touch of sadness in his chest at the premature loss she had suffered. Then a startling, highly unpleasant realisation brought him out of his chair and sent him rushing to his desk.

Impatiently he flipped through the papers until he found Nicky's note. As he reviewed it, a scowl settled on his face.

Hell and damnation! He *had* remembered the dates correctly. Nicholas, Sarah, their children and all the rest of the Stanhopes and Wellingfords—all of Elizabeth's family—had departed for Europe, it appeared, barely a week before Everitt Lowery's passing. The family party was not due to return to England for another three months at the earliest.

There was no help for it. Despite his vow never to willingly place himself again in the same room with the lady who had so shaken his world, that lady was Nicky's sister-in-law. With her family out of reach, Nicky would expect Hal to call on the widow, ensure that her husband's lawyer and man of business had her financial affairs well in hand and, in Nicky's stead, offer to assist her with anything she required.

Going back to his chair, Hal sighed and downed a large swallow of the wine. Please heaven, let Lowery have left a decent will and employed a competent man of business. The Wellingfords had been nearly penniless when Nicky married Sarah, so Hal knew Elizabeth probably hadn't brought much of a dowry to her marriage. He hoped Lowery's finances were such that he'd been able to leave his widow a comfortable jointure.

Of course, that didn't mean she couldn't easily run herself into dun territory. As Hal recalled, a woman's response to both joy and calamity involved the acquiring of a large number of new gowns, bonnets, pelisses, footwear and the nameless other fripperies females seemed so fond of. That had always been his mother's way and he had no reason to expect that a woman as stupendously beautiful as Elizabeth Lowery would react any differently.

With it having been six weeks since her husband's demise, he'd best gird himself to call on Mrs Lowery immediately to make sure she wasn't already having to outrun the constable. Lowery's fatherless son didn't need to have his mama land them in debtor's prison.

Taking another deep draught of wine, he recalled sardonically the bulging armoires in his mother's several dressing rooms. Only the gigantic size of his father's fortune had allowed Hal to achieve his majority—and assume control of his mother's finances—with that lady still possessing a sizeable portion. Unless Lowery had tied up his funds carefully and appointed a vigilant trustee, if she spent her blunt as freely as Letitia Waterman, Lowery's lovely widget of a wife could swiftly exhaust a modest competence.

Fulfilling his duty as Nicky's stand-in shouldn't be that burdensome, he reassured himself. He'd probably only need to visit the widow once, after which he'd be able to deal directly with Lowery's man of business. Besides, it had been a very long time since he'd seen Elizabeth.

Having weathered seven Seasons' worth of beauties posing, posturing and pouting before him, he was doubtless no longer as impressionable as he'd been that long-ago afternoon. Besides, 'twas likely that, over the years, memory had exaggerated the incident. Wary as he was of winsome women, surely when he met Elizabeth now he'd experience only a mild appreciation for her striking loveliness.

After all, a man could appreciate a masterpiece of art without aching to possess it.

Hal took a deep breath. He could do this. And he would…tomorrow, he decided. Tomorrow he would meet Elizabeth Wellingford Lowery again.

Chapter Two

$\mathcal{A}$s early the next morning as Hal imagined a fashionable lady might be receiving—which meant nearly afternoon—Hal arrived at the Lowery town house on Green Street. To his relief, since he wished to get through this interview as quickly as possible, as soon as the butler read his card, he was shown to a parlour with the intelligence that the lady of the house was occupied at present with another caller, but would see him shortly.

Telling himself to breathe normally, Hal paced the small room to which he'd been shown, silently rehearsing the speech he'd prepared. If he took his time and didn't panic, he should be able to avoid stuttering through the few lines that expressed his condolences, offered his assistance in Lord Englemere's stead for the duration of her family's absence, and asked the direction of her late husband's man of business so he might consult this gentleman without having to intrude again upon her privacy.

As Hal made his third circuit of the room, running a finger under a neckcloth that had grown unaccountably tighter than when he'd tied it several hours ago, a soft scuffling sound caught his attention. Halting by the doorway, he peered out to see a small boy standing in the hallway, a metal toy soldier clutched in his hands as he cast an apprehensive glance over his shoulder at the stairway behind him.

When the boy's eyes lowered from his inspection of the stair landing, his gaze met Hal's and he gasped. Tightening his grip on the soldier, with another quick look up the stairs, he whispered anxiously, 'You won't tell Nurse I'm down here, will you?'

Stifling a smile, Hal gave a negative shake of his head.

Relaxing a bit, the boy said, 'I shall go back up directly. Only…only the general lost his arm, and I thought Mama would want to know.' He held up the toy, showing Hal the torso and the detached limb.

A lady's drawing room was no place for a young boy, as Hal knew only too well. He ought to save the lad a scolding by encouraging his immediate return to the nursery. But looking down at that small woebegone face, he couldn't make himself utter the words.

'I was ever so careful, but the arm just…came off,' the lad continued earnestly. 'Papa could fix him in a trice, I know, but Papa…' The boy's voice trailed off and he swallowed hard, tears appearing at the corners of his blue eyes. 'Papa has…gone away. He always told me I must never disturb Mama in her studio, but she would want to know about the general, don't you think? He is my best friend.'

Suddenly a vivid memory engulfed Hal, so searing it robbed him of breath: a pudgy little blond boy weeping in a hallway, denied entry to his mother's room. Exiled to the nursery, watched over by an unfamiliar, dragon-faced woman who rapped his knuckles when he cried and told him he should be ashamed of blubbering like a girl. Who refused his pleas to speak with his mother, informing him that Mrs Waterman was too busy to see a whiny little boy.

Lowery's son looked to be about the same age Hal had been when he'd lost his father. He'd never forgotten, could feel vestiges still of the loneliness and devastation he'd suffered.

A deeply buried, smouldering anger welled up to swamp his reluctance to meet Elizabeth Lowery. He might not be the paragon of scintillating drawing-room conversation his mama wished for, but he could make sure this little waif wasn't shunted aside and neglected, as he'd been. Whether the boy's beautiful mother wished to deal with him or not!

Without further thought, he stepped into the hallway and went down on his knees beside the child. 'Hal Waterman here. Your Uncle Nicky's best friend. Let me see your soldier. Then we'll tell your mama.'

The boy's expression brightened. 'Uncle Nicky talks about you all the time. I wish he was here. Mama cries and cries. She says Uncle Nicky has gone away too—' Sudden alarm clouded the lad's face. 'Uncle Nicky will…come back, won't he?'

'Yes,' Hal assured him. 'Travelling in Italy. Be back soon. But I'm here.' Gesturing towards the soldier, he said, 'Let me look? Maybe I can fix him.'

'Could you?' the boy breathed. 'That would be capital! Then you would be my new best friend!'

If not that, at least the champion of his interests, Hal resolved grimly—until Nicky could take over, of course. Carefully accepting the toy and the arm the boy held out, Hal bent to inspect the mechanism that attached the limb.

Meanwhile, in her studio down the hallway, for the last hour Elizabeth Lowery had been going over the household accounts. She'd found the books in her husband's desk yesterday, along with enough cash in the chest to satisfy her disgruntled servants, but Sands informed her that he and the cook must soon purchase additional provisions. She would need to peruse the books to determine how much more cash to obtain from the bank.

Sighing as she tried to total a column of figures detailing the costs of tallow candles, flour, lamp oil, coal and a long list of similar household necessities, Elizabeth wished she had paid more attention to her governess's lessons on mathematics. With her older sister Mereydth and younger sisters Emma and Cecily in the room—the girls two and three years her junior and bubbling over with lively conversation—she'd usually been able to escape Miss Twimby's attention. Daydreaming through the lesson, she'd merely bided her time until she could abandon her books and return to her charcoal and her paints.

'Twas no use; she'd lost track of the total again. With a huff of frustration, she pushed the book away. Such an interesting pattern the figures made, flowing down the page in her husband's neat hand. The three at the edge of the page, turned on its side in her current viewing angle, looked like a bird seen at a long distance, its wings curved in flight. While the seven at the bottom reminded her of a tall crane, balanced on one skinny leg, bill facing into the wind as he stood at the edge of a marsh.

She was smiling at the image when a tap sounded at the door. The portal opened to reveal Sands, but before the butler could utter a word, a swarthy, powerfully built man shouldered past him into the room.

'Needn't announce me like some toff,' the man said as he strode in. 'Smith's the name, ma'am. I'm here at the behest of my employer, Mr Blackmen. And since my business is with the lady…' he looked back at Sands '…you can take yourself off.'

Despite the intimidating stare the intruder fixed on him, Sands held his ground, looking at Elizabeth. Lifting a hand to signal he should remain, she said coolly, 'I don't believe I am acquainted with a Mr Blackmen, sir. Perhaps you have mistaken your errand.'

Smith gave a crack of laughter. 'Not likely. Old Blackmen, he don't tolerate mistakes. And you might not be "acquainted", but I guarantee your lately departed ball-and-chain was. Knew the boss right intimate, Mr Lowery did. If you know what's good for you and your little boy, you'll let me tell you what he sent me to say. A personal matter, so you'd best send old long-nose there packing.'

Alarmed—but also angered—Elizabeth hesitated. On the one hand, she didn't relish being left alone with a man who looked like a ruffian out of a tenement in Seven Dials. But if the matter were sensitive, perhaps she should receive his message in private.

Swiftly making her choice, she nodded at Sands. 'You may wait in the hall.'

The butler bowed. 'As you wish, madam. I shall be outside the door.' Despite his advancing years and the fact that the visitor outweighed him by several stones, Sands gave Smith a challenging look. '*Directly* outside the door, if you should need anything, ma'am.'

While the butler bowed himself out, Smith laughed again. 'As if I couldn't snap that old coot like a twig if'n I wanted! Got to credit him for gumption, though.'

'Perhaps you could just deliver your message,' Elizabeth interposed, unnerved and appalled by her unwanted visitor's vulgarity.

'Let me just do that, then,' Smith said affably. 'I can see your late husband had a hankering for pretty things.' He looked Elizabeth up and down, the insolent inspection making her want to slap his face.

'Didn't always have the blunt to purchase his niceties, though,' Smith continued. 'Which is where my employer came in. Always there to help a gent who's a little short of the ready, for a modest return, of course. I'd guess your man meant to pay back what he'd borrowed, but then—' he made a swiping motion at his neck '—cocked up his toes afore he could make good on his expenditures. Now, my employer being a soft-hearted man, he gave you a month after the funeral for grieving. But now he's wanting his blunt.'

Mr Blackmen must be a moneylender, Elizabeth surmised, consternation flowing through her. Why would Everitt resort to borrowing money? Were dealings with a cent-per-center even legal? If they were, could she be held accountable for repaying the debt? And, if so, where was she to obtain the funds?

Desperately trying to mask her distress beneath a façade of cool uninterest, she said, 'I know nothing of these transactions. You shall have to take this matter up with Mr Scarbridge, my husband's man of business.'

Smith made a rude noise. 'Scarbridge—that incompetent? Seeing how deep he's in River Tick hisself, I doubt he'd know a groat about handling anyone's finances—if he was to leave off his gaming and whoring long enough to try, that is. No, little lady, my master intends to settle this business with you personal.'

This was too much—she simply couldn't handle one more disaster. An almost hysterical anger burning through her alarm, she snapped, 'Do you expect I know any more than Mr Scarbridge does? I'm neither a solicitor nor a banker. You waste your time here, sir! Good day.'

Smith's genial expression hardened. 'I wouldn't be so quick to run me off, Mrs High-and-Mighty,' he said, advancing on her. 'Don't expect you'd be so high in the instep if the magistrate was to come calling, ready to haul you and that boy of yorn off to Newgate.'

Her momentary flash of bravado extinguished, Elizabeth gasped. Newgate! Could this awful Mr Blackmen truly have her imprisoned for debt? Her mind slammed from panic to anger and back like a child's ball tethered to a string.

What should she do? Nicky was a peer; he would know. Oh, why did he and Sarah have to be away now?

'No need to get yourself into a pelter,' Smith said, recalling her attention. He gestured around the room. 'Got lots of fancy things here—that silver inkpot, them vases on that shelf, those marble heads of soldiers over there by the divan. Fetch a pretty penny, I'd wager. Lowery paid enough for 'em.'

'Those are classical Greek, my husband's pride,' Elizabeth protested.

'His pride, eh?' Raising his eyebrows, Smith leaned across the desk and put his hand over hers. With a moue of revulsion, Elizabeth tried to snatch it back.

Laughing softly, Smith seized her fingers, tightening his grip until his nails bit into her skin. 'You kin lose the fripperies…or yer house. Or,' he said in a deeper tone, his dark eyes heating as he stared at her, 'we could deal in another commodity.'

His gaze fixed on her bosom, he lifted his free hand to tug at a strand of golden hair. 'You're a fine-looking woman. My master might like that—or I might.'

No one had ever looked at her or talked to her so crudely— as if she were some Covent Garden strumpet procured for his amusement. 'My husband would kill you for speaking to me so!' she said furiously.

'Lucky for me he's already dead then, ain't it?' Smith replied.

Renewed outrage drowning her fear, Elizabeth wrenched her hand free. 'Get out!' she cried, her voice shaking with indignation and rage.

Smith made her an exaggerated bow. 'I'll leave—for now, Mrs High-and-Mighty, but I'll be back. You can bet the golden curls on your head on it.'

As if concluding a normal business call, Smith pivoted and walked with a jaunty tread to the door. Opening it, he gave her another mocking bow before shutting it behind him, leaving Elizabeth appalled, outraged…and thoroughly alarmed.

Chapter Three

Hal had just finished his inspection of the Lowery boy's soldier when a door further down the hall opened and closed. 'That's Mama's studio,' the child said, excitement in his eyes. 'Mayhap she's done now. Let's go see!'

Hal tried to ignore the sinking sensation suddenly spiralling in his gut. He was rising to his feet when a swarthy man in a freize coat, hat pulled down low over his eyes, brushed past them, a frowning Sands in his wake. Without a backward glance, the man exited through the door the butler hurriedly opened for him.

'Now!' the boy said urgently, tugging on Hal's hand. 'While Sands is busy!'

Hal tried to summon the words to tell the child that although he might scurry in to visit his mama, Hal ought to wait for the butler to announce him. But when the boy looked up, a pleading look on his face as he whispered 'Please', against his better judgement, Hal allowed the boy to lead him down the hallway.

Hal had barely time enough to wonder why such a rough-looking gent had been paying a call on Mrs Lowery before the child had him at the doorway. One rapid knock later, the boy pushed open the door and hurtled into the room.

'Mama, Mama, look at the general!' he cried as he ran in. 'He's hurt. We need to fix him!'

Halting on the threshold, Hal looked over at the woman he'd not seen in so long. When Elizabeth Lowery glanced up from her son and saw Hal, he felt as if all the air had suddenly been sucked from the room.

She wore a simple black gown, a harsh shade, his mama said, that robbed the colour from a lady. But not from Elizabeth. The midnight hue rather emphasised the fairness of her hair, gleaming gold in the pale light from the window. The flush of peach at her cheekbones set off the cream of her face and the blaze of her eyes, deep cerulean like the noon sky at midsummer. The oval face with its pointed chin was a touch fuller than he remembered, while a few tiny lines at corners of her eyes imbued it with character.

This was no flawless ingénue, poised to begin life, but a vibrant, experienced woman who had lived, loved and laughed. A woman who stole his breath just as easily as she had seven years ago, while the force of the connection he felt to her froze him in place on the doorstep.

Amid the rush of sensation, one disjointed thought emerged: she was even more beautiful now than the first time he'd seen her.

While his pulse thrummed in his ears and he struggled to breathe, Hal dimly noted the child holding the soldier up to her, his words tumbling over each other as he tried to explain what had happened to his toy.

Rising to her feet, Elizabeth Lowery hushed her son with a gesture of her hand. 'David, you are being impolite. First you must introduce your visitor.'

Hal forced his body into motion and found his tongue. 'Hal Waterman, ma'am,' he said, bowing. 'Nicky's friend. Just returned from the north and read of your loss. My sincere regrets.'

'He's going to be my friend, too, Mama,' the boy interrupted. 'He says while Uncle Nicky is in It-tal-lee he can fix the general for me.'

'David, you mustn't impose on Mr Waterman,' his mother reproved. 'And what are you doing down here? Where is Nurse? And Sands?' Rubbing her hands together distractedly, she gave Hal a tremulous smile. 'I do apologise, Mr Waterman. You must think you've stumbled into Bedlam.'

At the subtle correction, the child drooped, his eyes lowering, his hand with the broken toy falling back to his side. 'I'm sorry, Mama,' he murmured. 'I'll go back up. But I thought you would want to know about the general. So we can fix him. Like Papa would.'

Elizabeth's eyes sheened and she took a ragged breath. 'I know, dearest. Papa fixed everything. We'll see what we can do, but later.' Giving her son a quick hug, she clasped his shoulders and gently turned him toward the door. 'Go back up now, there's a good boy.'

His small shoulders hunched, David nodded. Chin wobbling, he walked towards the door.

The child's anguish, clearly visible on his woebegone face, burned through Hal's haze of bewitchment. In the figure of Elizabeth he could almost see his own mother, brushing him off, sending him away, too obsessed by her own wants and needs to spare the few moments necessary to comfort a distressed child.

Sympathy—and anger—reviving, he held out his hand as the boy walked past him. 'Still be friends,' he said, taking the small fingers in his large ones and shaking them. 'Come back and fix the general.'

The boy's eyes widened. 'You will?' he asked. When Hal nodded, a smile broke out on his face. 'Then you will be my new best friend!'

'David, you mustn't trouble Mr Waterman—' his mother objected behind them, but Hal silenced her with a shake of his head. 'No trouble. Glad to do it. Until later.' He gave David and his soldier a salute.

Giggling, the boy returned it before scampering from the room. Setting his jaw with firm purpose, Hal turned to face Elizabeth Lowery.

Trying to mentally regather the now-scattered bits of the speech he'd rehearsed, Hal said, 'Sorry to intrude, but know your family is away. My best friend, Nicky. He'd want me to act for him. Check with your man of business, help in any way I can.' Champion the interests of your son, he added silently.

'My...my man of business?' Putting her hands to her flushed cheeks, Elizabeth laughed disjointedly and her lips trembled. 'You're terribly kind, Mr Waterman, but I couldn't bother you with our problems.'

Hal frowned. Something wasn't right here. One of the few benefits of his verbal affliction was that his enforced silence had made him a keen observer of the people and events around him. Suddenly he recalled the rough man in the freize coat. 'Did previous caller upset you?'

Tears gathered at the corners of her lovely eyes and she pinched her trembling lips together. Swiping a hand over her eyes impatiently, she said, 'Well...yes, but I cannot ask you to—'

Hal waved a hand, his mind already going over the implications of a bully-boy tough calling on a lady at her home. 'Pretend I'm Nicky. Here to help. 'Tis what Nicky would do. Sarah, too.'

She seemed genuinely distressed. Maybe that excused her brushing her son aside—this time, Hal thought, still studying her.

Her tear-glazed eyes inspected his face. 'Are you sure?' she asked. 'You're right, I would turn to Nicky, were he available. I know I ought not to involve you, but I truly have no idea what to do. And Nicky and Sarah have both spoken so often and so highly of you, that, although we are but little acquainted, I feel as if I know you.'

Hal shrugged. 'Simple. Do anything for Nicky. Nicky do anything for you. Family. Besides, son's new best friend.'

That earned him a feeble smile. Finally she nodded. 'Very well, I shall tell you.'

'What did the man want?'

'Though it seems incredible, the caller, a Mr Smith, claims my husband borrowed money from his employer, a Mr Blackmen. Money he now wants back, with interest, if I correctly understood his implication. He said if I do not pay him, he could have my son and I evicted from this house and sent to Newgate.'

Her eyes went unfocused as she stared into the distance. Bringing her arms up, she crossed them over her chest and hugged her shoulders. 'He said he might…' Her voice trailed off and she shuddered.

Viewing that defensive pose, Hal had no difficulty imagining what the brawny interloper might have demanded of this beautiful, vulnerable woman who'd had only an elderly servant to protect her. That some low-born ruffian dared even imagine he could despoil Elizabeth Lowery's genteel loveliness sent fury rushing through Hal's veins..

If the miscreant had so much as touched Elizabeth, he was a dead man.

'Did he hurt you?' Hal demanded.

Evidently startled by the volume and intensity of his voice, Elizabeth jumped, her gaze darting back to Hal. 'N-no. He…he only frightened me a little, as I'm sure he meant to do.'

'Sure you are unharmed?' Hal persisted, already envisioning his hands around the tough's thick neck.

He must have looked as fierce as he felt, for her eyes widened and a smile quirked her lips. 'There is no need to track him down and tear him limb from limb, I assure you.'

'Won't bother you again, swear it. Check my contacts at Bow Street. Take care of him.'

Her wry smile gentled. 'Thank you,' she said softly. 'I feel safer already. To reiterate, he said his name was Smith and his employer a Mr Blackmen, although I cannot be sure those are their actual names. He said that Mr Lowery had borrowed money to fund his antique purchases.'

She frowned, her gaze thoughtful. 'My husband delighted in his collection. I know he bought several fine new statues just the month before his…his death. Shall I make a note for you of what he purchased and when?'

Hal gave a negative shake of his head. 'No need. Have it here.' He pointed to his head. 'Not much conversation, but good memory,' he said, his mind racing through the possibilities.

Bow Street knew most of the moneylenders. Even if the man had given a false name, Hal was confident they could run him to ground.

If Lowery had indeed borrowed money from a usurer, there was no legal way the lender could recover more than the principal. Whatever that sum had been, Hal would repay it at once to ensure Mrs Lowery received no further friendly little visits. If upon review the Lowery estate hadn't the funds to reimburse him, he knew Nicky would pay him back when the family returned from their holiday.

And despite Elizabeth Lowery's reassurance that she was unharmed, he still intended to pay a little visit on the man who'd invaded her house today.

'I don't know why Everitt would resort to consulting a money-lender,' Mrs Lowery's troubled voice recalled him. 'He's always been an avid collector—' she gestured toward several marble busts on the shelves in the studio that even to Hal's untrained eye looked particularly fine '—but I had no idea we were in financial difficulties.'

'Man of business said nothing?' Hal asked. 'When he called to read the will?'

Her eyebrows winged upward in surprise. 'He hasn't called.

Nor, to my knowledge, has there been a reading of the will. I suppose Everitt had one, but I know nothing about it.'

'Who is solicitor?'

'Mr Scarbridge.'

'Eustace Scarbridge?' Hal echoed, astonished and taken aback.

'Do you know him?' Elizabeth asked. 'He is—was—a distant cousin of Everitt's. They attended Cambridge together. Though I don't believe Everitt consulted him very much.'

Unsure what to reply, Hal remained silent. Eustace Scarbridge. He barely refrained from groaning. So much for his happy vision of paying a single visit on the bewitching Elizabeth and being able to conclude the rest of his dealings about the Lowery estate with the deceased's solicitor.

Hal was not surprised Lowery hadn't consulted Scarbridge often. He would have to have been dicked in the nob to have confided anything of importance to a man Hal knew to be a gambler and a ne'er-do-well always looking for a high-stakes table at which to lose his blunt—if he wasn't throwing it away on some expensive barque of frailty. Hal hadn't even known the man was a solicitor, rather eloquent evidence in itself of the amount of time Scarbridge spent pursuing his supposed vocation.

Hal considered himself as reverent of the bonds of kinship as anyone, but he couldn't help damning Lowery for feeling so constrained by them that he'd not retained a solicitor worthy of the name.

'Should Mr Scarbridge have called?' Elizabeth asked anxiously, recalling Hal from his consternation. 'I'm sorry to keep asking questions, but as I suppose is quite obvious, I know nothing about finances. Or anything else useful,' she added with a twisted smile.

She looked weary and cast-down, almost as woebegone as her son. 'You know the state of household accounts,' he replied, wishing to encourage her.

She brightened imperceptibly. 'I was just looking over them. And I have paid the servants.'

'Know balance? After expenditures for house, mourning clothes.'

Her momentary look of confidence faded. 'I've only begun to look over the accounts and…I'm afraid I'm not very good with numbers. Besides, Sands, our butler, took care of ordering the wreaths and mourning dress. I already had some older gowns that would do, so I have no idea what all the necessities cost.'

'Old gowns?' Hal echoed, astounded. His mama never missed an opportunity to expand her wardrobe. For the death of a close relative or acquaintance, she invariably purchased at least half a dozen new gowns, plus bonnets, scarves, stockings, pelisses and slippers to match. After all, she'd told him on the last occasion, styles had changed since she'd last worn mourning, and he couldn't expect her to appear in public shabbily dressed.

Mrs Lowery, however, looked distressed. 'Are you thinking I should have purchased new ones? I assure you, I meant no disrespect to Everitt. Perhaps I should have made the effort, but I was already so beside myself, I couldn't bear the thought. Shopping is so taxing, all the material so lovely, with so many different textures, weaves and colours 'tis nearly impossible to choose.'

'Mama has same problem,' Hal replied. 'Chooses one of everything.'

That elicited a brief smile, though Hal's reply had been entirely serious. 'And it's so time-consuming. My husband and his cousin Miss Lowery, who lives with us, have always been kind enough to handle those purchases for me. Miss Lowery delighted in discussing the latest fashions with Everitt, who was always willing to escort her to the dressmaker's. Since I care little about what I wear, as long as 'tis comfortable, I've been happy to let them.'

'Don't like to go to the shops,' Hal repeated. Staring at her incomparable loveliness, he just couldn't get his mind around that incredible statement.

'No,' she admitted with another apologetic shrug. 'I expect it was unkind of me to foist such a…a feminine matter off upon my husband. He…he spoiled me dreadfully, you see,' she said, her voice hitching.

A beautiful woman who didn't delight in spending a man's blunt. Hal shook his mind away from that conundrum back to the matter at hand. 'First, I'll call on Scarbridge. See what he knows.'

'What of the loan?' she asked. 'Mr Smith said he would be back.'

'Won't be. I'll take care of it.'

'But what if Mr Scarbridge tells you there's not enough money to repay the loan?'

The anxiety in her eyes cut at his heart. Wanting to reassure her and unable to voice a sufficient number of appropriately soothing words, without thinking, Hal stepped over and took her hand.

Immediately he realised what a bad idea that was. He looked at it, her small slender fingers, gloveless as if she'd just put down one of her paintbrushes, clasped in his big ones. Her skin softer than he'd imagined, the feel of it sending shivers of fire straight to his loins. Her scent, some attar of roses that reminded him of the flowers he'd had planted in the gardens back at the Hall, wafted through his nostrils and clouded his head.

He wanted to wrap her in his arms, tell her everything would be all right, that he would protect her from every danger, watch over her and guard her with all the strength he possessed for the rest of his days.

All after the mere touch of her hand. This was going to be even worse than he'd feared; a death knell of warning tolled in his brain.

He released her fingers and staggered back a step, his heart pounding so hard, he knew she must be able to hear it. 'Will take care of it,' he managed to mumble. Desperately he made her a bow and turned to go.

'Mr Waterman,' her voice recalled him. Urgently needing to escape, he halted long enough to look back over his shoulder.

'Thank you for offering to protect us. I don't feel quite so alone and helpless now.'

'Pleasure,' he replied. As he paced toward the exit, he tried to ignore the little glow her words had ignited in his heart.

Thoughtfully Elizabeth watched the big man walk away. She rubbed her hand, which still tingled strangely.

She wasn't sure what to think. She did feel much less anxious, as she'd told him. Though she probably shouldn't have confided in him, since, despite being Nicky and Sarah's good friend, he was no more closely related to her than Sir Gregory.

Still, as he'd assured her in that odd, clipped way he had of speaking, he was a *family* connection, while Sir Gregory was merely a friend of Everitt's. Though she had dispatched a note telling Nicky and Sarah of Everitt's death right after the funeral, she had no idea when or even whether her missive would find them. She knew Mr Waterman was right in asserting that Nicky would expect his best friend to assist her until he returned himself.

Though Mr Waterman had seemed almost…hostile when David first brought him in, her heart warmed as she recalled the scene. Even if she'd not heard glowing avowals of his character from her sister and brother-in-law, she would have trusted Hal Waterman based simply on the way he'd treated her son.

He'd knelt down to David's level, coaxed a smile to his solemn little face, then actually made him giggle. How her heart had leapt to hear it! After this awful, interminable month, poor David was desolate for attention, hungry for the company of a man upon whom he could depend.

Even as she was.

She did feel she could depend on Hal Waterman to handle the distressing matter of Mr Smith and the loan. Now that she thought about it, she recalled Nicky telling her Mr Waterman had a keen mathematical mind and was an expert in matters of finance and investment. Quite likely not even Nicky himself would be better situated to resolve whatever tangle Everitt had left in their financial affairs.

So she would be seeing Mr Waterman again. The idea made something stir within her. Though she'd felt nothing but grief and regret for so long, she wasn't sure just what.

Probably it was that he presented such an arresting figure— she could almost feel her fingers itch with impatience to find a brush. Though he was taller and broader of shoulder than any man she'd ever met, he carried himself with an athlete's easy grace. The muscles of his thighs and calves revealed by his knit breeches and form-fitting boots attested to time spent in the saddle, while the abdomen beneath his plain waistcoat appeared firm and flat. As for his face, with his golden hair worn just long enough to curl over his brow, a high forehead, well-formed nose and square jaw, he reminded her of the Roman bust of Apollo her husband had recently acquired.

Although with his size and air of authority, she would rather paint him as Zeus, king of the gods. For a moment, she smiled at the idea of ordering him to strip off his garments and dress in a toga, the better for her to capture the likeness.

Something about the image made her feel suddenly overwarm. She reached up a hand to fan herself. Hal Waterman was quite as attractive as he was arresting, she realised.

He found her attractive, too, she knew. By now she was used to seeing the interest flare in men's eyes when they looked at her. She could identify every degree of attraction, from the gentle love and respect that had always shown in Everitt's, to the slavish eagerness to impress of some of the young men he'd sometimes brought to dinner, to the hot-eyed lust in Mr Smith's that she'd found so disconcerting and repellent.

That might have made her current situation more difficult, except that the masculine appreciation in Mr Waterman's eyes had not made her feel at all uncomfortable, overlayed as it was by a quaint shyness and a respect bordering almost on reverence. With utter certainty she knew that admire her as he might, he would never say or do anything to distress or discomfort her. Even the clasping of her hand that she'd found so oddly disturbing had been meant only to reassure.

Yes, she could depend upon him utterly. And if something else tickled at the edges of her consciousness, some little niggle in the pit of her stomach she couldn't quite identify, she needn't regard it.

Mr Waterman promised to keep her and David secure until Sarah and Nicky returned. For that favour, she would owe him her warmest appreciation.

Chapter Four

Still shaken from his encounter with Elizabeth Lowery, Hal returned to his bachelor quarters on Upper Brook Street. Feeling the morning's events called for stiffer reinforcement than a glass of wine, he headed straight for the brandy decanter in the library.

The satisfying bite of the liquor burning its way to his belly helped relax the knots in his nerves. Breathing easy for the first time since leaving the widow's presence, he tried to shake his mind free of her lingering spell.

All right, so she was still beautiful. Dazzling, even. And, yes, he burned as fiercely to possess her as he had the first time he'd seen her. Except now, moved by her plight and that of her fatherless son, he also wanted to protect them and ease the small boy's misery.

He could handle his lust. For six years now he'd had a comfortable, mutually agreeable arrangement with a big-hearted lady he'd met at one of London's most exclusive brothels and who now resided in a discreet house on Curzon Street he'd purchased for her. Sweet Sally would keep his masculine urges slaked.

He'd just have to work on leashing his emotions.

It was unfortunate that Lowery hadn't entrusted his business affairs to someone capable of managing them. It appeared that Hal was going to have to tap his contacts and do some investigating to determine exactly how things stood so he could restore the Lowery finances to good order before turning everything over to Nicky upon his return.

Which meant he would probably see a lot more of Elizabeth…far more than was good for his heart or his senses. Hearing himself sigh at that conclusion like an infatuated moonling just up from Oxford, Hal straightened and squared his shoulders.

All right, so it was unlikely, given her professed dislike of shopping—a description Hal still had a hard time believing—that Elizabeth Lowery had got her household into financial difficulties. But just because, unlike his own mama, she didn't visit the shops more regularly than she did her son's nursery didn't mean she was born to bear his children.

If he tried to focus his visits to Green Street on spending as much time with the boy and as little as possible with the widow, he might still escape this tangle intact. Surely he could manage to remain sensible for the two-or-so months remaining until Nicky came home?

He had just knocked back the last measure of brandy when a tap sounded at the door and his valet Jeffers entered, bearing several boxes.

To the unspoken question of his lifted eyebrows, Jeffers said, 'Your lady mother called while you were out.'

Hal groaned. 'Praise God I was out.'

Jeffers smiled. 'Having called so early on the expectation of finding you at home, Mrs Waterman was…less than pleased to discover you away. It took a glass of Madeira and some of Cook's best biscuits to convince her you'd not deliberately conspired to have her quit her bedchamber at nearly dawn and go out in the early morning damp so prejudicial to her complexion, all the while knowing she would fail to find you here. Though she did condescend to leave these packages, I believe it would be accurate to infer that you are still in her black books.'

'Always am anyway,' Hal mumbled.

Jeffers nodded sympathetically. 'Quite.'

'What's in 'em?' Hal gestured to the boxes. 'Know you've looked.'

Jeffers cleared his throat. 'Mrs Waterman purchased some garments that she felt might assist you in updating your wardrobe to present a more fashionable appearance.'

Hal rolled his eyes. 'How bad are they?'

Jeffers opened the first box. 'Wellington pantaloons are quite stylish now,' he said, shaking out the garment and holding it up.

Grimacing, Hal inspected the long pants that featured side slits from calves down to ankles, where they fastened with loops and buttons at the heel. 'Not so bad, but keep my breeches.'

'Very good, sir.' The valet opened the next box, and with a determinedly straight face, held up a waistcoat.

Alternating blue and yellow stripes, each nearly three inches wide, met Hal's incredulous view.

'Mrs Waterman said it was all the crack,' Jeffers informed him.

Hal snorted. 'Don't doubt. On man my size, look like curtains out of bordello.'

The valet's lips twitched. 'I believe this last item meant to avoid that by giving you a more…slender look.' He removed the garment from its box and held it out.

'What the—?' Hal exclaimed.

''Tis a Cumberland corset,' the valet explained. 'The body contains whalebone stays, which, once placed about the waist, cinch in with these strings…'

Hal nipped the garment from his servant's hand, looked it over briefly—and burst out laughing. After a moment, Jeffers lost the battle to maintain an expressionless demeanour and started laughing as well.

Finally containing his mirth, Hal wiped his eyes and tossed the corset back in its box, where it collapsed in a clunk of whalebone.

'I'd give 'em to poor, but poor not sapskulled enough to wear 'em. Take 'em, please.' Hal stacked the boxes and handed them back to Jeffers. 'New, and if know Mama, highest quality. Suppose you can sell 'em somewhere.'

'Should I place the money in the household accounts?'

''Course not. Abominations yours now. As you well know, you damnable pirate. Sold enough of Mama's gifts over years to fund retirement.'

Jeffers grinned. 'Thank you, sir, 'tis very generous.'

'Off with you,' Hal said, grinning back. 'One thing, Jeffers…'

Already carrying away the boxes, the valet halted. 'Sir?'

'Catch you wearing that waistcoat, you're discharged.'

Jeffers swallowed a chuckle. 'If I should ever don a garment even remotely resembling that waistcoat, sir, you may have me taken straight to Bedlam. Oh, Mrs Waterman did mention she hoped you'd have the manners to return her call.'

Hal sighed as he watched the heavily-laden Jeffers walk out. That was surely the purpose of his mother bringing gifts—besides her unslakeable urge to make purchases, of course. She knew that should she not find Hal at home, he would be obligated to call and thank her for her kindness.

At which time she would probably chastise him for his ingratitude in not wearing the new trousers and waistcoat. Recalling the latter, Hal grimaced. He'd suffer a hundred jawbonings before he'd wear a monstrosity like that.

Did Mama really think that a whalebone contraption and one hideous waistcoat could turn him into the pattern-card of fashion she wished him to be? Or was she merely trying to irritate him beyond bearing?

Unhappily, he was going to have to call on her and find out. Best do it first thing this afternoon and get it over with, before he went to Bow Street to investigate Mrs Lowery's unsavoury caller.

Setting his lips in a grim line at the prospect, Hal tugged the bell pull to call for luncheon.

Several hours later, after dressing with a care that would doubtless be lost on a lady who was anticipating lace-tied pant legs and a boldly striped waistcoat, Hal presented himself at the large family manse on Berkeley Square. Holmes, his mother's butler, showed him to the Green Parlour, assuring him his mother had been anticipating his call and would receive him directly.

Palms already sweating, Hal propped one shoulder against the mantel, hoping his mama's social schedule was full enough that the time she'd allotted for this visit would be correspondingly brief.

He heard the door open, heralding his mother's arrival, and took a deep breath. As Mrs Waterman swept into the room, Hal walked over to make his bow and kiss his mother's proffered hand.

'Lovely gown, Mama. Look enchanting.'

As, in truth, she did. Through arts jealously guarded by that lady and her dresser Hayes, though she was well passed her fortieth year, Letitia Waterman contrived to appear decades younger. Her intricately arranged blonde curls were as bright, her body as slender and her pale skin almost as unlined as when she had been the brightest new Diamond in society's Marriage Mart, a society over which she ruled still.

One of the scores of beaux she'd dazzled her first Season had been Hal's father, Nathan. And since, though the Watermans were untitled, the family was related by blood or marriage to half the great houses of England and possessed more wealth than most of them put together, it hadn't been thought surprising that, from the scores of offers she'd reportedly received, she had condescended to bestow her hand upon Nathan Waterman.

Hal sometimes wondered if his father had ever regretted that.

'Thank you, dear.' His mother's eyes, blue where his were grey, inspected him before she made a small moue of distaste and waved him to a chair. 'I see you failed to avail yourself of the more fashionable garments I selected for you.'

'Sorry, Mama. Most kind of you. But not my style.'

'That's precisely the point, son,' she replied, a touch of acid in her tone. 'I was attempting to replace "no style" with something more befitting a man of your stature, but I see that, once again, you have rebuffed my attempt.'

There was no point answering that, even if Hal were tempted to try to make an explanation. She'd only interrupt his laborious reply, wincing slightly as if his halting speech pained her, which he supposed it did.

Really, son, must you be so blockish? Her oft-repeated reprimand echoed in his head. *Just state what you mean!* If only it were that simple, Mama, he thought.

It wasn't that he didn't immediately formulate a reply. He just couldn't get the words out. Not for the first time, he regretted that humans didn't communicate by note.

He was an eloquent writer, all his Oxford professors had agreed. He'd even gained somewhat of a reputation penning amusing doggerel for his friends' amateur theatricals. And, though he'd never admit it to anyone, occasionally he still wrote sonnets like the ones that had earned him high marks in his composition classes.

Though his mama, were she aware of this talent, would probably find it as shocking as his financial pursuits. A gentleman was prized for his clever, amusing drawing-room conversation, not for sitting alone scribbling verse.

She covered his silence by asking Holmes to pour wine before turning back to him, a smile fixed on her face.

Apprehension immediately began churning in Hal's gut. He

knew that smile. Mama wanted something from him, and past experience warned it wouldn't be anything he had the remotest desire to give.

Hal waited grimly while the butler served them and then withdrew. As soon as they'd each had a sip, his mama put down her glass and smiled again. Hal braced himself.

'It's been weeks since I've had you to escort me anywhere. All that travelling about in the north, inspecting some dreadful earthworks or other.'

'Canals, Mama.'

His mother waved a dismissive hand. 'It sounds distressingly common. Is it not enough that you must dirty your hands dealing with those Cits on the Exchange? A gentleman simply shouldn't engage in anything that smacks of trade.'

From the frown on her face, Hal surmised that another of society's dragons must have been tweaking his mother—jokingly, of course—about her unfashionable son's even more unfashionable activities. He thought again what a sore trial he must be to her…even though his 'unfashionable' activities maintained the fortune she so delighted in spending.

He considered apologising, but, true to form, she continued on without pausing to let him reply. 'Well, enough of that! I expect I shall soon be seeing much more of you, for I've recently met the most charming young lady. Such beauty! Such presence! I simply had to make her my newest companion. I'm positive that once you meet her, desire for her company will lure you away from your tedious pursuits back into the *ton* gatherings where you belong.'

Gritting his teeth through that speech, Hal barely refrained from groaning aloud. Would Mama never give up? Unfortunately the Marriage Mart each year churned out a never-ending supply of new maidens on the hunt for a husband. Most of whom, he thought sardonically, seemed fully prepared to overlook his taciturn nature and unfashionable proclivities in order to get their lace-mittened hands on the Waterman wealth.

'It just so happens that my dear Tryphena is visiting this afternoon. I'll have Holmes escort her in so you two can become acquainted at once!'

Just wonderful, Hal thought glumly. He could try to tell his mother that he didn't wish to meet her latest protégée, or that he needed to leave immediately on a matter of pressing business. But he knew he couldn't utter enough words to argue with her, that she would easily overwhelm his limited powers of expression in a torrent of rebuttal and in the end, simply refuse to accept any answer but the agreement she wanted him to utter.

After seven years at this game, he'd long since learned it wasn't worth his breath to try to dissuade her.

So he simply sat, sipping his wine and wondering how long he'd be condemned to remain before Mama would allow him to escape, while Mrs Waterman chattered on about the exquisite taste, superior accomplishments and well-connected family of Lady Tryphena Upcott.

All too soon, Holmes announced the arrival of the young lady herself. With resignation Hal rose to greet her.

The girl entering the room appeared a bit older than Hal had anticipated. Then the name clicked in his consciousness.

Daughter of an earl, Lady Tryphena had been several Seasons on the town without becoming engaged. The gossip at Hal's club said she was too high in the instep to accept a gentleman of less than the most exalted rank, from whom, apparently, no such offer had yet been forthcoming. Perhaps, Hal thought, after ending three Seasons unwed, she'd decided great wealth would be an acceptable substitute for elevated title.

With her excellent family connections and exacting standards, it was small wonder Mama favoured the girl. Perhaps since Hal had rejected her attempts to saddle him with a chit fired straight out of the schoolroom, she thought to have better luck with an older candidate.

Though not up to his mama's usual guage of flawless beauty, Lady Tryphena was attractive enough. Her dark eyes were large, if not brilliant, her face pleasant, her light brown tresses charmingly arranged and her afternoon dress doubtless in the latest kick of fashion.

Hal bowed over her hand. 'Charmed.'

'Charmed to meet you, too, Mr Waterman,' Lady Tryphena replied.

'I've just been telling my son that we're counting on him to escort us to all the most select functions this Season,' his mama said, indicating with an elegant turn of her wrist that they might be seated.

Hal took care to select a chair as far from Lady Tryphena as possible.

'That would be delightful,' the girl said as she perched beside his mother on the sofa. 'I'm sure you will know just which entertainments will be the most glittering. Mama has always said you possess the most discerning intellect of any lady of the *ton*.'

Mrs Waterman smiled and patted Lady Tryphena's hand. 'How very kind of you both. Indeed, I've just received an invitation to Lady Cowper's ball for Friday next. It will be the most important event of the beginning Season. Hal, you will be free to escort us, I trust.'

Heart sinking, Hal scrambled to think of an excuse. While he rapidly examined and discarded reasons that would prevent his appearance at this choice social event, Lady Tryphena said, 'There's sure to be dancing, of course.'

'Naturally,' his mother replied.

Lady Tryphena looked Hal up and down, her gaze as assessing—and faintly disapproving—as his mama's. 'He does own the proper attire.'

'Of course he does. But I shall send his valet a note just to make sure. Though looking at my son you might not always be able to credit it, Jeffers is quite competent.'

Astounded, Hal realised the ladies were discussing *him*…as if he weren't even present.

Lady Tryphena didn't look convinced. 'Dancing pumps, too? He doesn't have the look of a man who possesses dancing pumps. Not that he actually has to dance—' her glance said she suspected he might cavort about the floor like a tame bear if set loose upon it '—but he should still be properly outfitted. In any event, I should be delighted to remain at your side, conversing with the gentleman waiting to speak or dance with you, for I'm sure you shall be immensely sought after, as always!'

His mother smiled graciously at that speech. 'Sweet child, how thoughtful you are! But you must dance as well. My son will be suitably attired, never fear. Besides, we can always purchase the appropriate footwear if necessary.'

This was the worst yet. His mama's previous candidates had all been too awed in her imperial presence to attempt much conversation, nor had they dared dart more than a few timid glances in his direction.

Perhaps he preferred ingénues after all.

A rising anger submerging his shock—and a hurt he should be long past feeling—Hal rose to his feet.

'Sorry, pressing engagement,' he said, interrupting the ladies' ongoing discussion of the best shops in which men's dancing slippers might be procured. 'Pleasure, Lady Tryphena. Mama.' After according them a bow he had no desire to give, he turned to stride from the room.

Apparently realising she had pushed him as far as she could, his mother made no attempt to stop him. 'Friday next, Hal. We'll dine here before leaving for the ball.'

Hot with rage, Hal didn't so much as nod. As he walked away, Lady Tryphena said, 'Is his speech always so oddly stilted?'

'It's a sad trial to me,' his mother said with a sigh.

'Well, if it pleases you, I shall certainly work on that! Perhaps with your help I can bring him up to snuff.'

The closing door cut off whatever reply his mother had offered. Too agitated to wait for the butler to return his hat and cane, Hal brushed past the startled footman stationed in the entry hall and quit his mother's house.

He'd arrived in a hackney, but at the moment he was too impatient to linger while one was summoned. Besides, a brisk walk might help settle his anger and dispel the lump of pained outrage still choking his throat. Thankful that he had a goal to achieve this afternoon—the investigation of Everitt Lowery's finances— he set off towards the City.

How should he proceed with his mother? He could simply fail to appear, but in the past that had generally resulted in an immediate summons accompanied by a jobation on his unreliability and lack of consideration for her feelings and sensibilities. It was usually easier to outwardly acquiesce to his mother's demands.

She knew she could win any verbal battle, so he no longer attempted any, but rather went through the motions of escorting her while according her candidate of the moment so little attention and encouragement that finally either the girl or his mother gave up. After which he would suffer through a painful scene where his mother would rant at him for his unfeeling, ungentlemanly behaviour and ingratitude at her efforts, then wail that she was destined to die abandoned and unloved, denied the comfort of a daughter-in-law and grandchildren, before finally weeping and declaring she meant to wash her hands of him for good.

Unfortunately, she'd never done so. But this attempt was her most embarrassing and humiliating effort yet.

Would she never give a thought to *his* needs and sensibilities? He laughed bitterly. When had she ever?

Less than a month after his father's death, at six years of age he'd been dragged off to Eton, still begging Mama not to send him away. At Eton, thank the Lord, he'd met Nicky, and in the harsh and often cruel world of schoolboys, eventually found a place.

He'd never cried for his mama again. The grieving lad's open wound of need for parental love had closed and scarred over. He'd come home as seldom as possible, often spending his holidays with his friends Nicky and Ned, then moved into a town house of his own as soon as the trustees of his estate gave its management over to him.

Yet in her self-absorbed, quixotic way, he knew his mother loved him, as much as she was capable of loving anyone. She always claimed to have missed him when he returned, first from Eton and then Oxford, and demanded to hear all his news. After a few minutes of his halting recitation, however, she'd interrupt to begin a monologue about fashion and gossip that lasted the rest of his visit. And he'd know that, once again, he'd disappointed her.

Even now, she chastised him if he called too infrequently, though his visits never seemed to give her much pleasure. Still, he supposed her continual efforts to 'improve' him and find him a suitable wife were her way of demonstrating affection, a misguided but genuine attempt to make his life better—according to her lights.

As Hal the boy had given up hoping for his mother's love and companionship, Hal the man knew 'twas impossible he'd ever gain her understanding or earn her approval. He just wished she would leave off trying to remake him into the sort of son she wanted.

Still unsure how he was going to avoid Lady Cowper's ball— but adamant that avoid it he would—Hal stopped at the first hackney stand he happened upon and instructed the driver to take him to Bow Street.

Chapter Five

Late that afternoon, Hal ducked to enter the low doorway of a ramshackle tavern deep in the district of Seven Dials. The unpalatable combination of hurt, humiliation, frustrated anger and lust that had simmered in him all afternoon settled to a slow, satisfying burn as he spied his quarry in the dim, smoky interior.

He crossed the dirty rush-strewn floor to seat himself at a rickety table against the back wall and signalled the innkeeper for a drink. Keeping his gaze carefully straight ahead, out of the corner of his eye he watched the swarthy man seated at the adjacent table.

Hal waited, every muscle tensed, but, after sliding him one quick glance, Smith returned his attention to his brew. Hal exiled a silent breath of relief. Apparently the man didn't remember brushing past him in Elizabeth's hallway during his little visit to Green Street. He'd be able to retain the advantage of surprise.

Of course, the other dozen occupants of the taproom were covertly watching Hal as well. Strangers seldom wandered into the heart of one of London's worst rookeries. And although Hal eschewed *ton* fashion and was dressed simply in a plain coat and breeches, the quality of his garments and his well-polished leather boots marked him none the less as a man of means.

Which meant, in this neighbourhood, as a mark who at the least should exit lighter of his purse, if he exited the premises at all.

The avaricious gleam in the eyes of the tavern wench who sashayed over to bring him his glass of blue ruin announced that she intended to get her share before the others pounced him. 'Tuppence for yer drink, guv'ner,' she said, leaning low to give him the best view of her assets. 'Fer another, I'll satisfy all yer wants.'

Hal slipped a coin in her hand. 'For drink.' Adding two more, he said, 'For not satisfying rest.'

After quickly thrusting the coins into her bodice, the barmaid shrugged. 'Just tryin' to be friendly.' Leaning closer, she murmured, 'Beings you be so generous, lemme advise ya to scarper outta here afor ol' Smith there calls out his bully boys. Otherwise, be lucky to leave the Dials with yer skin, much less yer fancy duds.'

Hal slipped another coin into the girl's hand. 'Thanks. Kind of you.'

The girl smiled, revealing cracked, stained teeth. 'Sure about them needs? Be a pleasure to handle a big…hearted gent like you.'

Hal patted her hand. 'You leave. Might get rough.'

The girl raised an eyebrow before sauntering back to the far side of the bar with a flagrant display of swaying hips that for a few moments captured the attention of every male in the room. After tossing the innkeeper a coin, she looked back at him.

Hal sent her a brief smile for the respite she'd offered him in which to make his escape. But he had no intention of leaving until he'd accomplished the purpose that, acting on the information he'd obtained from his friend Mason at Bow Street, had led him here.

Grimacing as the raw bite of the liquor scalded his throat, he swallowed a sip of the blue ruin and waited.

Soon enough, his patience was rewarded. Obviously unable to resist what he considered easy prey, from the table beside him, Mr Smith leaned closer.

'See you're a stranger, mate,' he said, spreading his gums in a semblance of a smile. 'Looking for someone? Be happy to help—for a small fee, a'course.'

Swiftly Hal reached down to snare the hand that had snaked over to snatch his purse. 'Robbery not very friendly,' he replied, pulling Smith's arm up on to the table and holding it trapped at a painful angle.

Smith's snarl of anger was followed by a yelp of pain, then the sound of bone cracking bone as Hal countered the right hook the man threw at him with an uppercut to the chin. Smith's eyes rolled back in his head before Hal dragged him up and pinned him into his chair.

'Shouldn't bother widows either. Understand?'

The mere idea of what this oily ruffian had no doubt threatened to do to Elizabeth Lowery made Hal's fury blaze hotter. Though he'd given the man a way to capitulate, a ferocious desire to punish Smith for invading her home, frightening her and besmirching her with his lecherous gaze made Hal hope the tough wouldn't avail himself of it.

Fortunately for Hal's turbulent emotions, a man didn't survive in Seven Dials by meekly conceding at the first setback. As Hal had expected, Smith snarled and jerked his head.

Four of the slouching inhabitants of the bar sprang up and approached them. Hal saw the flash of at least two blades before, with a roar of satisfied rage, he leapt to his feet, slammed Smith against the wall, then channelled all his strength and outrage into a swift right jab to Smith's kidney followed by a left uppercut to his jaw.

He released Smith, who slid unconscious to the floor, and turned towards the next attacker, sliding a blade of his own from beneath his sleeve. His blood pumping, ferocious satisfaction stretching his lips into a mirthless smile, he poised on the balls of his feet, daring the man to attack.

Meanwhile, the reinforcements Mason had recruited for him jumped from their positions all around the room to head off Smith's other three accomplices.

Men didn't survive Seven Dials by being stupid either. With his leader inert on the floor and the blade-wielding Hal grinning at him like a demon, the tough facing Hal backed away, then broke and ran for the door. The other three, cut off from escape, slinked back to their chairs.

Hal strode to the bar and dropped several coins on it. 'When Smith wakes up, tend him,' he told the innkeeper. 'Goes to Green Street again, finish him. Tell him that.'

Rapidly bobbing his head, the man gathered up the money. 'Certainly, yer honour. I'll surely tell him.'

'Right pretty work,' the barmaid murmured, brushing her full breasts against his sleeve. 'If'n you ever git back here, remember me.'

Though his hand hurt and his knuckles were bleeding, Hal made her an elaborate bow. 'Pleasure, ma'am.'

Feeling much more cheerful than when he'd entered, Hal strode out of the tavern, his confederates filing out after him. 'Appreciate help,' he told Mason's assistants, who nodded before melting away down the alley.

Hal crossed the dim street to the corner where Mason awaited him, passing him a purse of coins under the guise of shaking his hand. 'All my thanks.'

Surreptitiously pocketing it, Mason said, 'I trust Mr Smith learned his lesson?'

'Studying it now,' Hal replied.

'No need to call a constable, I suppose?'

'Come here if needed one?' Hal asked.

Mason chuckled. 'Probably not. Nor should we linger with night starting to fall.'

Nodding at that truth, Hal followed the Bow Street man through the warren of alleyways until they reached an area where the buildings looked like they might survive the next windstorm and the pedestrians no longer passed by with a huddled, furtive air.

'Hopefully you've discouraged the enforcer, but I'm afraid nothing can be done to inhibit the moneylender. Blackmen is still entitled to the return of his principal and could bring a motion against Mrs Lowery.'

'Won't come to that,' Hal assured him. 'Worked out repayment. Thanks for help.'

'Always a pleasure to contribute to the education of a gentlemen like Mr Smith,' Mason said before heading off.

His hand throbbed and Jeffers would likely go into apoplexy when he saw the bloodstained coat, but otherwise Hal felt clearheaded and confident. Normally he avoided violence; as a small boy set upon by bullies when he first came to school, he had a sharp dislike for larger, stronger individuals who attacked the smaller and weaker.

'Twas Nicky who'd come to his defence all those years ago, Hal recalled, thereby earning Hal's immediate gratitude and respect. 'Twas Nicky as well who'd taught Hal the rudiments of self-defence and looked after him until Hal found his feet, earning him his eternal devotion and friendship.

Conscious of his potential to injure opponents who lacked his size and strength, when he grew older Hal abandoned pugilism for the intricacies of the foil, where the need for quickness and dexterity neutralised his advantages of height and reach. Only once before had he deliberately set out to pound a man unconscious—when Nicky's Sarah had been pursued by a baronet of vicious reputation who'd tried to hurt her.

In that case, as in this, the punishment he'd allotted had been well deserved, though today he'd needed Mason's kind assistance. Without reinforcements at his back, the confrontation at the tavern might have ended differently.

It helped to have friends in low places, he thought with a grin. If Mama considered his colleagues on the Stock Exchange vulgar, she would have fainted dead away had she seen his confederates this afternoon.

Hal had almost reached the respectable part of Covent Garden when the sound of jeering caught his ear. Down an alleyway, he spied several boys laughing as they pelted rocks toward something hidden behind a stack of rubbish.

Immediately transported back twenty years, Hal turned and charged down the alleyway at them, roaring. Within seconds the startled boys scattered.

Hal halted by the pile of rubbish, but instead of the skinny child he expected to find, a thin, mangy dog cowered under the shreds of some old playbills. Just a puppy, he quickly ascertained, mayhap the runt of some litter.

An intelligent animal, it appeared, for though Hal was almost three times the size of its erstwhile attackers, sensing a rescuer, the little dog immediately limped over to him. Whining and wagging its skimpy brush of a tail, the dog tried to wind itself around his ankles.

'Down!' Hal commanded before the animal could jump up and plant its filthy paws on his knee. Recognising the voice of authority, the mutt flattened himself on to the alleyway beside Hal, his tail still wagging.

With a sigh of exasperation, Hal looked down at the muddy prints already marring the shine of his boots. Probably Jeffers would find claw marks gouged in the leather as well. As he gazed down at his footgear, dark canine eyes gazed back up at him hopefully.

What did the silly dog expect him to do? Hal wondered. Though he'd scared off the animal's attackers, there would be nothing to prevent them from tormenting the animal again later.

In the fading light he could see several cuts on the dog's ears and face where the rocks had nicked him.

If the animal escaped these assailants, he'd likely only encounter others. Or starve.

Hell, Hal thought, sighing again. His coat was probably ruined already and as for his breeches, he could always fall back on the Wellington pantaloons Mama had sent him. Kneeling down, Hal picked up the little dog and cradled him against his coat. Yipping excitedly, the animal tried to crawl up and lick his chin.

'Still!' Hal commanded, holding the dog motionless. With a canine sigh, the dog settled against his chest, that pathetic tail still wagging against Hal's arm.

What would he do with this little dog? Hal wondered. Even washed up and with a bit more meat on his bones, the animal would never win any prizes for beauty. He supposed he could have the dog sent down to his country estate.

But as he reached the hackney stand, another thought occurred and he smiled. Homely or not, once the animal had been fed and groomed, Hal wagered he knew someone who would be thrilled to welcome the little dog as his new best friend.

Chapter Six

Late the next morning in her studio, with a welcome feeling of accomplishment, Elizabeth put down her brushes and took off her apron. Glancing in the little mirror over her workbench as she tidied her hair, she smiled at her reflection, more cheerful than she'd felt since the awful evening of Everitt's demise.

Perhaps it was knowing she need not fear a return call by Mr Smith or the reassurance of having turned her financial matters over to hands much more competent than her own, but, whatever the reason, Mr Waterman's visit had energised her. She'd spent a delightful evening with David, reading to him, playing with his soldiers, even teasing him into laughter. As she tucked him in that night, they'd hugged each other tightly and, despite shedding a few tears, for the first time since Everitt's death she'd felt with deep certainty that somehow they were going to be all right.

Then, when she'd checked on Miss Lowery this morning, she'd found the older woman sitting in a chair. After a month during which her husband's cousin had scarcely left her bed, her continuing weakness and lethargy such a contrast to her normal cheerful energy that Elizabeth had begun to fear she might lose dear Amelia, too, she'd been thankful almost to tears at that lady's improvement. They'd shared a cup of chocolate, after which she'd had to command Miss Lowery most insistently to remain in her room and make no attempt to resume her household duties until the doctor certified she was fully recovered.

And now she'd just finished the most productive painting session she'd had in months. Inspired by the loveliness of the sunlight playing on and through the mist—or more often, London's frequent fog and smoke—over the London rooftops, she'd begun a study of a city scene of the adjacent houses. For the first time, she felt she'd captured the grey mist's airy, swirling character.

Perhaps, after nuncheon, she might even take David for a walk to the park.

She was about to exit when a knock sounded and Sands bowed himself in. 'Sir Gregory Holburn to see you, ma'am. Shall I bring some refreshment to the south parlour?'

'Sir Gregory?' she echoed, surprised. 'Y-yes, I suppose. Tell him I shall join him in a few minutes.'

Although Everitt and the baronet had been close friends, she hadn't expected him to call again so soon, she thought, frowning. Recalling Mr Smith's disturbing visit and what she'd learned yesterday about Mr Scarbridge's incompetence, apprehension tightened in her gut. Had Sir Gregory come to warn her of some new disaster?

Anxiety quickening her steps, she decided to dispense with changing her old, worn painting gown for a more suitable dress and went instead directly to the south parlour.

Sir Gregory rose as she entered and came over to kiss her hand. 'Dear Lizbet, how lovely you look.'

Despite her anxiety, Elizabeth had to stifle a smile, for the pained expression on the meticulous Sir Gregory's face as he cast a glance at her frayed and rather shapeless gown was anything but admiring. She probably should have changed her dress.

Meanwhile the baronet escorted her to the sofa and seated

himself beside her. 'I didn't mean to inconvenience you, but my schedule today being so full, I took the one chance I had to call. I heard some news at my club last night that, I must admit, rather distressed me.'

Elizabeth's amusement evaporated in an instant. 'What news?' she asked, her anxiety reviving.

'Perhaps 'tis only a hum, for I cannot picture you and that great oaf in the same room, but I heard that Hal Waterman had called, offering to look into Everitt's financial affairs.'

'Yes. Have you heard there were irregularities?'

'In Waterman calling upon you? 'Tis not precisely irregular, I suppose, but—'

'No, no,' she cut him off impatiently. 'Irregularities in Everitt's finances. I've only just learned that Mr Scarbridge, his solicitor, is a complete incompetent. Heaven knows, I know nothing about finance!'

'Well, I should hope not!' Sir Gregory exclaimed. 'You, dear lady, have no need to trouble your pretty head over complicated matters that were best left to your husband's discretion.' He cast a mildly reproachful look at her dress. 'All the financial expertise you require is knowing which dressmakers create the gowns that best display your beauty.'

'Indeed,' Elizabeth said flatly. Somehow that caveat seemed to have escaped the notice of the tough who'd come to threaten her. Apparently Sir Gregory was more pained by her choice of raiment than by the possibility that the estate's finances might be in total disarray.

Before she could decide whether or not to tell the baronet about Mr Smith's alarming visit, Sir Gregory said, 'I must confess to be feeling somewhat…slighted. I would have hoped that if you felt the need for someone to look into your finances, as Everitt's closest friend, you would have asked me.'

'Did you know Mr Scarbridge was incompetent?'

'Of course.'

'Then why did you not warn me? How am I to protect myself and my son when I have no idea what…obligations are currently being pressed against Everitt's estate?'

Sir Gregory patted her hand. '*You* protect yourself and your child? My dear, you needn't even consider attempting something so alarming! I know how cast down you've been by Everitt's demise, but remember, you've not been left entirely alone and friendless. I fully intended to visit Mr Scarbridge and see what needed to be done once I completed the my own estate business. Everitt was a gentleman, after all. If there are obligations against his estate, the creditors can wait until I have time to deal with them.'

At least one of them wasn't prepared to wait, Elizabeth thought. And though she frankly avowed that she knew nothing about wills or finances, she wasn't sure she appreciated Sir Gregory's cavalier dismissal of her ability to protect her son.

Still, it was vastly comforting to know that in addition to Mr Waterman's competent assistance, she might count upon Sir Gregory as well.

Though she still must consider it fortuitous that his friendship with Nicky had propelled Mr Waterman to come forward, for his sense of urgency in setting the estate to rights seemed to exceed Sir Gregory's. Indeed, he must have begun asking questions immediately if the baronet had already heard of his investigations.

'With you at present so preoccupied, I should rather think you would find it very convenient that Mr Waterman offered to attend to my small affairs. You will not need to put yourself out after all, Sir Gregory.'

'You misunderstand, dear lady! Any service I can render you would be a pleasure!' he protested. 'Besides, though I've heard Waterman is quite competent, I'm not sure of the…propriety of him investigating your husband's finances. There are no blood ties between you, after all, and, as a new widow, you must be careful of appearances.'

Since no blood ties existed between herself and Sir Gregory, his meddling in her affairs wouldn't be any more proper. But though she'd certainly not intended to do so, apparently she'd wounded his feelings, so she refrained from pointing this out.

Instead, she replied, 'It's true that we are not blood kin. But you may recall that my sister Sarah is married to Mr Waterman's best friend, Lord Englemere, who recently took his family and all my siblings on a Grand Tour of the Continent. Before he departed, he asked Mr Waterman to assist me with any difficulties that might arise during my family's absence.' Which was not precisely true, but close enough that it should soothe Sir Gregory's injured sensibilities and his concern over propriety.

'Oh. Well, no, I hadn't been aware of the connection. That would render his calling upon you entirely proper, I suppose.' Somehow Sir Gregory didn't look as relieved by the knowledge as she might have expected.

'Nicky—Lord Englemere—has also told me on several occasions that Mr Waterman is most astute in matters of finance. Englemere and my sister hold Mr Waterman in the very highest regard, so you may rest easy knowing that everything dealing with the will and the estate will be handled by someone of absolute skill and integrity.'

'As I already said, I have no reason to question either Waterman's skill or integrity. However…well, how can I put this delicately? He isn't the best *ton*. 'Tis said he often keeps quite common company and involves himself personally in financial dealings that a gentleman ought to leave to the bourgeois tradesmen bred to handle them. I just hope that association with him won't taint you with the odour of the shop.'

Had she any desire to figure upon the *ton*'s stage, Elizabeth supposed such a warning might give her pause. But since she'd never had the least interest in society, Sir Gregory's caution left her unmoved…except once again to amusement. The baronet's countenance was so grave, as if Mr. Waterman's fashionable failings were of genuine importance, that she had all she could do not to smile.

'I shall be on my guard,' she replied, working to keep the mirth from her expression.

'In addition, competent though he may be, I fear you will hardly be able to comprehend any information Waterman tries to convey. It amazes me that anyone manages to understand his cryptic utterances. Even his mother, dear lady, confesses she finds it difficult to grasp his meaning. Indeed, 'tis almost beyond believing that he could be the son of the incomparable Letitia.'

Elizabeth's momentary humour faded. Apparently Sir Gregory did not much like Mr Waterman. Regardless of the reasons for his disapprobation, Elizabeth was becoming rather annoyed by his subtle disparagement of a man who was not only highly esteemed by her sister's family, but whom she herself found to be sympathetic, helpful—and quite attractive.

'How disappointing for Mrs Waterman,' she said, an edge to her voice. She'd never met Mr Waterman's mother, but she could not think very highly of a lady, incomparable or not, who would publicly disparage her son. 'Though I find her difficulty somewhat surprising. I myself had no trouble whatsoever in understanding Mr Waterman.'

'Truly?' Sir Gregory blinked, clearly taken aback. 'Well. You always were rather observant for a female. But,' he gestured to the mantel clock, 'my time remaining is short, so let us proceed to a more pleasant matter! I understand there was a sad accident a few days ago. As distressed as the lad already is at losing his papa, I thought he might appreciate this.'

Sir Gregory picked up a wrapped parcel from behind the sofa

and handed it to Elizabeth. 'Go ahead, open it. If it meets your approval, you can give it to the boy.'

Inside the wrapped package, Elizabeth found a new toy soldier, all gleaming paint and shiny brass. 'How considerate of you, Sir Gregory!' Elizabeth exclaimed. The gesture was even more impressive when one considered that the baronet was not a man used to dealing with children.

Though she still could not approve his unkind words about Mr Waterman, Sir Gregory could have chosen no better way to redeem himself in her eyes than by this kindness to her child. 'How can I thank you?'

'I take it you do approve, then? To bring you pleasure, ma'am, is all the thanks I desire.'

The fervour of his gaze made her a little uncomfortable. 'How did you know about David's broken soldier?' she asked, looking down at the soldier.

'Oh, I have my little sources,' Sir Gregory said with a chuckle. 'I sent my valet out to find a replacement. I'm pleased he chose something suitable.'

Though she shouldn't have expected a busy man like Sir Gregory to take the time to visit a toy seller personally, her enthusiasm dimmed a trifle. 'Yes, he did very well.'

'Shall we summon the boy and let him have his treat?'

'If you can spare the time, then, yes, I would be happy to.' At Sir Gregory's nod, Elizabeth rang the bell pull to summon Sands and have him fetch David from the schoolroom.

While they waited, Elizabeth prompted Sir Gregory to talk about his visit to his estate. A few minutes later, Sands ushered in her son.

Though his widened eyes showed his surprise at finding his mother had a visitor, David made Sir Gregory a proper bow. 'Good day, sir,' he said politely. 'Sands said you wished me to see me, Mama?'

Elizabeth's heart swelled with motherly pride at David's impeccable behaviour before a man she knew he disliked. Indeed, it filled her with gladness just to look at him, so grave and correct as he addressed them both.

Dropping a brief kiss on the top of his head, Elizabeth said, 'Yes, my dear. Sir Gregory has been kind enough to bring you something, and I thought you ought to have the opportunity to thank him personally.' She handed him the toy soldier.

Solemnly David regarded the toy. With a smile Elizabeth could tell was forced, he bowed again to the baronet. 'Thank you, Sir Gregory.'

'You're quite welcome, my good man,' Sir Gregory said in the over-hearty manner of adults who aren't accustomed to conversing with children. 'Capital little soldier, eh? No need to fix the old one now. Toss him in the dustbin!'

'Oh, no, sir!' David's eyes opened wide with alarm. 'I could never do that. Papa gave him to me. And he's a general, not just a soldier. General Blücher.'

'Ah, I see. Sentimental value. But one soldier's as good as another, eh? Except on a battlefield, perhaps.' Sir Gregory chuckled at his own joke.

David did not look amused. 'They are not alike,' he replied, frowning. 'General Blücher was the head of all the Prussian soldiers. Napoleon might have won Waterloo, Papa said, if General Blücher hadn't come with his men. This soldier—' he held up the baronet's gift '—is a Royal Irish Dragoon guardsman. They didn't fight at Waterloo.'

'Perhaps,' Sir Gregory said, clearly beginning to lose patience. 'But it's only play, son. Would you rather have a working soldier or a broken general?'

David set his chin. 'I want *Papa's* general. Besides, Mr Waterman is going to fix him. I don't need yours!'

Tears in his eyes, the boy tossed the soldier to the floor and ran out of the room.

Aghast, Elizabeth watched the door slam behind him. In many ways, David seemed so mature for his age, sometimes it was hard to remember he wasn't yet seven. Still a baby, really, and aching for the father he missed so keenly.

Embarrassed none the less, Elizabeth turned back to the scowling baronet, who was staring at the rejected toy. With a nervous smile, she went over and picked it up.

'I'm dreadfully sorry. I know when he's calmer, David will prize the gift. You must excuse him, he's still so overwrought—'

'Poor behaviour shouldn't be excused, Lizbet, regardless of the circumstances,' Sir Gregory said blightingly. 'You do the child no favour by indulging him just because he had the misfortune to lose his papa. Society will judge him on his comportment—which, I am sorry to report, in this instance was sadly lacking. But now I must go. Do be on your guard about Mr Waterman. I shall call and check on you later. Madam.' After giving her a stiff bow, Sir Gregory walked out.

Elizabeth exhaled a trembling breath. She understood only too well how the mere thought of discarding a prized toy his father had given him, an object that represented many hours the two had spent together, Everitt spinning stories about Waterloo, David hanging on every word as they manoeuvred his soldiers in mock battle, would upset her son. It must seem to the boy almost like suggesting he toss away the memory of his father. Small wonder he'd taken Sir Gregory's well-meant gift so badly.

But it was a gift and it had been well meant. Sir Gregory was correct. Some time later she would have to reprimand David and bring him to realise that his behaviour had been unacceptable. Worse still, she was going to have to induce him to apologise.

How she'd bring that about, with David already so ill disposed towards Sir Gregory, she'd worry about later. With a sigh at having the day that had started out so promising turn suddenly sour, Elizabeth set off to soothe her son and coax him down for nuncheon.

Chapter Seven

Two mornings later, trying to quell the nervousness in his gut, Hal rang the bell at Mrs Lowery's Green Street town house. Truly, he'd rather face down a dozen Mr Smiths in some low dive in Seven Dials than meet one Elizabeth Lowery in her drawing room.

The butler who answered the door informed Hal that his mistress was presently working in her studio and ushered him to a salon to wait while he informed Mrs Lowery of his arrival. Hal's request that Master David be summoned from the schoolroom to see him in the interim was unusual enough to surprise a momentary raise of eyebrows from the butler before Sands bowed himself out.

A little shamefaced, Hal paced the parlour. David having mentioned that his mama always worked in her studio in the morning, he'd deliberately timed his visit for this hour. He'd wanted a respite after he arrived in the house to settle his nerves and a chance to visit the boy before he subjected himself once again to Elizabeth Lowery's unsettling presence.

When he was finally ushered into her office, he must be able to concentrate on getting out the words to accurately describe the state of Lowery's finances. He could not let himself be distracted by the rose scent that wafted from her or the mesmerising blue of her eyes that beckoned him to halt in mid-syllable and simply gaze into them. Or the perfection of her skin that made him burn to feel the silk of her face beneath his fingertips…

Catching the direction of his thoughts, he shook his head. He'd have to do better than this. He had but to recall her and his body began hardening, his mind losing its grip on his purpose in coming here. For a few panicked seconds, he considered bolting from the house.

But he couldn't do his duty by running away and delaying wouldn't make confronting her any easier. He'd never shied from dealing with difficult situations—witness the last seven years of handling his mother—and didn't intend to let Nicky down by starting now.

As he rallied himself, he heard the rapid patter of approaching footsteps. A moment later, David burst into the room, the broken soldier dangling from one hand.

The glowing look on the boy's face as he skidded to a halt just inside the threshold temporarily dispelled all Hal's misgivings. 'Oh, Mr Waterman!' David exclaimed. 'You came back!'

Once again, Hal was catapulted back to a time when he had been small, grieving and friendless. It was worth all the difficulties he would encounter being around the boy's mama to bring that look of pleasure and relief to the child's face.

''Course. Promised I would.'

The boy's excitement faded. 'I made Mama angry,' he confessed. 'About the general. I didn't mean to. But Papa's friend Sir Gregory wanted me to throw him away and take a soldier he brought me instead. It wasn't a general, just a soldier, not even a Waterloo soldier. I…I threw it on the floor.' The boy hung his head.

'Mama read you a scold?'

David nodded. 'She says I have to 'pologise to Sir Gregory. I did thank him for the soldier. But I don't want it. I don't want anything from him. I wish he would stay away.'

'Father's friend, you said?' Hal asked.

Looking suddenly apprehensive, David gazed up at Hal. 'Are you going to be angry with me, too?'

Hal shook his head. 'No. Ladies want you to be polite, though. Family friend. Trying to help.'

'That's what Mama said. But I don't like him. He never looks at me when he talks. He looks at Mama, and his eyes get all funny. 'Sides, you are going to help until Uncle Nicky comes back, aren't you? Mama said you would.'

'Promised, didn't I?'

'You'll be my friend, like Uncle Nicky?'

Hal could imagine only too well what it meant to the boy right now to have a man upon whom he could depend. Would that one had appeared in his life at such a juncture! He stuck out his hand. 'Friend.'

Solemnly the boy shook it. 'Best friend. Are you going to fix the general now?'

'Try to.'

'How? May I watch, please?'

Hal nodded as he withdrew a coil of wire and a pocketknife from his waistcoat. Accepting the toy the boy handed him, he motioned David to follow as he took the soldier over by the window to work in the grey morning light. Quickly he removed the broken wire that attached the toy arm, inserted and secured a new one.

'See if it moves correctly now,' Hal said.

Eagerly the boy jiggled the arm. 'It works!' he declared. 'Thank you! Papa would be proud of you!'

Hal chuckled even as something twisted in his stomach. Whatever his financial failings, Everitt Lowery had been a good father to his son, one who had obviously lavished on the boy both time and praise.

The image flashed into Hal's mind of a tall blond man, his features blurred by time, calling out encouragement as Hal brought his first pony to a trot. The impression vanished before he could bring it fully into focus.

'Let's go show Mama!' David said, holding the toy up with both hands. 'She won't be angry any more when she sees how you well you fixed him.'

At that moment, Sands reappeared at the door. 'Mrs Lowery will see you now, Mr Waterman.'

'See?' David said. 'We can go in.'

Trying to gird himself against the inevitable shock of his response to Elizabeth Lowery, Hal took the hand the boy offered and walked with him down the hall.

After the butler announced him, Hal followed David into the studio, the child fairly dancing with excitement as he ran to his mother. 'See, Mama, Mr Waterman came back! And look, he just fixed the general for me!'

Mrs Lowery turned and curtsied to Hal's bow. Once again the sheer loveliness of her flowed over him in a wave of sensation he felt in every nerve.

It was easier this time, he tried to tell himself. At least he expected the response, while David's eager chatter gave him a few moments to bind up his ravelling wits.

'How kind of Mr Waterman,' Elizabeth said as she inspected the toy. 'You thanked him properly, I trust.'

'Oh, yes, Mama. I'm ever so grateful. He fixed him almost as good as Papa. And he says he will be my friend until Uncle Nicky comes back.'

'That is handsome indeed,' his mother said, flashing Hal a smile of gratitude. 'He is doing both of us a great service, so you must promise not to tax him too much.'

David was silent for a moment. 'Does that mean I can't ask him to play soldiers with me?'

'He will probably be too busy, son. He has a house and many duties of his own, besides the ones he has undertaken for us.

Besides, I am not certain I should allow you to play with the general right now. Remember what we talked about.'

David grimaced. 'I was very rude to Sir Gregory and I cannot play with soldiers again until I 'pologise to him. Not even the general?' he asked with pleading eyes.

'I think you must leave the general with me,' she replied. With a heavy sigh, David gave her the soldier.

'Thank you, son. Now, Mr Waterman doubtless has matters to discuss, so back to the schoolroom with you. And no more sneaking away from Nurse!'

'But I didn't—' the boy protested.

'No arguments, if you please,' his mother cut him off. 'Make your bow and leave like a proper young gentleman.'

Though Hal knew he probably should stay out of any dispute between mother and son, fairness compelled him to attempt to intervene. By the time he assembled the words, David had already dipped him a bow and headed to the door.

The sad expression on the boy's face as he looked over his shoulder one last time at the toy now reposing on his mother's workbench fired an anger that propelled Hal into speech. 'Didn't sneak down!' he burst out as the door shut behind David. 'Asked Sands to fetch him. So I could repair toy.'

Clearly surprised, Elizabeth fixed that vivid blue-eyed gaze on him again. 'You…sent for David?'

Hal struggled to focus on his ire and keep his words moving forward. 'Yes. Shouldn't take away favourite toy.'

'How very kind of you! I will apologise to David for misjudging him. But I didn't keep the general for that reason. You may not know, but he—'

'Rude to Sir Gregory,' Hal interrupted. 'Told me. Impolite, but only child. Probably be rude myself, try to take away something of my father's.'

'Believe me, I understand the reason for his attachment to the toy! Still, though I cannot thank you enough for repairing it, it does not seem proper that I reward his bad behaviour by allowing him to play with the general until he has made amends.'

Made amends for a social transgression—when all the boy was struggling to do was keep the memory of his father from fading into the featureless blur that was all Hal had left of his own.

Sudden strong emotion overtaking him, Hal felt the words rise in his throat, almost tumbling out in their urgency. 'Keep others, then, but let him have general. He's a boy, not pattern-card to sit in Mama's drawing room. Let him be boy! Needs tutor, dog, pony. Needs to go outside, not be banished upstairs. Needs mother to leave her room—' Hal's voice rose as gestured around the studio '—and pay attention to him!'

Hal halted, perspiring and red-faced after having delivered perhaps the longest speech of his life. In the sudden silence, Elizabeth Lowery stared at him, her lips open in an *O* of surprise.

How had he let himself get so carried away? Hal wondered, now aghast. He'd intended only to make sure Elizabeth Lowery didn't, in her grief, neglect her son. He shouldn't have let his simmering resentment over his own mother's treatment propel him into lecturing her about David's upbringing, a subject about which he really knew very little.

In any event, he should never have spoken thus to a lady. After that clumsily delivered tirade, she'd probably think him as blockish as his mother did and have Sands eject him from the house. Miserably he waited for her to skewer him for his effrontery and dismiss him.

It took Elizabeth a moment to recover from the shock of Mr Waterman's unexpected verbal attack. How dare he! No one had ever raised his voice to her like that! But even as she began to formulate a frigidly polite response, she saw Mr Waterman mop his brow, his expression of distress suggesting he'd been as surprised by his outburst as she was. Before she spoke, he made her a deep bow.

'So sorry! Shouldn't have ripped up at you,' he said, looking almost as shame-faced as David had after she'd scolded him for his rudeness to Sir Gregory. 'Not my place. Lost my father about the same age, though. Remember what it's like. Leave now, if you prefer.'

As taken aback as she'd been, there could be no mistaking Mr Waterman's genuine regard for her son. He'd sought him out, listened attentively to his concerns, even gone out of his way to fix the toy David prized so dearly. Struggling as she was to try to help her son deal with the sudden disappearance from his life of the father who'd been his boon companion, how she could she resent or reprove him for speaking out on David's behalf?

'On the contrary, please stay. I admit your…rather forcefully expressed opinion gave me pause for a moment, but I see in it a kindness towards David that I very much appreciate. I grew up surrounded by sisters, my only brother scarcely much older than David when I married, so I know very little about a boy's needs. I should be very grateful for your advice.'

For a moment Mr Waterman simply stared at her. 'Not angry?'

She shook her head. 'No, I'm not angry. Only deeply touched by the attention you've given David.'

'Want…my advice?'

His tone sounded absurdly questioning for a man as competent and commanding as Mr Waterman. Then she recalled Sir Gregory's—and apparently his mother's—disparaging descriptions. Perhaps, being so halting of speech, he didn't often have his opinion solicited.

'Yes, though I hesitate to impose upon you more than I already have. But you seem to understand David so well already, perceiving how much he valued the general and then being clever enough to repair him. You mentioned that he ought to have a tutor and a pony. He seems so young! Are you sure he is ready for that?'

Waterman nodded. 'Boys his age sent to Eton. Rode first pony when I was five. Look into one for you?'

'That wouldn't be too much trouble?' When Mr Waterman shook his head, she continued, 'Then, yes, please do. Although…are you certain I can afford it? What have you discovered about the estate?'

The tentativeness seemed to fall from him in an instant. 'Called on Scarbridge. As expected, had no files. Or none that remembered. Sure husband had will. Part of settlements when married, Nicky would have made sure. Probably among papers in office. Allow me to look?'

'Of course. What of Mr Smith and the debts?'

'Blackmen is moneylender. Obtained total of what owed. Substantial. Also checked with bank. Lowery Manor let to tenants. Mortgage on unentailed part.'

Fear coiled in Elizabeth's throat. 'That Smith fellow said Mr Blackmen wanted the loan repaid immediately. Is there enough in Everitt's account at the bank to do so? Must the mortgage be repaid as well? Oh, I wish I knew more about what to do!'

'Don't worry!' Mr Waterman stepped towards her, as if to take her hand reassuringly, then halted.

Her nightmares over landing in Newgate revived by his report so far, Elizabeth wished he hadn't stopped. Indeed, with an urgency that was more than just a need for comfort, she wanted to throw herself against his chest, rest her head on his wide shoulder, let him bind her with arms that looked strong and competent against the tall, hard length of his body. A heated urgency coiled deep within her.

'Mustn't worry,' he repeated, recalling her attention. 'Took care of Smith. Will take care of Blackmen too.'

Curiosity momentarily derailed her other concerns. If he

wished to, she imagined the massive Mr Waterman could project an ominous presence his brevity of speech would only reinforce. She hoped the despicable Mr Smith had been thoroughly intimidated!

'Manoeuvre rental funds, current balance in accounts,' he was continuing. 'Need to find ledgers in office. But can continue to live in manner befitting gentlewoman. One not overfond of shops.'

It took her a moment to notice the slight quirk of his lip, the sudden sparkle in the clear grey eyes in a face whose expression remained sombre. He'd made a joke! she realised incredulously.

She burst out laughing. Mr Waterman looked startled before a slow grin tugged at his lips.

'I think I can promise you that,' she assured him. 'Feel free to work in Everitt's library whenever you wish. If there is anything else I can do to assist you, please don't hesitate to ask.'

'Work there now, if you permit. Check on pony later. Tutor too?'

'Are you sure it wouldn't be too much trouble? I must admit, I haven't any idea where to begin.'

'Remember when Nicky found tutor for his son. And pony. Check his contacts.' Mr Waterman shrugged. 'Not too bright, but know about boys.'

'Not bright?' she echoed. 'On the contrary, I think you are enormously clever—and very intuitive. You accurately assessed David's needs after just one meeting! And you seem to have made good progress already in sorting out the estate, even without the ledgers I hope you will find in my husband's office.'

His grey eyes searched hers for a moment, as if trying to ascertain whether or not she was mocking him. Apparently convinced by the sincerity of her expression, he looked quickly away, the tips of his ears pinking. 'Kind of you,' he mumbled.

From his awkwardness at receiving her praise, she surmised he was not accustomed to compliments. She recalled once again Sir Gregory's scornful assessment of him, a belittling judgement apparently shared by his own mother. Had his slowness of speech led that lady to assume he was slow of intellect also?

The kernel of outrage she'd felt upon first hearing of his mother's disdain swelled until she found herself blurting, 'Have you always spoken with such brevity?'

Bright colour suffused Mr Waterman's face. Mentally kicking herself for embarrassing him, she said, 'Pray disregard the question! 'Twas both impolite and prying.'

He waved away her apology. 'Sorry. Know I speak like block. Was worse, though. Used to stutter. Nicky helped. Taught me to concentrate on main thought.' He gave her an apologetic look. 'Still mostly incomprehensible.'

'Not in the least!' she countered. 'I have no difficulty at all understanding you.' Recalling the effusive compliments showered upon her by the friends Everitt had sometimes brought home to dinner, she chuckled. 'Indeed, in a society where many chatter on to great length about nothing, 'tis refreshing to encounter a gentleman who expresses only what is most important.'

Once again his eyes searched hers, catching her gaze and holding it while he assessed the honesty of her statement. 'Thank you,' he said quietly.

Something trembled in the air between them, something almost palpable that sent a little shock through her, made her breath hitch and her pulse accelerate.

My! He certainly had an odd effect upon her, Elizabeth thought, hastily dropping her gaze. Whatever might cause that?

Though he projected an aura of mastery when dealing with finances, in other matters he seemed to completely lack that overconfident masculine arrogance so many men displayed around females. Perhaps it was the unusual combination of absolute competence and disarming humility that struck her so.

Nor, widow or no, was she immune to the masculine appeal

of that impressively tall, well-made physique, she acknowledged, feeling another little quiver.

'You are most welcome,' she murmured, still unsettled.

'Should get to work. Have Sands show me library now?'

'Of course. I've delayed you far too long.' She reached over to tug the bell pull. 'Ask Sands for anything you might require. And thank you again. I'll never be able to adequately express my gratitude for all you are doing for David and me.'

He bowed deeply. 'Pleasure.'

Sands knocked at the door so quickly, Elizabeth suspected he must have been lurking outside. After instructing the butler to conduct Mr Waterman to the library, she watched him walk out.

Perhaps she missed the company of a quietly attentive gentleman more than she realised, for she regretted having to send Mr Waterman off. Despite her slight discomfort over the disconcerting way he affected her, everything else she'd discovered about him excited either her admiration or curiosity. The little glimpses his curt speeches had given her into his character left her wanting more.

So he'd lost his father as a young boy. No wonder he felt such a deep sympathy for David. She was glad she would have the benefit of his advice, since growing up in similar circumstances ought to make him an excellent judge of how best to compensate David for the fatherly care of which fate had suddenly deprived him.

How sad, though, that Mr Waterman's mother had obviously not filled the gap for him. She tried to imagine David lost in grief, a severe stutter preventing him from being able to easily communicate his needs and feelings, watched over by someone who looked upon his affliction with distaste and disdain. Her mother's heart twisted.

She recalled how he'd blushed at her praise. She smiled. It was bad of her, but she'd quite enjoyed making him blush. It pleased her to know she could excite a strong reaction from him. And it seemed to her about time that he received the compliments he deserved for his kindness and his unselfish assistance.

Her smile faded. She might have a few things to say, mama to mama, should she ever encounter the incomparable Letitia.

Had Mrs Waterman been so distraught over the loss of her husband that she'd shut out her little boy all those years ago? It seemed she must have, to have elicited so strong a reaction from Mr Waterman today. Did he suspect she would become equally neglectful of David? Was that why he'd railed at her?

She'd just have to prove to Mr Waterman that she recognised *her* son's needs and was determined, in spite of her inadequacies and her own distress, to meet them.

She smiled wryly to herself. She wasn't sure why having Mr Waterman's approval should matter to her, but it did. She was glad that the necessity to go through the papers in Everitt's library would require him to call here for the next few days. With an anticipation that was beginning to equal her son's, she looked forward to becoming better acquainted with Mr Hal Waterman.

Chapter Eight

As he laid ledgers in orderly stacks on Everitt Lowery's desk a short time later, Hal found himself smiling. He, tongue-tied, blundering Hal Waterman, had made the incomparable Elizabeth Lowery laugh. Despite his cryptic wording, she'd understood his little joke—and found it funny.

Who could have anticipated such a miracle?

She'd surprised him in other ways as well. Having gritted his teeth, expecting to have his character and behaviour shredded for his presumption in criticising her, he'd been astounded that, instead, she'd thanked him.

He could only imagine how, with her razor-sharp wit, Mama would have left him bleeding on the floor.

But then, he was discovering that, despite her astounding beauty, Elizabeth Lowery was not very much like his mama after all. She cared little about dress, seemed completely uninvolved in society and, like her sister Sarah, she was kind. And though she'd claimed to be ignorant of how best to help her son, she was without question deeply committed to working out how to do so.

She'd even called him clever. Him, clever! Of course, Nicky and Ned often told him so, but that was concerning such masculine affairs as hunting, fencing or horsemanship. Without being arrogant, he knew he was excellent with a foil, a dead shot with any weapon, a tireless rider and skilled in all the attributes men considered important. 'Twas just in the polite society of ladies that he felt clumsy and backward.

No female had ever even hinted she found him intelligent. Probably intimidated by his size or put off by his monosyllabic speech, behind their fans and polite words they regarded him with expressions that said they thought him a dolt or a dullard. Like Mama did.

The mantel clock chimed, reminding him he had work to do here before going on to a meeting with several brokers in the City. He needed to focus on the task at hand, not linger here daydreaming of earning another smile from Elizabeth Lowery.

The canal project that had occupied him in the north was to open a new phase and he intended to buy in from the beginning. Transportation was the key to the further development of the British economy, a means to deliver raw materials to the mills that could turn them into finished goods and bring the products of England's fertile fields and small workshops into the cities, benefiting both the country folk and the burgeoning urban population.

Horse-drawn transport was the way of the past. Rather than refuse to acknowledge that and try to hang on to practices that must change, there was both economic benefit and profit to be made in investing in the future.

He paused, ledger in hand as the idea suddenly struck him. Even without as yet possessing all the papers he needed to get a complete view of the Lowerys' financial condition, he knew he must persuade Mrs Lowery to sell some of her husband's excellent antiquities collection. The proceeds of that sale would pay off the debts Lowery had accumulated and supplement the widow's income until the estate's crops came to market.

He'd intended to use the modest fees from the rental of

Lowery Manor to cover the repairs and improvements to that property; since apparently Lowery hadn't inspected his estate in some time, there would inevitably be matters that needed attending to. Hal tried not to think unkindly of a man who'd not only borrowed beyond his means, but had neglected to properly oversee the assets he possessed.

But if enough remained after the estate's needs were met to fund an investment in the canal project, over the next few years Mrs Lowery might see large returns. Based on the performance of the shares he'd bought in the last project, such an investment might ensure that Elizabeth Lowery could live comfortably for the foreseeable future, whether or not she chose to remarry.

Young and beautiful as she was, she probably would wish to marry again, Hal thought. And, no, he must not let himself even consider that prospect.

She seemed to have genuinely loved her much older husband and would probably spend the full year society dictated in mourning him. If she then decided to remarry, Hal knew there would be a host of eager contenders to the hand of the beautiful Elizabeth.

Men who truly were gallant and witty and all those things ladies so prized. The only asset he possessed in feminine eyes, his wealth, didn't seem to hold much appeal for Elizabeth. He mustn't forget that kind and appreciative as she was of his assistance, Elizabeth Lowery would never look twice at a man like Hal Waterman.

He'd dreaded coming here today. He needed to cling to that sense of dread. Elizabeth the merely beautiful was dangerous enough to his peace of mind. He dared not imagine the damage that could be done to his well-ordered life by a lady who not only captivated his senses, but whose intelligence, kindness and thoughtfulness worked their way insidiously into his mind and heart.

And then there was David Lowery. He liked the boy and wanted to help him, but he shouldn't get too attached. Nicky would be back soon and would fill the gap in the boy's life that the loss of his father had created.

He needed to finish this work for the Lowerys and remove himself from their life…before he found himself craving to stay.

Whistling a cheerful tune as he returned after a successful session with the brokers, early that evening Hal trotted up the steps of his bachelor quarters on Upper Brook Street. He'd have some wine and change his garments before meeting at his club with Lord Montague and Lord Chelmsworth, two peers who, like Hal, were keenly interested in investing in the latest economic innovations. Hal was confident that after hearing details of the new project, both gentlemen would wish to buy shares.

With the last of the financing guaranteed, he could then travel north to consult with the engineers and get the project underway. His spirits lifted further at the idea of escaping London and returning to his element, negotiating the advances with the local banks, clambering in and out of earthworks with the engineers as they inspected the progress of the work, even taking a hand with a shovel himself from time to time, and, finally, the incomparable excitement of watching scaled drawings and his own vision slowly become reality.

He'd pledged a little more today to the broker than he'd originally calculated. If he could convince Elizabeth Lowery—or her trustees, for he still expected to turn up a will directing that Lowery's affairs be turned over to someone more competent than Eustace Scarbridge—he would sell the extra shares to the Lowery estate.

He'd be proud to report to Nicky upon his return that he'd not just straightened out the tangle in which Lowery had left his finances, he'd also made investments to allow the widow a sizeable income for the rest of her days.

He sighed. At least he'd leave Elizabeth Lowery something

pleasant to remember him by, once Nicky returned and Hal had no excuse to see her again.

As he entered his town house, the footman stationed at the doorway held out a note. 'From Mrs Waterman, sir,' the man said. 'She said it was urgent.'

Hal's cheerful mood took an immediate downturn. Whatever Letitia Waterman wanted was always urgent. Stifling a desire to curse, with thanks Hal took the note and continued up to his bedchamber.

'Twas an invitation—a summons, really—to dine at Berkeley Square. Checking the mantel clock, Hal thought he would have enough time to call on his mama—hopefully before her protégée arrived—present his excuses and still meet his friends for dinner.

This time he would not let her browbeat him into remaining. He must also, he recalled, somehow manage to weasel out of the obligation to escort her and Lady Tryphena Upcott to that damned ball.

His good mood now ruined—at least until he could escape his mother's clutches and leave for his club—Hal rang for Jeffers and poured himself a large glass of wine.

Less than an hour later, Hal paced the floor of his mother's elaborate drawing room. He should have expected it would be impossible to see his mother early, that she would still be completing her *toilette*. He only hoped Montague and Chelmsworth didn't consume all of their dinner before he finally arrived.

Every minute he lingered increased the chances that Lady Tryphena might arrive before he could take his leave. When Holmes finally announced his mother's entry, Hal was so relieved, he was actually glad to see her.

'Hal darling, you are early!' his mama said, giving him her hand to kiss. 'Lady Tryphena and Lord Kendall should be here shortly. I thought we could have a cosy dinner and perhaps go on to the theatre.'

'Sorry, Mama, can't,' Hal said, holding his mother's gaze steadily. 'Glass of wine, then leave. Might have managed if invited earlier,' he added.

It never failed to irritate him that his mama, who claimed to be so meticulous about social niceties, thought nothing of summoning him at the last minute. As if he could never be committed to something of more importance than whatever she wished him to do.

'Leave?' she repeated, frowning. 'Surely your evening plans can accommodate having dinner with your closest kin.'

'Prior business,' he informed her.

She made a moue of distaste. 'Can you not confine meeting with Cits and merchants to daylight hours? Evenings should be reserved for mingling with your peers.'

'Are peers, actually,' he replied. 'Chelmsworth and Montague. Dining at White's.'

Since both men held seats in the Lords, she couldn't find fault with their breeding or the fashionable *ton* location. But his mama wouldn't give up that easily. Hal waited to see what other objections she could manufacture.

'I suppose I must approve, for once, your choice of company,' Mrs Waterman allowed reluctantly. 'We'll have to forgo the theatre, then. Send a note to White's and tell them you'll join them later.'

Hal shook his head. 'Waiting dinner for me. Most impolite, send excuse at last minute.'

He had her there, Hal thought. Apparently conceding the point, she said, 'Oh, very well. It would not do to give offence to men of their prominence. Perhaps you can spare the time to have some sherry with your mother?'

Ignoring her sarcasm, Hal took the glass Holmes handed him.

He'd managed, with less difficulty than he'd anticipated, to avoid having his evening commandeered. Now he hoped his luck would hold and he could make his exit before Lady Tryphena arrived, sparing him the need to converse with her. That comment about her helping Mama to improve his speech had not yet lost its sting.

'But I am most disappointed,' his mother continued. 'I had counted on having you and Lady Tryphena become better acquainted before Lady Cowper's ball. Since you seem to have grown so exacting about your social obligations, 'tis fortunate I solicited your escort for that so early.'

So that was the reason behind the last-minute invitation. Euphoric as he was to have a valid excuse on this occasion, unfortunately he hadn't yet come up with anything as foolproof to escape the ball. His mother would hardly deem his preference for dining at his club and playing a few hands of piquet a sufficient excuse to refuse her invitation. Still, one way or another, he intended to wiggle out of it, so he might as well incur her censure immediately by beginning to lay the groundwork.

'Not sure. New investment pending. Have other consultations. Best not count on me.'

'Business consultations,' his mother said, dismissing those with a sniff. 'I forgive you for tonight, since Lords Chelmsworth and Montague are both men of impeccable birth. But if I understand you correctly—never an easy feat—you're saying that for the night of the ball, you haven't a prior engagement with anyone of equal stature.'

In the face of her direct probing, Hal tried to think of some reasonably truthful positive reply—and failed. 'No,' he admitted at last.

'Tradesmen and bankers can be put off to another day. So, shall we say seven?'

Only desperation could have tumbled such an idea into Hal's head. But anything was better than suffering through an evening in the company of Lady Tryphena the bring-him-up-to-snuff. 'Not gentlemen,' he said. 'Lady.'

His mother put down her glass and stared at him. 'You have a previous engagement with a…a *lady*? Someone of gentle birth? Then why do I not know of her? Who is she?'

'Nicky's sister-in-law, Elizabeth Lowery.' Seeing that dreaded gleam appear in his mother's eyes, Hal's discomfort intensified. 'Not what you think!' he added. 'Recently widowed. Nicky away, just helping out.'

The last thing he wanted was to bring his mama down upon Elizabeth. The idea of her descending with imperial condescension upon Green Street, subjecting Mrs Lowery to a pointed interrogation about her intentions towards Hal and assessing her value as a potential daughter-in-law, was almost as humiliating as envisioning Lady Tryphena attempting to correct his speech.

His mother stared into the distance, mentally running through her catalogue of the *ton*. 'Everitt Lowery's widow. Yes, I remember now seeing the announcement in the paper. I don't recall ever meeting his wife. She must not figure much in society.'

'Lives very secluded,' Hal hastened to confirm, watching hopefully as the interest in his mama's eye faded.

'Then rearrange your call for later. Being widowed and living in seclusion, it cannot matter much to her which evening you assist her.'

'Does,' Hal responded determinedly. 'Family event,' he continued, embroidering as he went. 'Wouldn't wish me to desert widow.'

Having on so many occasions compelled Hal's assistance by invoking her status as his poor widowed mother, even Letitia Waterman wasn't inventive enough to find a way to fault that laudable sentiment. It appeared his last-minute ploy might work after all.

His mother's frown deepened. Accustomed to getting her way

in all things, Letitia Waterman wasn't pleased to be outmanoeuvred, especially by her slowtop of a son.

Knowing he'd better escape before she devised a more effective counter-attack, Hal hopped up.

'Must go. Not keep Montague and Chelmsworth waiting. Pleasure, Mama.'

'Surely you can remain a little longer. Lady Tryphena should be here any moment and will be most distressed to miss you. And I cannot be happy about Englemere entangling you in family business he ought to be taking care of himself. 'Tis greatly presumptuous of him when I most especially wanted you to attend Lady Cowper's ball.'

Might his mother be a tad jealous of his devotion to his friend? Hal wondered. He'd never thought she cared a fig that he'd spent so many of his school holidays at Englemere Hall. If it had irritated her, 'twas probably just that she'd missed having him at her beck and call.

'Be other balls,' he replied, intending to hie himself north before he could be called upon to escort her to any. 'My regrets to Lady Tryphena and Kendall.' Bowing deeply, with a huge sense of relief, Hal headed for the door.

His departure came none too soon. As his hackney rounded the corner from his mother's house, he spied Lady Tryphena alighting from another carriage in front of it.

Thank heavens he had escaped her…both this evening and for the Cowpers' ball! Hal's sense of euphoria dimmed, however, when he recalled the stratagem he'd used to buy his freedom.

He'd claimed he was to escort Elizabeth Lowery to a family party. Although he was certain she wouldn't accept an invitation to go out—it being too soon after her husband's death and it being Hal who was asking—he was still going to have to make her an offer. He didn't mind playing fast and loose with the facts, but he couldn't reconcile it with his conscience to have avoided his mother's company by employing an outright lie.

Still, the embarrassment of stumbling through a sure-to-be-quickly-refused invitation to Elizabeth Lowery had to be less humiliating and uncomfortable than spending an evening with his mother and Lady Tryphena, Hal reasoned, none the less already dreading the awkwardness of having to tender one. Resolutely he turned his mind from that unpleasant prospect to the much more enjoyable thought of spending the evening with convivial men who shared his interests.

And trying, as he did so, to squelch an irrational flare of hope that Elizabeth Lowery might actually accept his invitation.

Chapter Nine

The next day at the same pre-noon hour as his previous visit, Hal arrived at Green Street, making a short stop at the mews behind the town house before ringing the front doorbell. This time, after informing Hal that his mistress was presently occupied in her studio, Sands seemed less surprised when Hal asked to visit with Master David while the boy's mother finished her morning's work.

Knowing that at some point he was going to have to deliver an invitation to Elizabeth Lowery, Hal's nerves were knotted even tighter than they'd been the previous day. Recognising that fact, he hoped to stay longer with David, both to distract himself and in anticipation of the pleasure his surprise would bring the boy.

David's mother would likely be less enthusiastic, but Hal believed her when she'd affirmed that she valued his opinion and wished to do what was best for her son. He was fairly confident that her concern for her son's happiness would overcome whatever misgivings the lady might harbour over the new addition to her household.

Once again his spirits rose as David fairly bounded into the room. 'Mr Waterman! Have you come to play soldiers? I don't have the army, but Mama gave me back the general. He's working wonderfully.'

'Glad to hear it. Must work in father's office. But other plans first.'

'Not now, then?' The boy's eager expression faded. 'Mama said you are very busy. Could you play later?'

'Work later. Come sit.'

Looking puzzled, the lad took a chair beside Hal and gazed up at him inquiringly.

'Growing into a man. Must prepare. Lowery Hall yours, learn to care for it. Begin formal studies.'

'Mama said I am to have a tutor. Will it be hard?'

'No, interesting. Make you wiser, stronger.'

The boy nodded solemnly. 'Mama says I must be strong, like Papa would want me to be.' His lips quivered. 'It's hard, though. I miss him so much.'

Feeling a pang of his own, Hal reached over to ruffle the boy's hair. 'Gets easier. Responsible, now father's gone. Help Mama. Take care of what's yours. Not expect Nurse or Mama to do it. Think you can?'

The boy puffed up his chest. 'I'm very 'sponsible. I'm strong, too. I can help Mama.'

'Start now, then. Ready?' Hal stood and motioned toward the door.

Looking mystified, the boy followed Hal from the room, down the hall and out the back stairs towards the mews.

'Are you going to show me your horse? He must be very big! I should love to have a pony. Aubrey got a brindled pony last year. He let me feed him a carrot when we visited Uncle Nicky at Christmas. I told Papa I was old enough to have a pony, too, but he said I'd have to wait. We just have the old carriage horse, 'cause Papa didn't like to ride and Mama is afraid of horses.

That's silly, don't you think? Horses are beautiful! When I'm grown, I shall have dozens!'

Smiling at the boy's chatter, which relieved him of the need to contribute anything to the conversation, Hal continued until they reached the small stable block which held, as David had told him, only a modest carriage and one ageing carriage horse.

And David's surprise.

'Have something for you. Must be very responsible, take care of him. Promise?'

Before the boy could reply, Hal led him inside the small stone structure. Upon spying his rescuer, the puppy dropped the piece of rope he'd been trying to tug out of the hand of a smiling groom and gambolled over to Hal, yipping joyously.

A few days of good feeding had added a bit of flesh to his bones and a bath had revealed fur of an indeterminate brown. With his perky ears almost healed of their cuts and his soulful dark eyes, the dog looked much more attractive than the night Hal had found him near Covent Garden.

'A puppy!' David exclaimed, bending down to stroke the little animal's back. 'Oh, thank you! I've always wanted a puppy. I shall take good care of him, I promise!'

'Your responsibility,' Hal cautioned. 'Feed him daily. Brush him, bathe him. Train him. Very important.'

'Down!' Hal commanded the dog, who was trying to jump up on his knees. The puppy dropped back to his haunches, the rapid brush of his tail stirring up the straw on the stable floor. 'Must be well behaved,' Hal continued. 'Otherwise, a nuisance.'

'Oh, yes, I want to train him! You'll teach me how?'

'Later,' Hal replied, smiling again at the boy's excitement. 'Get to know him first.'

'What is his name?'

'Your dog now. You name him.'

'What do you think? A name is very important, isn't it?'

'See size of paws? Going to be big. Needs big name.'

'How about "Max"? Do you think he would like that?'

Hal nodded. 'Good name.

'Max!' David called, catching the puppy, who'd been running in circles around his legs, nipping at his shoelaces. 'Your name is Max now,' he told the animal, tilting the dog's head so the puppy looked up at him. 'You shall be my dog and you will learn to be very obedient and I shall be proud of you.'

As if agreeing with that statement, the dog barked and licked David's chin. 'That tickles!' David cried, rubbing his chin and laughing. Sitting down on the stable door, he let the puppy crawl into his lap, barking and licking him.

His heart warmed by the boy's delight, Hal tossed the watching groom a gold coin. 'Help boy with dog.'

'Be proud to do it, sir,' the groom replied, catching the coin and slipping it inside his shirt in one smooth motion. 'A pure pleasure it is to hear the little master laughing again. Pup's a cute one, too.'

'My thanks.' Satisfied that the dog's care wouldn't be an imposition on the household, Hal turned and walked toward the house.

'Mr Waterman!'

Halting in mid-stride, Hal looked back. David, with the puppy nipping at his heels, ran up to him.

'Thank you, thank you so much! I just know Max is going to love it here.'

'Be good friend to you.'

'As good a friend as you are. And…do you think I could call you "Uncle Hal"? You are Uncle Nicky's good friend and so that makes you almost like an uncle, doesn't it? Aubrey calls you uncle and you're not really his uncle either.'

Something in Hal's chest twisted as he looked down at the eager young face gazing up at him. He loved spending time with Nicky's son Aubrey and Sarah's friend Clare's offspring as well, but all these children possessed both a mother and a father who cherished them. He had never felt quite so needed as he did at this moment, bathed in the glow of David's admiring gaze.

He held out his hand. 'Uncle Hal.'

Giving a whoop of glee, David shook it. 'Thank you, Uncle Hal. C'mon, Max, let's go play with your rope!'

Smiling, Hal watched the two run off. David was so hungry for masculine attention, so appreciative of small kindnesses. It might be harder than he had anticipated, Hal thought as he re-entered the house, to turn the care of the boy back over to Nicky.

By the time Hal had returned to the parlour, the pleasant aura generated by the interlude with David and the dog gave way to a return of dread. Since putting off unpleasantness never diminished it, he'd determined upon arriving here today that before going to the library, he would meet with Elizabeth, confess what he'd done, and deliver the damned invitation.

Hopefully, she would be as kind as she'd been the day he'd had the effrontery to criticise her, refuse him quickly and let him return to his work with a minimum of embarrassment. He had only a few more ledgers to inspect, if the ones in the library represented all that Lowery had kept, and once he'd finished his perusal of them, he should have a complete enough picture of the Lowerys' financial condition to be able to recommend to Elizabeth how she should proceed.

Calling to the footman on duty in the hall, he asked the man to inform his mistress that Hal requested to see her at her convenience.

She didn't keep him waiting long. Hal felt the change in the air, the subtle wafting of her rose scent, before he turned to see her enter the room, her glowing beauty making it seem as if light itself had entered the chamber.

She was so lovely, it made him ache, while the brilliance of the smile she turned on him made it agonisingly difficult to think. Fortunately, the rituals of greeting were so ingrained the words came automatically to his lips. After an exchange of courtesies, he took the chair she offered.

'Are you making good progress through the ledgers? Is there anything else I can do to help?'

'Hope to finish today. Suggestion to think about, though.'

'And that is?'

'First, must sell some of husband's collection. Regrettable, but necessary. Review it, decide what can part with.'

She nodded. 'I had expected that. Indeed, I've already prepared a list of those pieces which I think might be easiest to sell. And if that was "first", then I expect there must be a "second". I hope you didn't save the bad news for last,' she said, her tone turning nervous.

He smiled, glad that he'd be able to reassure her. 'Not bad. Investment proposition. Suggest use some of rental from Lowery Hall to buy shares. New canal project. Should show handsome return.'

'I know no more about canals than I do about finance, but if you recommend it, it must be a wise move.'

'Previous venture highly profitable. Expect this one will be. Secure your, David's, futures.'

'Are you sure?' Her eyes lit. 'That would be wonderful! Ever since that horrid Mr Smith's visit, I've been so worried, wondering whether we would be able to pay off the debts and still be able to fund David's schooling. And the mortgages on Lowery Hall! Everitt always preferred living in town, but David might not. I should like him to be able to terminate the lease on Lowery and return to the estate that is his birthright, should he so desire.'

Hal nodded. 'Details to work out. But by time old enough to decide, should have choice.'

Elizabeth shook her head, setting her golden curls dancing. 'How can I thank you enough?'

Silk shimmered just so in the sunlight, Hal thought. Would her curls feel like silk, were he to run his fingers through them?

Would the touch of her face be like satin against his palms, if he could cradle her chin in his hands as he longed to do?

Trying to stifle his always-simmering desire, Hal mentally shook himself back to the task at hand. It was so tempting to say nothing and bask in the light of her presence a few minutes longer before proceeding to the library. He hated to have to utter the confession that would extinguish the grateful glow in those blue eyes and turn her smile to a look of distaste or scorn.

None the less, it was time to confess. He'd start with the easy one—Max. 'Brought David present. Puppy. Boy should have dog.'

Her eyes widened. 'A puppy? Oh, my! Yes, you did tell me he ought to have one, but I must confess I didn't expect you to find him one so…speedily. Everitt didn't keep dogs and we never had them about the house growing up. I…I expect I shall learn to adjust.'

'Won't be in house. Stay in stables. David train him. Teach responsibility.'

Hal paused, suddenly recalling his joy at receiving a puppy of his very own from Nicky upon his first visit to Nicky's home, Englemere Hall. Hal's own mama believing that dogs didn't belong in the house of a gentlewoman, he'd never had one before—and had never been without one since, though, with his city lodgings so small, he left the dogs at his country estate.

The unquestioning loyalty and affection of that small animal all those years ago had helped fill the deep void of loneliness in his heart. 'Something to care for, care for him,' Hal explained.

Elizabeth nodded. 'A friend and companion. Yes, I can see it could do him good. How thoughtful you are! Please accept my deepest thanks.'

'One more thing,' he made himself say.

She smiled again, her expression warm, almost…tender. 'And that is?'

'So sorry, terrible idea, but done. Can't unsay it. Problem. With my mother.'

'Can I assist in some way?'

She seemed so concerned and eager to help, which made it that much harder to keep going. Gritting his teeth, Hal forged ahead. 'Wanted me at ball. Lady Cowper's. Didn't want to go. Said I had previous engagement.' He took a deep breath. 'With…with you.'

When Elizabeth remained silent, Hal's courage dropped to his boot tips. 'Couldn't lie. So must ask. To…to go out. Somewhere. There, done it. Can refuse. Meant no disrespect to you or Lowery,' he added, resisting the urge to tug on his restricting neckcloth.

Feeling sweat trickling down his back, he turned his face from her quizzical gaze and prayed for her to refuse him quickly.

'If I understand correctly,' she said after a moment, 'your mother wished you to escort her to Lady Cowper's ball and you refused, saying that you had a previous engagement to accompany me…somewhere?'

Wishing desperately to escape, Hal nodded.

Elizabeth Lowery laughed—not a brittle, scornful sound, but a lilting music that made a listener want to laugh with her. 'How very bad of you! Is she such a tyrant, your mama, that you must tell so great a whisker to escape her company?'

Hal nodded again. 'Desperate measures. Has new protégée. Wants to marry me off. Wealthy, you know.'

'So she is chasing you about with the parson's mousetrap in hand.'

'Has been for years. Rules Marriage Mart. Awful place.' He shuddered, recalling all the awkward, miserable, embarrassing evenings he'd spent at Mama's behest, enduring her exasperated looks and the increasingly bored expressions of the ladies she meant him to charm.

'It must be dreadful,' she agreed. 'I must confess, one of the reasons I accepted Everitt's offer was to avoid having to endure a London Season. The mere thought of being inspected and talked about and judged by roomfuls of society's highest sticklers, all of them looking for something to criticise, absolutely terrified me.' She shrugged. ''Tis silly for a grown woman to have to confess it, but I'm still quite shy.'

Hal shook his head to make sure he'd heard her correctly. 'You—shy?'

She nodded, her cheeks pinking. 'A terrible failing, I know, which I've never overcome. After Sarah married Nicky, there was discussion of bringing all us sisters to town. Then after church one Sunday I overhead the squire's wife saying she knew I'd never "take" in London, such arrogant airs I gave myself, never deigning to speak to my neighbours. I was so distressed! Though she was correct in observing that I seldom talked with anyone outside my own family, 'twas not because I felt superior! I decided upon the instant that if someone who'd known me all my life could think that about my character, I…I couldn't face the prospect of all the censorious eyes I'd meet in London.'

This beautiful, enchanting creature was worried that society would reject her? The notion was so incredible, Hal could find nothing to say.

She gave him a wry smile. 'I'm afraid I'm a terrible coward. I'd much rather retire to my studio, immerse myself in my paints and canvas and emerge only into the indulgent company of my family.'

'Wrong, though,' Hal said. 'Society not censure. Society embrace you. Be Diamond.'

'Sounds rather hard and cold,' she said. 'But, let us return to your dilemma. Not feeling you could reconcile it with your conscience to tell your mama a complete lie, you now feel compelled to tender me an invitation?'

Hal's trepidation returned. 'Yes,' he admitted.

'I've scarcely left the house since Everitt died,' she said, the amusement fading from her eyes. For a long moment she stared into the distance, sadness settling on her face. Then she shook her head and said briskly, 'But I suppose it's time I ventured forth. After all, it cannot be as bad as you enduring an evening upon the Marriage Mart with your mama's protégée in tow. So, where was it that you had engaged to accompany me?'

'You…you want to go?' Hal asked incredulously.

'I would be honoured to have your escort,' she said softly, her blue gaze catching his and holding it.

Hal's chest expanded until wasn't sure he'd be able to grab a breath. Of course, Elizabeth was merely grateful for his help, and kind enough to wish to assist him out of his difficulty with Mama. But the very thought of escorting her, of walking into some public place with her hand on his arm…

Elizabeth Lowery beside him in a carriage, her rose scent wrapping around his head. Her golden curls brushing his shoulder, the warmth of her body radiating toward him, her lips, the delicious curves of her body but inches away… The rush of images made him dizzy with anticipation and desire.

He tried to beat his thoughts back into order. She saw him not as a man, but as Nicky's friend, that was all. Someone as safe and companionable as…as the elderly cousin who still lived with her. He mustn't make of it any more than that.

'Where…want to go?' he asked at last.

'Did you have no place in mind? I confess, I've gone abroad so seldom in London, I have no idea.'

'Theatre? Go early. Take David.' With the boy as chaperon, surely Hal would find it easier to control his riotous senses and rampaging imagination. Besides, he enjoyed the boy's company and David was old enough that he ought to begin experiencing more of the city.

'You wouldn't mind?' she asked, her face lighting. 'That would be wonderful! I'm sure David would love such a treat. How very kind you are! So, when was this ball you couldn't bear to attend?'

'Next Friday.'

'Then,' she said, her eyes dancing, 'David and I would be delighted to confirm our *previous* engagement to attend the theatre with you next Friday.'

Still scarcely able to believe she'd accepted him, Hal nodded. 'Next Friday. Good. Well, better get to work.'

She stood, signalling Hal to rise as well. 'I hope your task progresses. Perhaps I should go meet David's newest best friend, don't you think?'

Shortly afterward, Hal found himself in the library, barely remembering how he'd got there, so filled with marvel was he that Elizabeth Lowery had agreed to ride out with him. He almost wished Mama could see them together. What a shock it would be to her to discover a woman of Mrs Lowery's incomparable loveliness on the arm of her doltish son!

Except that her seeing them together would be a very bad idea indeed. He'd deliberately encouraged his mama's erroneous assumption that Mrs Lowery was a dowdy older lady of no social importance. If Mama ever discovered Elizabeth was, in fact, young, well bred and extremely beautiful, any number of unpleasant consequences might follow.

She could be jealous, seeing Hal's attendance on someone of Elizabeth's youth and loveliness as a threat to her dominance over her son. She could resent Elizabeth for causing Hal to slight her current favourite. Worst of all, she might descend upon Green Street to conduct the inquisition Hal had previously imagined with dread.

No, best that Mama be safely ensconced at her *ton* society ball while he squired Elizabeth Lowery.

And despite the restraining effect David Lowery's presence with them should have upon his desire, if Hal wanted to be assured of keeping his lustful urges under control, it would be advisable to pay a visit to sweet Sally the night before their excursion to the theatre.

Chapter Ten

Three days later, Elizabeth sat in the schoolroom, watching David with his puppy. Proud of the skills Mr Waterman had assisted him in training Max, David had persuaded her to let him bring the dog into the house just this once so he might demonstrate Max's achievements.

'Sit, Max,' David was commanding. His tail wagging, the puppy settled his hindquarters on the floor and looked up at her son hopefully.

'Good boy,' David said and fed the dog a titbit. 'Uncle Hal said I should reward Max each time he does what I tell him. He said after a while, Max will want to obey me even if I don't give him treats.'

'It seems to work,' Elizabeth observed. 'Should I lay in a stock of sweetmeats before your tutor arrives, to reward you for doing your lessons?' she teased.

'Of course not, Mama,' he replied seriously. 'I shall do my lessons because I am 'sponsible. Uncle Hal says I have to be strong and wise and learn to take care of what is mine, like you and Lowery Hall.'

Though Elizabeth wasn't sure she approved of the informality of her son calling Mr Waterman 'Uncle Hal', David had been so excited when he told her he'd been given permission to do so that she hadn't had the heart to forbid it. Indeed, after years of second-hand acquaintance through Nicky and her sister, so well did she feel she knew the man that she herself often thought of him as simply 'Hal' and had to be careful not to slip up and address him so.

Weaving himself around David's ankles, Max barked, obviously wishing to recall his master's attention. 'Good boy,' David said, dropping another treat into his mouth.

Who was training whom? Elizabeth wondered with a chuckle. Then a knock sounded, followed by the entrance of the butler. Her momentary flare of excitement subsided when Sands announced, 'Sir Gregory is below, ma'am. Shall I tell him you will receive him shortly?'

Elizabeth glanced at her worn painting gown, now liberally adorned with puppy hair. 'Yes, I'll join him as soon as I change into something more suitable.'

'Please, Mama, can Max stay here a little longer? I'll take him back to the stable before nuncheon, I promise,' David asked.

'Since you are doing such a good job, I suppose he can remain a little longer. Just this once.'

'Thank you, Mama! Uncle Hal says that in the city a dog should stay outside, but if he is well behaved he can come in the house sometimes.'

'Well, if "Uncle Hal", says so, then I suppose it must be true.' Giving David a hug, she walked out.

Her son had certainly taken to Mr Waterman, she mused as she crossed the hall to her chamber. His conversation now was frequently punctuated with 'Uncle Hal said…'

While her maid helped her change into a morning gown, Elizabeth let her thoughts wander around the fascinating topic of Hal Waterman.

Chary of speech as he was, Mr Waterman seemed to have had

no difficulty communicating a great deal of useful advice to her son. Though his kindness and the attention he showered on her son filled her with gratitude, Elizabeth hoped David wasn't growing too attached to him.

After all, Mr Waterman was merely discharging the obligation he felt he owed Nicky. Once her sister and brother-in-law returned, there would be no reason for him to continue his almost-daily visits. At that point, David would probably transfer his need for masculine attention to Nicky without missing too keenly the loss of Mr Waterman's comforting presence.

Not being a small boy who simply needed the guiding hand of any concerned gentleman to ease him through his grief for his late father, she wasn't sure she would be equally successful at not missing Mr Waterman.

Elizabeth dismissed her maid and sat at her dressing table. Not quite ready yet to meet the meticulous Sir Gregory, she studied her reflection, idly twisting one blonde curl around her finger.

She had to admit she would have preferred that it were Mr Waterman who'd asked for her. She'd not seen much of that gentleman these last few days and had to confess herself a bit jealous that though he seemed always to find the time during his trips to Everitt's library to stop and visit with David and Max, he did not always call upon her. Unfortunately his other obligations seemed to occupy his afternoons and evenings, so that he usually came by in the morning while she worked in her studio.

She'd recently taken to beginning her painting sessions earlier, that she might finish in time to catch him for a brief conversation before he left.

She always had a valid reason to stop by the library, of course. First it was to propose that, if Mr Waterman could reconcile it with his conscience, he escort them to an afternoon performance at Astley's on the day of Lady Cowper's ball rather than to the theatre, David being more apt to be awake and alert at that earlier hour. At his tender age, her son would likely find the equestrian displays more enthralling than the stage, and if they took David for ices after the performance and made a meandering journey home, they would still retain Hal late enough to provide him with an excuse to avoid his mama's event.

Another day she'd had a question about finances; on another she'd wished to inquire about his progress. Still, she had to admit to herself that it was more her desire to come into his presence for a few moments than a truly urgent need to consult him that led her to seek him out.

No, Hal Waterman would certainly not miss her company as keenly as she would miss his. From what she gathered of the little he'd told her about his investments, he was a busy man who would probably be grateful to be relieved of the burden of tending the affairs of one modestly situated widow of no social importance.

Though, sadly, somehow his mother had so mishandled her relationship with her son that he seemed to dread spending time with her, as a mother herself she could appreciate the woman's apparent eagerness to see her son happily married and settled. Absurdly shy as he appeared to be with women, possessed as he was of wealth, an impressive lineage and a compelling personal presence, at whatever point he decided he was at last ready to marry, his mama would doubtless have no difficulty assembling a large selection of beautiful, charming, well-bred, rich heiresses to tempt him.

Dismissing an unpleasant flash of what, she realised with some chagrin, had to be jealousy, she could only hope the lucky lady who eventually won his affections was intelligent enough to appreciate her good fortune.

Judging by his panicked avoidance of his mother's latest matrimonial candidate, however, Mr Waterman was nowhere near ready to step into the parson's mousetrap. Indeed, she ought to be grateful to his mother for inspiring the desperation that had led to his invitation.

Though at first the idea of appearing in public with anyone other than Everitt had seemed impossible, by the time Mr Waterman tendered his invitation, she was feeling more equal to the task. With Hal performing the role of escort, she was now quite looking forward to it.

Though she told herself most of her pleasure was the delight of being able to watch David enjoy one of London's most famous spectacles, she was honest enough to allow that the idea of spending time in close proximity to Mr Waterman also inspired an undercurrent of purely sensual anticipation. Her shattered heart still grieved for her dear Everitt, but as a young woman in her prime, surely she couldn't be faulted for being susceptible to the pull of physical attraction.

The idea of Mr Waterman's broad shoulders pressed into the carriage seat beside her, his tall, commanding figure looming over her as he helped her in and out of the vehicle, his well-formed knee perhaps brushing hers in the small space of the Astley Amphitheatre's benches caused a pleasant tremor deep within her. She imagined looking up at his handsome profile, outlined by the torches as the horsemen galloped across the arena. Watching the movement of those sculpted lips during his occasional comments…feeling the touch of those big hands stroking her cheek…

Along with the loss of sharing everyday thoughts and experiences with her husband, she missed the whole range of physical tenderness. Everitt's touch on her arm as he guided her through a doorway. The feel of his fingers tangling in her hair as he teasingly pulled on a curl. His arms around her, the warmth of him as he lay next to her in their bed.

She smiled as she recalled how horribly anxious and embarrassed she'd been on their wedding night. Nervous, fearful, wondering if in marrying this kind man she'd always looked up to as the dearest of family friends, she'd made a terrible mistake. How gentle he had been with her that night, telling her she mustn't worry, that he was still the Everitt who had always cherished her, that he did not mean to make her his wife until she felt quite ready.

He'd proceeded to do nothing more alarming than hold her close all through the night. Honouring his promise, he'd delayed taking her body until she'd grown almost comfortable with the idea of being touched so intimately.

His lovemaking had always been gentle, caring, reverent, even after he'd taught her how to experience pleasure in their union. In addition to the comfort their joining gave him, she missed that pleasure, too.

Though there had been little enough of it their last months together. She frowned as she recalled how he had several times begun, and then ceased, to make love to her, his face growing pale and still as he leaned back upon the pillows, a hand at his chest. She'd urged him to visit a doctor, but he'd laughed at her fears and told her that it was some mild complaint that would pass, nothing which needed to concern her or cause him to visit a sawbones who would only dose him with some disgusting concoction and charge him a huge fee before sending him home.

Why had she not insisted? How could she already be feeling lust—she might as well name the attraction for what it was—for another man when she'd failed her own husband so badly? Actually be imagining the touch of another man's hands, with Everitt not even two months dead?

Distressed and guilty, Elizabeth smoothed the mangled curl back into place with trembling fingers.

Suddenly she was glad that Sir Gregory, not Hal Waterman, awaited her below. Thrusting her hands into the gloves Gibbons had set out for her, Elizabeth rose and went down to meet her caller.

Sir Gregory rose as she entered the blue salon. The approval in his eyes as he bowed over her hand made her glad she'd taken the time to change and tidy her hair.

'Lizbet, I'm delighted to see you looking so much more relaxed and refreshed than at our last meeting! By the way, I brought some flowers for Miss Lowery, which, with your approbation, I hope, I've already directed Sands to convey to the invalid's room.'

'How very kind! I am better, Sir Gregory. Just in these last few days, I've felt less anxious, almost able to believe there will some day be a future for me and David.'

'Of course there will be, my dear!' he said, patting her hand. 'Though you cannot help but be low at times, Everitt would not want you to bury yourself away, for ever mourning him. He would urge you to seek a new path, new activities…and new companions to brighten your life, as soon as you felt able. Young David gets on well, too, I trust? And Miss Lowery continues to recover?'

A guilty pang struck her at Sir Gregory's innocuous words about moving on. Which led her to suddenly realise that David had yet to apologise to the baronet for his rudeness over the soldier. Best that she induce him to perform that unpleasant task as soon as possible.

'Yes, Miss Lowery is improving and David is doing better as well. He much regrets his outburst and would like a chance to apologise.'

'I'm glad to hear it—and pleased that you are conscientiously instructing him in proper comportment.'

As Everitt used to, she thought with another pang. 'I do try. Shall I send for him now?'

As Sir Gregory nodded, she opened the hall door and summoned a footman to go fetch her son.

'Though your family saw fit to call on someone else to assist with settling Everitt's financial matters,' Sir Gregory said when she returned to her seat, 'I hope you'll not forget that I would be honoured to assist you with anything else of which you may have need.'

His avowal brought Elizabeth absurdly close to tears. Sir Gregory might be a bit pompous, but he was an accomplished gentleman of impeccably good *ton*, one whose shrewdness, efficient management of his property and broad influence in society Everitt had often praised. He might not be at ease with children, but he meant well, bringing a soldier for her grieving son and flowers for the recovering Miss Lowery.

'Thank you, Sir Gregory,' she said softly. 'I shall certainly remember.'

Would it not be a relief to turn to him about such problems that arose as she struggled to master all her new responsibilities? Sir Gregory, who treated her with genteel reverence, who like Everitt wished only to relieve her of any matter that distressed or concerned her.

Sir Gregory, who did not arouse in this very new widow any disloyal thoughts or shameful desires.

They had just finished sipping the wine Sands brought when David entered. To Elizabeth's relief, he walked straight to Sir Gregory and bowed.

'Good morning, sir. Please let me 'pologise for being rude during your previous visit. The soldier you brought me is very fine. Thank you for your thoughtful gift.'

Though Elizabeth could tell the words were well rehearsed, the baronet seemed to perceive them as delivered with perhaps more contrition than they actually contained. 'I accept your apology and you are welcome,' he said approvingly. 'Come sit for a minute with your mama and me.'

Frowning, David said, 'I should go back and study my letters. I shall have a tutor soon.'

'Indeed, 'tis time that you begin formal schooling,' Sir Gregory agreed.

'Mama also says that children do not belong in a lady's drawing room,' David added hopefully.

Sir Gregory laughed and gave Elizabeth an approving look. 'So they do not, in general! But I expect this once your mama will permit you to remain.'

Elizabeth knew her son would rather not sit stiffly in a chair while the adults sipped their wine, especially as one of the adults was the baronet. But Sir Gregory had never before sought out her son's company, and he had been very gracious about accepting David's apology. Though she suspected the baronet had no more desire to entertain a child than her son did to remain, if their guest was doing his best to be sociable, she decided David could manage for a short time to return the favour.

Ignoring her son's urgently appealing glance, she said, 'I'm sure David would be honoured to remain and demonstrate how correctly he can behave.'

After a grimace at that less-than-subtle reminder, with a little sigh, David subsided into a chair.

'So, what will your tutor be teaching you?' Sir Gregory asked. 'A good grounding in the classics, I hope.'

'Mr Waterman says I should learn to manage Lowery Hall,' David replied.

Sir Gregory opened his lips as if to speak, then closed them. After clearing his throat, he said affably, 'Becoming a competent manager of your property is essential, but you need to be learned as well. A gentleman should have a good understanding of mathematics, science, literature and natural philosophy as well as possessing more practical skills.'

'Mr Waterman says a true gentleman takes care of his 'sponsibilites first.'

Sir Gregory's genial expression faded. 'My, who would have expected the taciturn Mr Waterman capable of uttering so many sentences together?' he said, an edge to his voice.

David raised his chin, a militant look on his face. 'Mr Waterman only says what's really important.'

'Indeed,' Sir Gregory said drily, setting down his glass. 'Now that I've assured myself that all is going well with you, I must take my leave.' He came over to press Elizabeth's hand. 'Let remind you, dear lady, that I am ever at your service, no matter the difficulty!'

Already moving towards the door, David said, 'Mr Waterman takes very good care of—'

'That's enough, David,' Elizabeth interrupted hastily. 'Thank you again, Sir Gregory, for your kindness. I will keep your gracious offer in mind.'

The three of them had just entered the hallway, David sketching a bow to Sir Gregory and heading for the stairs, when a small brown dog appeared on the landing above, pursued by a breathless housemaid. Spotting his master, Max started to bark, paws skidding down the wooden steps in his haste as he descended.

In her agitation before coming to meet Sir Gregory, Elizabeth had totally forgotten she'd let David keep the puppy in the schoolroom. No wonder David had been so anxious to return there.

David threw his mother a panicked look before shouting, 'Stay, Max!'

Evidently her son's attempts to instill in Max the concept of 'stay' had not yet fully succeeded, for, ignoring the order, the puppy lunged down the remaining stairs and galloped toward them.

An expression of distaste formed on Sir Gregory's face as he watched the mongrel rapidly approaching them. 'Stop!' he commanded.

It appeared that word had not entered into Max's vocabulary either. Though he slowed as he edged around them, too wary of the hostile Sir Gregory to attempt to approach his master, once past them he scurried toward the service wing.

'Max, come back!' David shouted as he raced after him.

Sir Gregory stood stiffly, staring in disapproval as dog and boy disappeared down the hallway. 'How did that animal get into the house? I didn't know David had a dog.'

'Mr Waterman brought him. He has been a wonderful companion for David,' she explained.

'Waterman again!' the baronet said with a sniff. 'I might have guessed. I warned you the man would be a poor influence! A city town house is no place for animals, which I would have expected even Hal Waterman to know.'

'Normally Max resides in the stables. I only allowed David to bring him in today so he might show me some of the tricks he's been teaching him.'

'It appears the boy—and the dog—are in need of more schooling. As is Waterman. Dogs in a drawing room! No wonder his poor mother can't manage to marry him off, despite his wealth.'

The mixed feelings she'd been entertaining about Hal Waterman dissolved into irritation at the baronet's scornful words. 'Mr Waterman may not be the best *ton*,' she retorted a bit hotly, 'but he understands the needs of a grieving little boy.'

'Probably because he never grew up himself. Now, I'll not disparage Waterman any further. I concede that the man has a good heart and probably means well. If David insists upon keeping the animal he's been given, though, it ought to be sent off to Lowery Hall. David needs to learn to become a gentleman, not be indulged by an overfond mother.'

'I'm not trying to indulge him,' Elizabeth said stiffly. 'Only to sympathise and understand his loss.'

'There, there, I don't mean to criticise! No one could expect a tender-hearted lady to know what a boy needs to become a man. That's why it concerns me that David appears so taken with Waterman, whom I would hardly recommend as a model of deportment to any young gentleman. A tutor is a good idea, by the way, for David ought to be preparing to enter Eton or Winchester.'

Her resentment at the baronet's criticism instantly dissolved in the face of a much greater anxiety. 'You mean…David should go off to school? Surely it's too early for that!'

'I know it will be difficult for you,' the baronet soothed, patting her hand. 'But he is by no means too young. David should be educated as befits his station and class, as Everitt would have wanted. Holding on to his leading strings while his schoolmates prepare to take up their responsibilities will be doing him no favour. He must be off to find his rightful place in the world. It would be better for you, too.'

Elizabeth shook her head adamantly. 'Sending David away might be best for him, but it would never be what I would choose for me.'

'Which is why you need a truly responsible gentleman to advise you on the many difficult decisions you must make in the coming months,' the baronet replied, his tone gentle now. 'Caught up in grief as you are, you cannot expect to make wise choices if you let emotion be your guide.'

Send David away! The very notion was like a knife to the heart. But she didn't want to wait so long that his schoolmates would taunt him as being a sissy, a mama's boy.

Oh, it was so difficult! The very idea of having to make such an agonising choice drained away her pitiful reserves of strength and sent panic coursing through her.

Though she had done better of late, it took only the suggestion of a real dilemma to bring home to her how inadequate she still was to handle life's crises, how far she was from recovering from the blow of Everitt's death.

She knew so little of the world outside her own home and family. Her emotions were still so easily touched, so turbulent and troubling. Maybe she should lean more on Sir Gregory. Certainly Everitt had trusted his opinion and valued his advice.

While she remained silent, the contradictory considerations whirling in her mind like the spokes on a carriage wheel, Sir Gregory drained his glass. 'I see you are still much moved. I never intended to upset you! But I feel 'tis imperative that you receive the conscientious advice that will help you make the wisest decisions.'

'I know, as Everitt's dearest friend, you have only our best interests at heart,' she said after a moment.

'If you understand that, I leave content. I shall check again on you soon, dear Lizbet,' he said, kissing her fingers. 'But if you need anything before then, only send me a note.'

Mutely she watched him depart, her thoughts and emotions more turbulent than ever. Was Hal Waterman truly a poor influence on David? Ought she to limit the time her son spent with him, limit the time she spent as well?

It would be a relief to distance herself from a man who tempted her to impulses and feelings she wasn't ready to experience…wouldn't it? Yet every service he had performed for her and David thus far had been so kind and thoughtfully done. 'Twas her own fault the puppy had ended up in the house, not his, after all. And she had felt so much more positive and confident since Mr Waterman had taken upon himself to watch out for them.

In addition, she'd just agreed to have him escort her and David to Astley's—a visit she had been looking forward to with some anticipation. Even if it would not be rude in the extreme to withdraw from the excursion at the last moment, it would be cruel repayment for all his goodness to them to deprive him of an excuse to escape the tender mercies of his disapproving, match-making mama.

Besides, it was his sense of duty toward Nicky that had sent Mr Waterman to watch out for them, and Nicky, a father himself, would never retain as his closest friend a man whose influence might harm a child. Perhaps Mr Waterman wasn't the paragon of *ton* graces Sir Gregory—and his own mother—would choose as the model for a growing boy, but he was honest, highly competent, kind—and David liked him, a factor that automatically made him more suitable than Sir Gregory as a mentor for her son.

Of course, Sir Gregory was highly competent as well. If she avoided the topic of Hal Waterman and his influence over her son, she could still ask his advice on other matters…couldn't she?

Enough! Elizabeth thought, weary of uncertainty. She'd go out to the stables and reassure David that she was not angry over the incident with Max. Then she would put this distressing matter of the two opposing gentlemen out of mind and let Friday's excursion with Hal Waterman take whatever course it would.

Chapter Eleven

The following evening, after one of White's excellent dinners, Hal took a seat in the card room, considering the rival merits of whist and piquet—and trying to avoid thinking that tomorrow he would escort Elizabeth Lowery and her son to Astley's.

Over the past few days he'd successfully evaded that alluring lady, timing his calls for earlier in the morning and barricading himself in the library after a brief visit with David. He smiled, recalling the boy's excited chatter and the endearing way he zig-zagged from entreating Hal to join in some game to a sombre-faced request that Hal school him in handling his ''sponsibilities'. Perhaps he'd figure a way to continue visiting the boy even after Nicky's return.

Having gleaned all he could from Lowery's ledgers, he'd just finished penning a meticulous account of the assets, liabilities and cash flow of the household along with a plan for meeting current expenses while accumulating the monies necessary for David's future schooling and the widow's maintenance. All that remained was to discover the still-elusive will, and he would have little excuse to continue his daily calls.

Except…though he'd successfully resisted the urge to seek

out Elizabeth, each of the last three days, she'd surprised him by stopping by the library. With her smile warming his heart, her beauty dazzling his senses, all the meticulously gathered figures in his head scattered like pheasants at a gunshot. He managed to do little more than nod and give monosyllabic answers to her questions. What a dolt she must think him!

Yesterday, however, she'd asked him to stay to nuncheon, an invitation so tempting he'd immediately refused. Once seated at table with her, basking in her beauty and listening to the lilting music of her voice, answering the surprisingly shrewd questions she asked about estate finances and enjoying the repartee between her and David, he feared he'd find it impossible not to linger for the rest of the afternoon.

And there was that much-anticipated, much-dreaded outing tomorrow. Having not had much luck thus far in taming the lustful imaginings continually sparked by the idea of spending hours in close company with the enticing Elizabeth, he probably ought to forgo cards in favour of an extended visit to his long-time paramour sweet Sally.

He'd about decided to do just that when an older gentleman stopped beside his chair.

'Mr Waterman,' the man said, bowing. 'Sir Gregory Holburn here. Might I beg the indulgence of joining you for a moment?'

At first surprised by this request from a man he only vaguely recognised, as he nodded and motioned Sir Gregory to a seat, his faint recollections clarified. 'Lowery's friend,' Hal recalled. 'Good man. Sad loss.'

'A sad loss indeed,' Sir Gregory agreed, motioning to a waiter. 'You will share a glass of wine with me?'

'Honoured,' Hal said, wondering what the best friend of the late Everitt Lowery wanted with him. Since David had mentioned the baronet's visit to the Lowerys—Hal recalled the affair of the soldier—Sir Gregory must know Hal was overseeing Lowery's estate. He hoped Holburn wasn't a gaming crony come to discreetly press a claim against David's inheritance.

Somewhat to Hal's annoyance, Sir Gregory proceeded first to chat about the latest *ton* gossip, a monologue in which Hal declined to participate and which he felt certain had nothing to do with Holburn's purpose in seeking him out. Not until they had nearly finished the wine—and Hal was about at the point of flatly demanding what the man truly wanted—did Sir Gregory finally mention the Lowerys.

'I understand that, at the behest of Mrs Lowery's family, you have undertaken to sort out the financial details of Everitt's estate.'

Taking a sip of his wine, Hal nodded. When he said nothing further, with a little grimace of exasperation, Holburn continued, 'From your reputation among the *ton*, I expect that you shall do a competent job of it.'

Hal suspected the baronet meant his reputation wasn't for being fashionable or well spoken. 'Hope to,' he replied.

'I'm sure Everitt would be pleased that the details of his estate are in the hands of one who is as well equipped as any barrister to handle them,' the baronet said.

The inference that Hal's talents were more suitable for a common working man than to one who belonged in the upper ranks of society confirmed Hal's initial feeling that Sir Gregory's opinion of him was less than admiring.

'Ought to be,' he said evenly. If Holburn were casting about for a reaction, he was tying a fly that wouldn't fish. After a dozen years of much more painful needling by his lady mother, the baronet's mild barbs barely pricked. Not sure why, or even if, Holburn was deliberating trying to bait him, Hal didn't intend to respond until he'd figured out exactly what the man was trying to accomplish.

'Well, I don't mean to be uncivil—'

'Do you not?' Hal interjected drily.

With an irritated glance, the baronet continued, 'But I must warn you I feel it would be best that you confine yourself to giving Mrs Lowery advice only in your field of expertise. I've already seen evidence of your meddling in other aspects of the household that cause me concern and, I believe, would have greatly concerned Everitt, too, were he here to observe them.'

'Were he here, no need to intervene,' Hal pointed out.

Ignoring the comment, Sir Gregory went on, 'Surely you realise that you are hardly a model for the sort of gentleman Lowery would wish his son to become. Introducing unsuitable animals into the household, encouraging Elizabeth Lowery to indulge her son in childish behaviour, insinuating yourself into the boy's life as some sort of expert upon every subject! Insofar as your actions influence Mrs Lowery to make poor decisions about her situation, your intervention, though perhaps well meaning, could well cause the boy and his mother serious long-term harm. I appeal to your sense of honour as a gentleman to refrain from monopolising the boy and putting forth opinions on matters concerning him in which you have neither expertise nor a valid concern.'

'You have valid concern?' Hal asked, hanging on to his temper with an effort.

'As Everitt's closest friend, of course I am concerned about the well being of his widow and son. I also feel that, in being so much better acquainted with the husband and father, to say nothing of holding a superior rank in society, I am much better placed to advise Mrs Lowery on the direction of her household than you are.'

'Indeed?' Hal drawled. 'Strange. Family didn't think so. Called on me.' Which wasn't precisely true, of course, but his initial vague feelings of distaste toward the baronet swiftly so-lidifying into genuine dislike as this diatribe continued, Hal couldn't help needling back a little.

The baronet gave a scornful harrump. 'Make light of it if you will, but 'tis no joking matter. Though I should have known you would refuse to act the gentleman. When have you ever, pray? Your conduct has for years been the despair of your mother…or so my intimate acquaintance with that charming lady led me to believe,' he added with something of a smirk.

So this self-important lordling had been his mother's *cicisbeo*—or more. Was that jibe about Mama meant to incite Hal to take a swing at him right here in the middle of White's, thereby demonstrating he was indeed the barbarian the baronet seemed to think him, an oaf ill disguised as a gentleman who did not belong among the elite of the *ton*?

If that were Holburn's aim, he was destined to disappointment. Hal had faced much more daunting threats to his self-control than the snide innuendo of one arrogant baronet. Shaking his head mournfully, Hal said, 'Poor Mama. Always attracted to flash over substance.'

While the baronet sputtered in outrage, Hal fixed an unsmiling gaze on Holburn and rose from his chair, signifying that their interchange was at an end.

Before he could bid Sir Gregory goodnight, one of Hal's best and oldest friends chanced to walk into the room. Spying Hal, Sir Edward Greaves quickly approached, hand outstretched.

'Hal! Well met! As you can see, I'm just in from the country and in need of sustenance and amusement. How about a hand of piquet after your friend leaves?'

'Leaving now,' Hal said. 'Obliged for the wine,' he said, sketching a bow to Sir Gregory.

Recovering his countenance, Holburn gave Hal an equally cold bow. 'Remember the advice,' Holburn said before straightening and walking away.

Ned, a self-proclaimed countryman who spent as little time in London as possible, gazed curiously from Hal's hostile expression to the baronet's retreating figure. 'Who was that?'

'Insect,' Hal said. 'Let's play cards.'

Obviously determining by the look on Hal's face that he didn't wish to discuss the encounter, Ned made no comment, instead hailing a passing waiter. 'I understand the canal project went well,' he said after he'd ordered a meal and a deck of cards. 'Made another thousand pounds since last I saw you? And what have you heard from Nicky?'

'Canal project goes well. Nothing from Nicky.'

'I dare say he's too dazzled by the wonders of ancient Rome and frazzled by co-ordinating a travelling party that includes nearly a dozen adults and several fractious children to find time to write. If I can squeeze enough from the shipment of wheat I'm here to sell, perhaps I'll give over the profits and let you work your money-growing magic on it. Farmer Johnson has a field adjoining my south pasture that I've coveted for years.'

With a little prompting, Hal was able to set his friend off expounding about his estate, cattle and crops. Somewhat guiltily according Ned only a modicum of attention, Hal worried over the purpose behind Sir Gregory's warning.

It was possible the baronet, as a well-meaning friend of the late Everitt Lowery, was honestly concerned that Hal, admittedly no paragon of fashionable gentlemanly behaviour, might encourage Lowery's son to follow in his unstylish ways. If so, the man was kind-hearted, if idiotic. At barely seven years of age, David Lowery was likely far too young to permanently adopt any man's behaviour as his model.

But Hal didn't think it was just that. There was an undercurrent of an almost—covetedness in the baronet's demeanour, as if Hal were poaching upon a preserve Holburn considered his own. Might the baronet feel insulted that Lowery had not named Sir Gregory as guardian of his home and property in what Lowery must have considered the unlikely event something happened to him?

Then he remembered a comment by David and the confrontation began to take on another meaning. 'He never looks at me when he talks,' the boy had said. 'He looks at Mama, and his eyes get all funny.'

With a flash of intuition as powerful as it was certain, Hal realised that what Sir Gregory Holburn coveted was not directing Everitt's Lowery's estate, but his widow.

Though he might resent Holburn's disdainful treatment and superior airs, he could hardly hold a fascination with Elizabeth Lowery against the man. Didn't Hal admire and revere and lust after her himself? Perhaps, sensing Hal's interest in her or fearing his privileged access to her, Holburn was attempting to warn off someone he thought might be a potential rival. Though with her so newly widowed, surely it was a bit premature to worry about that.

As he trolled his memory for titbits about Sir Gregory, an anger much greater than that induced by the baronet's snide comments began to build in his chest.

Though Hal spent as little time as he could manage in fashionable society, he was still aware of what transpired there. He now recalled that Sir Gregory Holburn, scion of a distinguished family and owner of several prosperous estates, though highly respected in society and much sought after by hostesses for his polished repartee and immaculate good manners, was not normally invited to the Marriage Mart functions Hal's mama favoured.

The mamas of society's hopeful maidens had long ago condemned Sir Gregory as a confirmed bachelor, unlikely to be tempted into matrimony by any of their daughters. Instead, over the years Holburn's name had been linked with a succession of beautiful and well-born matrons, both widows and married ladies whose husbands either turned a blind eye to, or never suspected, their little affairs.

Was Sir Gregory trying to get Hal out of the way so he could make Elizabeth the object of his gallantry? With her family gone, did he mean to deprive her of any advice and counsel save his own so that he might trade upon her innocence and vulnerability to persuade her to become his next *chère-amie*?

The mere thought of Sir Gregory sliding his body against hers on the sofa, coaxing the grieving widow to lean upon his shoulder while he stroked lecherous fingers down her peerless soft cheek and murmured soothing words into her ear, filled Hal's head with a red film of rage.

Not until he felt liquid coursing over his fingers did Hal realise he'd clutched his wineglass so tightly the fragile stem must have snapped. With an oath, he dragged a handkerchief from his waistcoat pocket, trying to barricade the pool of wine and glass on to the tabletop.

'Hand uninjured?' Ned inquired as several alert servants rushed over to attend to the breakage.

Looking down at his fingers disgustedly, Hal noted two small cuts. 'Nothing to signify.'

'I know I sometimes prose on about farming until it drives a listener to distraction, but I've never before had one destroy a wineglass,' Ned said lightly. 'Care to talk about it?'

'No,' Hal replied, knowing that, even if he could get out the words to express the turmoil of fury, doubt and jealousy swirling in his head, he couldn't share so damaging and unproven a suspicion about another gentleman, not even to a friend as close as Ned Greaves. 'Sorry about inattention, though.'

Ned said, waving a deprecating hand. 'You'll remember, I trust, that my advice and assistance are yours should you wish them. Shall we have that game? If you're going to be distracted, I might as well profit from it!'

Hal forced his mind from the conundrum of Elizabeth Lowery and Sir Gregory Holburn. He'd need to be much calmer before he could think over the situation sensibly.

It wasn't wise for him to embroil himself any further with—or care too deeply about—the Lowery family. Nicky would be home soon to take over guarding the best interests of his nephew and his sister-in-law. What Elizabeth Lowery chose to do then—whether remarry or take a lover—was really none of Hal's business.

But until Nicky returned, Hal couldn't help but believe it was his duty, no matter how painful it might be for him to distance himself later, to continue guarding them now. If he could somehow confirm his suspicions that Sir Gregory *was* trying to trade upon Elizabeth's grief and loneliness to coax or coerce her into a premature intimacy, he would have to do something to prevent it.

Doing something almost inevitably meant that tomorrow would not be the only day he'd be spending in close proximity to Elizabeth Lowery. Given that unnerving thought, Hal decided that as soon as he'd lost enough blunt to make Ned happy, he'd pay that visit to Sally.

Chapter Twelve

Several hours later, his purse lighter by an amount that greatly gratified Ned, his anxiety unmitigated by the quantity of wine he'd imbibed, Hal exited a hackney at an elegant town house in Chelsea.

Hal took a deep breath and mounted the stairs, a measure of calm descending on his troubled spirits. Every time he crossed the threshold of this house, he congratulated himself again on his good fortune in meeting Sally Herndon and his good sense, having swiftly recognised her for the gem she was, in persuading her to leave the select brothel in which he'd discovered her.

The town house he'd bought for her had become more a home to him than any other dwelling he owned, a place where he could count upon finding not just physical pleasure, but also a concerned listener, a thoughtful sounding board for his ideas, and shrewd, practical advice whenever he solicited it.

Perhaps he'd first seek some of the latter, since he was currently too disturbed and agitated to feel amorous, he thought as he went into the sitting room adjoining Sally's bedchamber. Before the evening was out, he trusted Sally's keen mind would soothe his worries and her skill and intimate knowledge of his body would lead them both to the nirvana of satisfaction and oblivion he craved.

He heard the soft swish of drapery and looked up. Clad in a satin dressing gown, Sally entered the sitting room, carrying herself with that innate queenly dignity that had caught his eye in Madame Lucie's parlour all those years ago. Taller than most women, her lusciously full figure and long, luxuriant fall of honey-coloured hair made her look every inch the courtesan. Yet one glance at her open, honest face, her intelligent eyes and rosy cheeks adorned with a sprinkle of freckles and Hal always saw the country girl of good yeoman blood she'd once been.

Evidently reading the tension in Hal's expression, she halted by the sideboard. 'Some port, Hal?'

'Please,' he responded, though thus far tonight wine hadn't been much help for the anxiety that plagued him.

She brought it over and gave him a kiss. He pulled her into a loose embrace and simply held her, savouring the clean lemon tang of the soap she used and the comfort of having her in his arms.

Gently she disengaged herself, pointed him to the sofa and went to pour herself a glass before joining him.

'I was afraid you'd run into difficulties, so long it's been since you've visited me. So, what is troubling you tonight?' she asked, concern in her blue eyes as she studied him over her wine.

'Twas one of the things Hal most liked about Sally. From the very first, she had treated him not as a protector who furnished her with a house and a wardrobe in return for providing him with the pleasures of the flesh, but as a friend whose company she enjoyed. She asked questions and displayed genuine interest in the answers she waited quietly for him to produce, never rushing him to respond or seeming impatient with his halting replies. With her, he never felt awkward and inadequate for taking as much time as he needed to get the words out. As a result, from very early n their relationship he had come to confide in her and solicit her opinion on more of his concerns than he'd ever voiced to anyone.

'Was there a problem with the canal workers?' she prompted, pulling him out of his reminiscence. 'I hear the lords in Parliament are worried out of their wigs about trade associations forming in the north. Wouldn't want commoners making demands of the toffs that own the enterprises, now would we? But I hope the dispute isn't harming your interests.'

Hal grinned at her. 'Been reading papers again.'

Sally smiled back. 'What else have I to do all day, after checking with the housekeeper and making sure the butler isn't robbing you blind? Despite my late profession, I come from industrious stock. I ought to pay you, my lord, letting me lounge about, doing nothing more taxing than tending my vegetables and reading all the periodicals you subscribe to for me. I'll soon have more education than a *ton* miss from some fancy lady's academy.'

Comparing the tone and expertise of Sally's conversation to that of his mother, a lady born, Hal said, 'Already have more. Common sense too. More valuable than education.' And wouldn't Mama have palpitations were she ever to learn her son had compared her unfavourably to a low-born country lass who'd come to London to ply the only profession left to a maid who'd lost her virtue!

Swallowing a chuckle, Hal said, 'Canal going well. Opening new phase. Put some money in for you.'

'How good you are to me, sir! The evening papers have been touting the prospects of canal ventures.' Giving him a quick kiss on the cheek, she laughed. 'I expect I'm the only demi-rep in London with blunt in investments.'

'One of few benefits of settling for simple man,' Hal said. 'Could have had titled lord.'

Sally shook her head, her expression turning tender. 'Even as a nodkin straight from the country, I knew the first time I met you that you was better than that whole lot of lordlings visiting Madame Lucie's. All them looking at me with lust in their eyes, smiling so nice all the while thinking I was no more than a toy for their pleasure. I'll never forget how different you treated me.' She angled her head at him. 'You remember what you said then?'

Hal shook his head and laughed. 'Sorry, don't. First time ever in brothel. Terrified, intimidated by all the ladies. Surprised managed to speak.'

'You stood on the edge of the room, so tall and handsome and serious, like one of them gods out of that mythology book you got me,' she recalled. 'Then you walked past the prettier, more experienced girls right up to me—tall shy Sally, fresh out of the country and probably still smelling of hay. You asked what county I'd come from, like I was some visitor to London instead of a tart in a brothel. I nearly swooned.'

Hal frowned. 'Are country girl. Never tart. How else survive after seducer abandoned you?'

'Well, 'tis good of you to think that, for most folks is ready enough to condemn! I am what I am and don't mean to deny it, though thanks to you I've not had to ply the trade since those early days. Nor, thanks to you, will I ever have to again! You've given me more for gowns and trinkets than I'd ever need, even invested money for me. But more'n that, you…talk to me. You never made fun of me wanting to educate myself nor scoffed at the notion of me reading them books and newspapers. When you came back to Madame Lucie's after that first night and said that you'd make her let me go if I wanted to come with you, I thought I was the luckiest girl in the world.' She leaned over to press his hand. 'I still do.'

'Been good for me too,' Hal affirmed fondly. 'Not just bedding me. Friend. Wise.'

'I'm not so sure about that last,' she said, shaking her head. 'So, what now? Counsel first…or comfort?'

Hal gazed over at her. She looked lovely, simply dressed as she always was, whether in modest, fashionable gowns indistinguishable from those of the *ton* ladies who would cross the street to avoid walking past her, or tonight in her ruffled satin wrapper. But with her firm breasts swelling beneath the dressing gown, her luxuriant hair tumbling over her shoulders and down her back, she also looked infinitely desirable. He felt passion stir.

But…he would be seeing Elizabeth tomorrow. If he enjoyed this night with Sally, slept replete in her bed, how could he face Elizabeth with the lemon scent of another woman still in his nostrils, seeped into his skin?

After downing a hasty swallow of wine to try to cool his fevered blood, he said 'Counsel. Have dilemma. Been standing in for Nicky with sister-in-law. Just lost husband. Finances in disarray. Sorting out. Sad little boy.' At the thought of David, he smiled. 'Brought him dog. But…husband's friend also calling. Sir Gregory Holburn. Widow lovely.' Just thinking of Holburn's possible perfidy transformed the heat of desire back to smouldering anger.

An avid reader of the London journals, Sally was more knowledgeable about *ton* society than Hal. 'You think he may be trying to persuade the grieving widow under his protection? A fine way to honour the memory of his friend!'

'Yes, suspect it. Accosted me tonight, warned me off. But how prove? How protect if prove? Maybe wants to accept Holburn. But loved husband, too soon for another.'

'Mayhap. But finding herself suddenly alone, bereft, uncertain what to do, she may grab the first support she finds. Lucky for her Nicky asked you to be there.'

'But not there all the time,' Hal replied, frowning. That was the heart of the dilemma. His first and strongest impulse after the confrontation with Holburn, to install himself on the sofa in the Lowery library where he might guard Elizabeth night and day, was in dire conflict with the imperative, almost as strongly felt, to protect his too-susceptible heart by spending as little time in the Lowery house as possible.

'Observe what you can when you are there,' Sally was advising. 'If it seems the lady favours the gent, then you shouldn't stick your nose into it. And since most likely this lordling isn't going to call when you're at the house, you should find an ally on the staff to tell you of his doings. There's sure to be a maid or footman happy to earn a coin by reporting what they know of their betters.'

Hal thought of the groom who'd seemed so pleased at David's delight in the puppy. But would a servant from the stables know enough of what transpired in the house?

'Try that. Still worried. Never gone into society. Sheltered whole life by family that loves her. Elizabeth a true innocent.'

Sally's eyes widened. 'Elizabeth?' she interposed.

'Elizabeth Lowery. Sarah's sister,' Hal explained. 'Afraid Holburn try to manoeuvre, manipulate her.'

Sally frowned. 'There be another danger. If Holburn treats her like his mistress, taking her about, buying her trinkets, especially so soon after her husband's death, society will think she's accepted his *carte blanche*, whether 'tis true or not. He could use that fact to coerce her consent.'

Anger flared into alarm. 'Damn!' Hal exploded, slamming his fist on the side table so hard the wineglass jumped. 'Hadn't thought of that. Easier to watch for, though. But how to protect if not sure?'

'You're so clever, I know you'll think of something.' Sally smiled at him, the slow seductive smile that never failed to turn his thoughts to mush and his body to flame. 'Just like I'm thinking of…something.' She ran her finger down his chest.

He was, oh, so tempted…but the image of Elizabeth's face danced behind his eyelids. Struggling to resist his body's demand that he succumb, Hal made himself pluck Sally's fingers from the buttons on his waistcoat. Shaking his head apologetically, he kissed her fingertips.

Sally's smile faded. 'You'll see the lady soon?'

'Tomorrow,' Hal confirmed.

Disengaging her hands, Sally rose and walked away. She tucked the dressing gown more firmly about her lush figure before turning back to him. 'So she's the one.'

'The one?' Hal echoed blankly.

Her expression infinitely sad, Sally nodded. 'All these years you stayed with me, every spring your mama throwing well-born ladies in front of you…well, at first I just figured you didn't want to be leg-shackled, leastways not to a chit of your mama's choosing. But for a long time now I've thought there must be…someone else. A lady who died or mayhap married another gent. Someone who kept you coming here while your friends went on to wed.'

Panicked denial rose in Hal. 'Not the one!' he insisted.

Sally raised her eyebrows. 'Is she not lovely, this Elizabeth?'

'Beautiful,' Hal affirmed with a sigh.

'Do you not admire her?'

Hal nodded glumly. 'Didn't want to. Thought she'd be like Mama. Isn't, though. More like you. Intelligent. Kind. Witty.'

'And you desire her?' Sally asked softly.

Hal felt his face flame. 'Yes,' he admitted gruffly.

Sally walked back to sit beside him. 'Then you must pursue her,' she said, gazing intently into his eyes.

'Too soon! Just lost husband. Besides, never want me.'

'Then she's a fool! You, Hal Waterman, are the best man any woman could ever have. You treat even a whore like a lady. I can only imagine how you'd treasure a real one.'

'You real lady, more than most I know,' Hal protested.

'Your mama, you mean. Wouldn't I just like to put a few words in that woman's ear! Hal, you are a man meant for loving.

I hear how you talk about Nicky's son and what he shares with his Sarah. You should have a family—a wife, sons and daughters to cherish.'

Sally was moving too fast. Hal didn't want to be swept along by the logic of her argument…didn't want to face what her conclusions would mean.

Before he could sort out his conflicting emotions well enough to try to counter her words, Sally said, 'This Elizabeth—she's been in your head for years, hasn't she?'

'Avoided her for years,' Hal admitted.

'You don't have to avoid her now. Heavens, she's not only available, it sounds like she needs your protection! Now, don't you go thinking I'm tired of you or wanting to look about for someone new—far from it. I'd be happy to go on as we have for ever. But…I see it in your face when you say her name… The wonder. The craving. I don't want to lie with you while you shut your eyes and pretend I'm someone else.'

Was that really what this visit was about? With his mind afire with Elizabeth, Hal couldn't be certain Sally's suspicion might not be right. Shame and distress adding to his anxiety, he hoped he spoke the truth when he replied, 'Wouldn't do that.'

Sally brushed his cheek tenderly. 'I know you wouldn't want to. So put that clever brain to figuring out how to woo the lady.'

Even if he accepted Sally's argument, it was too soon. He shook his head. 'New widow. Not fitting.'

'You've waited all these years. Stand by her now and wait a little longer. If she's got half the wits God gave a goat, once her heart's free from grief, she'll want you too. And if she doesn't…' Sally gestured around the room, 'You know where to find me. Don't let the doubts that, excuse my plain-speaking, your witch of a mother put in your head keep you from pursuing her. There's nothing sweeter than giving yourself body and soul to someone you love with all your heart.'

As she had loved the soldier who had seduced and left her? Hal wondered. But dare he believe what she was urging? That if he were a patient, considerate, and loyal friend to Elizabeth, he might have a chance to win her?

Did he really want that chance?

Attempting to peel away the misconceptions, fears and avoidance that had characterised his many-year fascination with Elizabeth Lowery, Hal tried to determine what he really felt.

As the barriers of doubt and denial dropped away, suddenly his mind cleared. Like a vista revealing itself once the morning mist burns off, he realised that, as he'd discovered over the last week that Elizabeth possessed a beauty of character to rival the beauty of the body that had enraptured him from the start, he'd lost to her what little of his heart she had not already captured the first day they met.

Which would explain why he'd kept finding excuses to put off visiting Sally, he who with his strong appetites usually spent most of his nights in her bed.

It was not just outrage at Holburn's possible treachery or a lustful need to possess. He did pine for Elizabeth. The hold she'd established over his soul that first afternoon had only strengthened over time. He might as well give up trying to protect from her the heart she already held.

Alarming as that thought was, where there was purpose, there was also hope. For the first time, he let the desire to win her he'd firmly stifled every time it struggled for expression cautiously emerge.

He could stand beside Elizabeth and protect her. He could wait while she grieved, let her come to know and appreciate him, endure the agony of uncertainty through the long slow process of discovering whether, in time, she could come to love him as he now admitted he loved her. Though he still dared not allow himself to envision the joy that would be his if one day she did give him her hand.

He came out of his reverie to see Sally watching him, tenderness in her eyes. 'Are wise. And friend dearer than you know.'

As she leaned over and kissed his forehead, Hal drew her back into his arms. For a long moment she clung to him before pushing him away.

After swiping a hand over the corners of her eyes, Sally gave him a little push. 'It's late, so you best be getting on. Go foil the villain and win the lady fair, like the heroes always do in them Minerva Press novels. If ever you want to talk, you know I'm ready to listen.'

Hal gave her hand a kiss and stood. He would miss Sally keenly…but she was right. Over the years he'd sometimes thought of marrying her, but something more than the horror of his mother and the discomfort of his friends, were he to do something so socially unforgivable, had always stopped him—the vision of Elizabeth he'd not even fully realised he was cherishing.

Nor did he feel right continuing to visit Sally now that he recognised Elizabeth embodied the dream he wanted to capture. Despite that, sadness and remorse twisted in his chest as he watched Sally, seared by his fondness for her and the conclusion that he must give her up. 'What of us? If pursue her, can't continue—'

''Course not,' she interrupted hastily. 'Don't you worry about me. Dear as we been to each other, I knew from the first it could never be permanent. You're not the sort of man to keep a mistress after he takes a wife. And scornful of society though you be, heaven knows you could never marry me! I've my friends and, thanks to your goodness, this house and some tidy investments. Maybe I'll buy a little place in the country.'

How brave and uncomplaining she was, sitting there smiling at him. He knew the break between them must pain her as much as it did him, yet she didn't cling to him or try to persuade him to change his mind. Indeed, it was she who'd made him face the truth and urged him to pursue the lady who held his heart. 'If problem, need me, call. And…thanks, Sally. Better woman than I deserve.'

She gave a watery chuckle. 'Probably I am, Hal Waterman! Probably I am.'

Hope firing a burst of energy, enthusiasm and excitement within him, he gave her one last kiss and set off across the room.

'Goodbye, Hal,' she called after him. As the door closed, he heard the merest whisper of something that sounded like 'my dearest love'.

Chapter Thirteen

Early the next afternoon, after destroying three neckcloths before he got his cravat tied to his satisfaction, sporting his newest coat and Hessians Jeffers had laboured to polish to a high gleam, Hal arrived at Green Street for his outing with Elizabeth and David.

After the dramatic revelations of the previous evening, he was more nervous than ever at the prospect of being in Elizabeth's company. He'd barely slept last night; all day his emotions had careened from an ecstatic desire to shout his love from the rooftops to a harsh self-rebuke that, despite Sally's kind words, it was highly unlikely the incomparable Elizabeth would ever come to feel similarly enraptured by cloddish Hal Waterman.

Understanding that the final resolution of his relationship with Elizabeth was unlikely to occur for many months yet, he knew he should act as he normally did. Yet by the time of his arrival, his thoughts and sensibilities were still in such chaotic disarray he wasn't sure he knew any longer what 'normal' was.

Thank heavens David would be with them! If he concentrated upon the boy, made sure everything went smoothly so that mother and son enjoyed themselves, and spoke as little as possible, he should manage to get through the afternoon without making a fool of himself.

Help her, befriend her, play the dependable adviser and casual friend she now thought him and nothing more, he told himself as he paced the blue salon, awaiting their arrival. Above all, stay fiercely on guard, lest the excitement and yearning that being close to her inspired in him should seep out in some expression of fervour or display of desire that might alarm or discomfort her.

His breathing halted and everything else in his world came to a standstill as Elizabeth entered the room. She was clothed all in black, of course, yet the apricot blush of her cheeks and the shining gold of her curls seemed so alive, so vital, in contrast with the dull mourning of her garments. His chest swelled with the sheer joy of her presence as he bowed to her curtsy.

'David will be down directly. He has been so excited, he could scarcely concentrate on his lesson this morning and so is just now finishing it. Thank you again for your kindness in offering this treat to him. And to me.'

Though her words were correct enough, she seemed somehow ill at ease, while the blue eyes she raised to meet his gaze looked wary.

Instantly Hal went on the alert. Now that the moment to appear in public with him had arrived, did she regret having accepted his invitation? He'd rather attend a dozen evening parties with Mama than have Elizabeth feel constrained in his company.

'Seem troubled,' he said, a sense of urgency pulling him out of his resolve to remain silent. 'Still go to Astley's? Not offended if changed mind.'

He couldn't forestall a rush of relief when her face cleared and she shook her head. 'No, of course not! David has been counting the moments until we could leave since he opened his eyes this morning. As I'm sure you must know, ever since you brought him

Max, my son thinks you hung the moon! I hope his exuberant chatter won't overwhelm you.'

Though Hal was more relieved than he should be that she intended to honour their engagement, to his penetrating eye she still seemed uneasy. He didn't wish her to accompany him just to please her son.

'Not overwhelm me. Enjoy his energy. Sure you equal to it?'

'I've been looking forward to the performance as well. If I appeared a bit…preoccupied, I apologise. Some trifling household matters, nothing worth speaking about.'

'Nothing too trifling. Good listener,' he encouraged, marvelling at the strength of his compulsion to eliminate any and all worries that brought a frown to the face of Elizabeth Lowery.

For a moment she looked away, her hands nervously pleating the fabric of her gown. 'Well…you did say you would advise me. With everything in his world having changed anyway, do…do you think it is a good time to send David away to school? You told me before 'twas quite normal for boys his age to go off to Eton. Though I must admit the very mention of it distresses me, I don't wish to keep him here if it will be detrimental to his future.'

Hal thought of David, the boy's sense of loss still so keen, his well being so fragile despite the love of his mother and the eager companionship of an energetic puppy. The years peeling away, he remembered another grieving little boy's reception at Eton.

He'd been large for his age, ungainly and shackled with the burden of stuttering. Some of the older boys had quickly chosen him as their chief object for ridicule, baiting him with rapid-fire taunts he could not summon the words to refute, mocking his tears of frustration and rage.

'Stoopid, stoopid, Waterman is stoopid!' Though it had been more than twenty years, Hal could recall with utter clarity the cadence of the chant, the sound of the disdainful voices telling him to 'cry, cry, cry, like Mama's baby boy'.

If only he had been. If only his mama had wanted him. But Elizabeth did want her son. There was no reason for David to face the trials he'd suffered.

'No!' he cried so fiercely, Elizabeth's eyes widened in surprise. 'Don't send. Lost father, don't make lose mother too.'

'You're sure? Painful as it would be to part with him, I know he must grow up and learn to stand on his own, take his place among other young men of his station.'

'Not man yet. Little boy still. Let him be. Grow up soon enough. Loves you. Let him.'

Apparently reading the distress that must have been evident in his eyes, her expression softened. 'Were you so very unhappy at school?'

He laughed shortly. 'Big for age. Clumsy. Boys make me run at them, trip me, laugh. Hanged myself if hadn't found Nicky.'

She pressed her lips together, blinking rapidly. 'How awful for you. I love David so very much. So…you don't think I would be "pampering" him or indulging myself to keep him here for a while longer?'

Hal shook his head emphatically. 'Loving him, not pampering. Loving him important. Most important thing in his world.'

She smiled shakily. 'That, I can easily promise.'

He nodded. 'Trust own instincts. Will know when old enough to go away. For now, just love him.' Then, wanting to comfort the distress he saw in her eyes, spurred on by emotion too powerful to resist, he took her hand, his gaze locked on her face.

Mr Waterman had told her before that he'd been sent away to school very young. But she'd not realised until this moment that the removal must have occurred very soon after his father's death, nor that the experience had been much more traumatic than he'd previously revealed. Her mother's heart, already troubled at the thought of losing David, welled up with sympathy for the desolate, grieving child Hal had been.

And then he took her hand.

There was nothing outwardly sensual or erotic in the gentle, almost reverent clasp of Hal Waterman's big fingers around her much smaller ones. Yet as he held her eyes with the ferocious strength of his gaze, a surge of physical awareness suddenly pulsed from the warmth of his handclasp throughout Elizabeth's body, resonating between her legs, making her breasts swell and her nipples tingle.

Every sense seemed to heighten. She was intensely aware of the heat emanating from his tall body standing beside her, the strong beat of his pulse against her fingertips, the barely perceptible sound of the curtains stirring on their rods in the breeze from the hallway. For the first time, she noticed the slight scatter of freckles across his cheekbones, the emerging blond stubble of beard, the sparkle of light in the grey eyes that darkened to blue-green at their centres. In the charged silence, she fancied she could almost feel the warmth of his breath against her lips.

The thought made her shiver, intensifying heat and need. An urge more primitive, more powerful than anything she had ever experienced or imagined flooded through her, demanding that she taste, explore. Her fingers itched to bury themselves in the red-gold silk of his hair while she rose on tiptoe and pulled him close enough to brush her aching breasts against his massive chest. She yearned to trace the outline of his lips with her own, tease open his mouth and capture the liquid plush of his tongue against hers, lose herself in the taste of him and the feel of his powerful arms encircling her.

So totally unprecedented and unparalleled was the feeling, she wasn't sure what might have happened next had the door not burst open as David rushed in.

'Uncle Hal, Uncle Hal, you're here! I'm so happy! Mama, I finished my lesson! Can we go now?'

Did Hal seem as shaken, as reluctant as she to break the contact between them? Struggling to master the shock, relief, and acute disappointment of David's timely—or untimely—interruption, Elizabeth none the less blessed the cheerful artlessness of her son as he chattered on to Hal about his delight at the forthcoming entertainment, giving her time to try to pull together her shattered thoughts and recapture a measure of calm.

David was already urging Hal toward the door. For good or ill, their impending excursion left her no time now to sort out the implications of this extraordinary reaction to Hal Waterman.

But like a stew taken from a boil and left to simmer at the back of the stove, while her nerves slowly settled to a semblance of normality, an acute awareness of him remained, shimmering at the edges of consciousness, occasionally sparking anew whenever he touched her.

She tried to blunt her reaction, telling herself that clasping her elbow to assist her in and out of the carriage and taking her arm to escort her to her seat in the stands at Astley's was mere courtesy, simple acts as polite and impersonal as his holding David's hand to make sure the child did not get separated from them in the throng pushing its way into the large oval amphitheatre.

But the flashes of warmth that sizzled through her body whenever she felt his hands on her continued unabated, both unnerving…and delicious.

In the back of consciousness her censorious mind warned that she ought to be appalled and distressed by this wanton reaction. But led on by the exuberant, milling crowd and her son's excitement, she was too energised by their emergence into the sun and wind of a brisk spring afternoon after long unhappy weeks indoors to tolerate any check upon her spirits. If her escort contributed a large part to the stimulating effect of this excursion, so be it. She intended to savour every pleasure to be derived from this afternoon and worry over its implications later.

And she was enjoying Astley's, much more than she'd expected. David had been shrieking with delight since the first performers took the sawdust floor, directing their troop of trained dogs through various tricks that culminated with the animals running offstage by leaping through rings of fire.

'Uncle Hal, do you think I can train Max to do that?' he asked eagerly.

'Needs to master "stay" first,' Hal responded. David must have confided to him the incident with Sir Gregory, Elizabeth thought, her gaze meeting his over the boy's head. Then Hal smiled, sending another tingle through her, almost as potent as those inspired by his touch.

David cried out and pointed, redirecting her attention back to the arena as a group of acrobats tumbled in. Some balanced flaming torches while doing intricate manoeuvres, somersaults and handstands; others juggled balls and other small objects, while a third group formed a human pyramid from whose peak the top man leapt to the floor, twisting and turning his body over and around before landing on his feet to the cheers of the spectators.

The featured equestrian events started next. The first riders galloped past while standing, kneeling or balancing upright on their hands. Other pairs approached from opposite ends of the arena and switched horses as they met in the middle; others rode tandem, one rider facing forward with the other balanced on his shoulders.

The noise of the crowd was too great for Elizabeth to be able to hear the eager comments David was directing into the ear Mr Waterman bent down to him, but Elizabeth expected she would soon be receiving a plea from her son for a pony of his own...as doubtless 'Uncle Hal' was now being entreated to teach David how to perform such tricks.

Although she herself was uncomfortable around horses,

whose tendency to shy or snort or rear unexpectedly she found disconcerting, she had to admire the sleek beauty of their glossy coats, the animals' speed and stamina and the great skill of their riders. As for David, the enthusiasm with which he clutched Mr Waterman's hand, his eyes shining and his face alight with excitement, brought a tender smile to her face.

Mr Waterman was right, Elizabeth thought. She should not deprive herself of these irreplaceable moments to enjoy her growing son. The world of scholarship and the time for living apart could wait until she felt both she and David were ready to move on to it.

As to when that would be, she would rely on her own judgement, as Mr Waterman had recommended. Her smile turned to a chuckle as she marvelled at the novel notion of Elizabeth Lowery, who had spent most of her life being guided by the opinions of others, deciding to proceed on so important a matter based on her own convictions alone.

Just as heartwarming had been watching Hal Waterman interact with her son. He had quickly adjusted his long stride to accommodate David's shorter one as he walked them to the carriage, then gave the boy a little extra toss as he helped him into that vehicle and the stands at Astley's, making David exclaim with delight. Throughout the afternoon, he'd displayed enormous patience, never seeming to tire of the continuous barrage of eager questions and comments with which David peppered him.

Recalling the easy grace with which he'd swung David to his seat and climbed up after them and his long, confident stride, Elizabeth marvelled that the man had ever been thought clumsy, so at home he now seemed in that large body he inhabited. Hadn't Nicky once told her he was a fencer? Perhaps that accounted for the fluidity with which he moved, the ripple of muscle in the arms that lifted her son so effortlessly.

Were his other limbs equally muscled? Elizabeth found herself wondering about the size and contour of his back, his legs, his torso. What a marvellous subject he would be to paint! To touch…

The hot, heady, giddy feeling intensified. Enough thinking about Hal Waterman's manly attributes! Fanning herself, she tried to direct her thoughts elsewhere.

All too soon for David's taste, the equestrian events ended and they joined the crowd exiting the amphitheatre. 'Thank you for sharing the experience with us, Mr Waterman,' Elizabeth said, warmed as much by the firm pressure of his hand on her arm as by her genuine gratitude. 'David, did you not enjoy the performance too?' she cued her son.

'It was wonderful!' David enthused. 'Better even than playing soldiers! Thank you so much, Uncle Hal. Oh, Mama, I do so want a pony. I want to stand on his back and ride at a gallop like the acrobats!'

Mr Waterman chuckled. 'Best learn on saddle first.'

'Can I have a pony? Please, Mama!'

Mr Waterman had already recommended that she provide one for her son. Giving Hal a pointed look that said 'now look what you've done!' she temporised, 'I expect you will have one soon enough.'

'Hoorah!' he cried, bouncing up and down. 'I'm almost as old as Aubrey when Uncle Nicky got one for him. I take good care of Max, don't I? I'll take good care of a pony too. You'll help me learn to ride, won't you, Uncle Hal?'

Not wanting her enthusiastic son to impose any further on their host, she cautioned, 'Now, David, you mustn't implore Mr Waterman to give up any more of his time. He's a very busy gentleman.'

'He's not too busy for me, are you, Uncle Hal?' David asked, turning his beaming face towards his benefactor.

Hal smiled and ruffled David's hair. 'Never, scamp.'

'See, Mama! Only say I may have one, please?'

'When Mama says so,' Hal cautioned the boy. 'Mustn't tease her.'

He nodded gravely. 'I won't, Uncle Hal, I promise. I'll be very patient. Capital!' he cried, giving another little leap. 'I'm going to have a pony!'

As they reached the hackney stand, Elizabeth recalled Hal mentioning that they might stop to get David ices after the performance. Not wishing to put him into a position to be implored by a pleading David if he no longer had the time or inclination to do so—which might very likely be the case considering he had just spent several hours with her energetic son, an endeavour one not used to dealing with young children might well find exhausting—she said, ''Tis growing rather late. I suppose we ought to return home.'

'No, Mama!' David protested. 'Not yet. We needn't go home yet, must we, Uncle Hal?'

Enjoying the outing and the tantalising presence of their escort even more than her son, Elizabeth had just as little desire to see the afternoon end, but she didn't wish to impose too far on their host's kindness. Damping down her own feelings of regret, she replied firmly, 'London has many wonders, my son. Now that you are growing older, we can explore more of them. But not today.'

'Best not go through Mayfair tonight,' Hal replied, giving her a significant look. He obviously wished to avoid even the rather remote possibility that they might encounter his mother. Which meant no ices at Gunter's. She suppressed a sigh. Home it would be then.

Before she could voice her acquiescence, Hal continued, 'Ever been to Royal Academy?'

'The Royal Academy of Art?' she asked, surprised. 'They sponsor an exhibition in the summer, don't they? Everitt sometimes mentioned bringing me to see it, but, with one thing or another, we never went.'

'Summer exhibition huge, impressive. Permanent collection smaller, but fine. Located in Somerset House, on the Strand. Not too far. Like to see it?'

'They have pictures, like the ones Mama paints?' David asked. 'I like her paintings. Can we go, Mama?'

'Have fine portraits. Gainsborough, Lawrence, Sir Joshua Reynolds. Student works too,' Hal said. 'Painter yourself, find interesting.'

How kind he was! Elizabeth marvelled again. Not only had he already offered them a treat her son would be sure to delight in, he'd evidently thought to discover a destination that would match her interests as well. The mere thought of viewing works by artists considered as the masters in their field sent her already high spirits soaring further.

'If you are certain it would not be an imposition, I would be delighted,' she said, smiling at him.

For an instant he stood very still, as if absorbing into himself the glow of her gratitude and enthusiasm, his ardent gaze once again capturing hers. 'Be honoured,' he said softly, the word like a caress.

A spiral of sensation started in her belly again, accelerating and intensifying as he clasped her hand to help her into the hackney. Savouring the intensity of the feeling, she held on a bit longer than necessity required while he handed her in.

David scrambled in after her, filling the carriage with questions about the building, the paintings and descriptions of his favourites among his mama's works, the most current being the sketch of Max she'd done for him the day before. And so, a short hackney ride later, Elizabeth found herself being handed down before a large, handsome building, its ground floor comprised of nine archways supporting a range of Corinthian columns surmounted by an ornamental balustrade.

'It's so big, Uncle Hal!' David exclaimed, looking upward in wonder. 'They must have even more pictures than Mama does.'

Smiling at David's awe, Hal said, 'Not just pictures. Government offices too. Clerk, courts, Navy, tax office. Visit here often. We go this way.'

Escorting them through the centre archway into a vestibule adorned with Doric columns, Hal led them to the entrance of the rooms occupied by the Royal Academy.

Hal walked in to consult with a man sitting just inside the doorway. After pressing a coin in his hand, Hal turned back to them. 'Students already gone for day. Locking up soon, but let us have half an hour.'

'Permanent collection in here,' he said, leading them down a hall flanked by sculptures and into an enormous room hung with canvases of all shapes and sizes. 'Exhibition here in summer. Walls covered floor to ceiling, hardly a space between. Artists from all over England, Europe. Impressive.'

Elizabeth stopped short inside the doorway, her eyes going wide with awe, amazement and then delight. For a moment she forgot everything, even the tantalising presence of Hal Waterman, overcome by the sheer majesty of artistic genius ranged on the walls before her.

Slowly she walked forward to pause before a landscape by Gainsborough…a portrait by Lawrence…another by Sir Joshua Reynolds. Oh, how she wished she had her pastels, or at least charcoal and a sketchbook! To try to capture something of the perspective, the posing, the Caraveggian play of light.

'President of Academy now,' Hal said, gesturing towards the portrait by Reynolds. 'Each member elected to Academy contributes one of best works.'

'They're magnificent!' Elizabeth said softly, finally finding her voice. 'I can't imagine what it must be like during the exhibition, with the walls completely covered.'

'Crowded,' Hal said.

She looked up, startled, to catch him smiling at her. He was teasing her! she realised. Making a little face at him, she continued walking down the room, studying how each artist had handled his subject, the choice of colour, the character of the brushstrokes. Oh, that they had hours for her to just stand and observe!

Seeming content to watch her, Hal kept pace with her slow promenade around the room, leaving at times when David tugged at his hand to take him to see some picture that had caught the boy's eye.

'Why that one great?' Hal's voice coming from behind startled her as she studied a Gainsborough portrait.

'See how natural and unpretentious the figure is, fitting so well into the pastoral landscape behind? How realistic, yet elegant the gentleman looks. And the light! How translucent and fluidly he applies the paint!'

'Mama, Mama, look at this one!' David ran over to take her arm. 'It's a storm!'

So it was, Elizabeth saw, surprised and immediately drawn in by the small canvas that portrayed a storm approaching a small boat at sea, dwarfing the vessel and the tiny figures manning it. In style and subject it was about as far from the academic elegance of the perfectly posed Reynolds portrait as an artwork could be, yet in its swirling imprecision was enormous power. She could almost feel the wind upon her face, the roiling of the waves, the desperation of the sailors reefing the sails. It reminded her a bit of her own efforts to capture the elusive breath of smoke above the London rooftops…only the present work displayed much superior skill and execution.

As she bent to try to read the label, Hal said, 'Work by William Turner. Former student here, now a member and sometime professor.'

'Mr Turner seems both audacious and brilliant,' Elizabeth said. 'I should like to see more of his work.'

Just then the man from the hallway entered, wagging a finger at Hal. 'Afraid we must go,' he said. 'Light fading anyway. Come back another time, if you want.'

'I should love it,' Elizabeth said, reluctantly taking his arm as he walked her slowly out of the room, pausing on the threshold for her to take one more longing, lingering glance back. Then, David loping beside them, they retraced their steps down the hallway.

'Mama's paintings are just as nice,' David pronounced. 'But I'm glad to go now. I'm hungry, aren't you, Mama?'

'We'll be home for dinner soon,' Elizabeth told him.

'But I'm hungry now,' David replied, looking up at Hal hopefully.

'Expect might find meat pastie on way home,' Hal said, holding his hand out to the boy. 'For 'sponsible young man soon to have pony.'

'Thank you, Uncle Hal!' David cried, beaming up at him. 'We can go, can't we, Mama?'

Still filled with a lingering wonder after her gallery visit, Elizabeth couldn't make herself reprove him as sternly as she ought. And she, too, was happy to linger in Hal's company as this magical afternoon faded into evening.

'Meat pies it shall be, then,' she said.

Chapter Fourteen

After leading them out of the Royal Academy grounds, Hal summoned a hackney and instructed the driver to set them down in Covent Garden. The square was bustling with traders hawking their wares, flower girls offering posies, and theatre-goers hurrying to reach their seats before the beginning of the evening's performances. After purchasing some meat pies from a vendor, they strolled the length of the square, enjoying the savoury taste of beef and crusty pastry and watching the activity around them. After reaching the hackney stand, Hal gave David a coin and told him to buy Elizabeth a bouquet from a flower girl.

'Important to show appreciation to ones we love,' Hal told the boy. 'Express thanks to those who care for us.'

David presented the flowers to her with a flourish. 'I hope you like the violets, Mama. I thought they were prettiest, just like you. And I do love you so!'

'As I love you!' Elizabeth replied and drew him close for a hug. As she cuddled David, over his back she saw Hal Waterman watching them. The tenderness and yearning in his eyes sent a little shock through her.

Was he thinking with regret about the motherly love he'd never had? Or…did he long for something more?

Then a hackney arrived and he was handing them up, putting an end to her speculation. There was no need to worry about beginning a conversation; David chattered through this drive as he had through the others, leaving Elizabeth to simply hold her bouquet, watch and enjoy.

Between herself and Hal Waterman, something sensual continued to sizzle, but that unnerving reaction was now overlayed by a calming sense of peace and happiness. At least for this moment, she refused to be upset or alarmed at the effect induced in her by the thoughtful, dependable, so very *masculine* man who had expressly crafted this wonderful afternoon for their pleasure.

Finally the long hours of fresh air and excitement began taking their toll. David's rapid chatter slowed and finally stopped as he leaned against her and dozed off.

'How can I thank you enough for this marvellous day?' Elizabeth asked Hal softly.

'Your, David's pleasure only thanks needed,' he murmured.

Though they lapsed into a companionable silence, still Elizabeth remained acutely aware of Hal sitting beside her, his size, strength, virility both reassuring and alluring. Blessing the near-darkness that allowed her to watch him more openly, she studied the angle of his head, his neck, the way the curls feathered over his collar. She marvelled at how his shoulders filled the space against the cushions, his large legs the narrow area between the forward and backward seats. The outline of his lips when he turned in profile sparked another little thrill, as did the thought of his bent knees, braced against the carriage seat so tantalisingly close to hers. A treacherous, dangerous desire continued to simmer.

She'd never watched a man like this before, she realised. Certainly she'd never looked at Everitt like this. What was happening to her?

A quick flash of panic made her wish the drive would end, that she might flee his disturbing presence. Yet the lure of him, the desire to remain close to him was more powerful still. She wished both that the excursion might be over and that it might never end. She could have eased further from him on the seat…but she didn't.

Indeed, she realised, she'd prefer to move closer still, while the lips he hadn't kissed, the nipples he hadn't even glanced at, burned.

She almost sighed with regret to have that alluring tension end when the hackney pulled up before her house. While she composed herself, Hal roused the sleepy David and helped him down from the vehicle.

After Sands ushered them in, she handed David over to the footman. 'Nurse will get you ready for bed,' she told David. 'I'll be up directly.'

'Thanks, Uncle Hal,' David said drowsily. 'And 'night. You're wonderful!'

Hal patted the boy's shoulder. 'You too.'

Her heart warmed by Hal's continuing kindness to her son, Elizabeth stood beside him and watched as the footman carried the boy upstairs. After he'd successfully reached the landing with his precious burden, she turned to Hal.

'I had hoped to ask you to stay to dinner, but…' Her voice trailed off. With David going up to bed and Miss Lowery still confined to her room and unable to accompany them, it wouldn't be proper. With a deep sense of disappointment, she knew she would have to bid him goodbye.

He nodded, as aware as she that his dining here unchaperoned would cause the servants to gossip. 'Another time.'

'I certainly hope so.' Now she should thank him and say goodbye—but she still couldn't seem to make herself utter the words. Nor did Hal voice them, as if he, too, didn't wish to put an end to this magical interlude.

He took one reluctant step towards the door, then turned back. 'Would you show me paintings? David very enthusiastic.'

She smiled. 'He would be, since I just completed a sketch of Max! After viewing the works of the masters, I'm not sure I want to let you view my poor efforts.'

'Gentle critic,' he reassured her with a smile. 'Would like to see them.'

Flattered that he'd expressed an interest in her work—even if it was probably just an excuse—one she welcomed!—for him to linger a bit longer—after a moment longer of hesitation, she nodded. 'All right, if you insist. But I warn you not to expect too much of me!'

He made a crossing sign with his finger, as if sealing a child's pact. 'Duly warned.'

Nodding to Sands, who'd been waiting to either relieve the gentleman of his coat or escort him back out, Elizabeth said, 'Take Mr Waterman's things and bring another brace of candles to my workroom. And ask Betsy to put these in water, please.' She set the violet posey down carefully on the hall table.

After turning over his coat, hat and cane, Hal followed her down the hall to her workroom. Though David had led him into her sanctum previously, she had received them at her desk near the door. Several of her paintings hung on the walls over the desk, but the canvases on which she was currently working were kept on easels by the north windows, not visible from the desk area.

The last of the daylight shone faintly through the large north windows as they walked in. Elizabeth paused to light several candles.

Now that Mr Waterman was here in her private space, poised to inspect the work that, except for her family, had been the central focus of her life, Elizabeth found herself suddenly nervous. Of course, it mattered not at all whether he admired her work. But she couldn't suppress a fierce hope that he would approve it.

She gestured to the large portrait over the desk. 'That one is of my husband, Everitt Lowery, painted last summer. The small piece below it is a colour study of some roses from our garden; the one to the left, a study of David I did last winter.'

His eyes widening, Hal approached closer to the paintings. 'You did these? Thought professional painter had. Likeness of David particularly fine.'

A rush of relief, gratification and delight filled Elizabeth. 'Thank you! I am rather fond of that portrait of David.'

Hal bent his head, studying it, then nodded. 'Captured angle of head, expression of eyes.' He turned to her and smiled. 'Almost hear chattering.'

Elizabeth smiled back. 'He does chatter! "How" and "why" and "when", until one can become quite weary with him! But you have been all kindness and patience.'

'Intelligent, interested. Like his chatter,' Hal affirmed. 'Have other works?'

'I've given most of the other oils to my family. A few are upstairs, but there are several more here, plus a number of drawings. If you would like to look?'

'Very much,' he said.

For the next half an hour, after a frowning Sands brought in two more braces of candles, Elizabeth showed Hal several more oil works, four sketchbooks full of pastel and charcoal drawings as well as the two unfinished oil paintings on which she was currently working, the cloudy rooftop and another portrait of David.

Hal examined them all with what seemed to be keen interest. Finally, she summoned Sands to bring wine and they walked back to sit by her desk.

'Work excellent,' Hal said, taking a sip of his wine. 'Much better than expected, meaning no offence.'

'None taken,' Elizabeth said. In addition to the ever-simmering connection between them, his enthusiasm for her work filled her with joy and gratitude. Sharing it with him seemed a fitting conclusion to the most wonderful day she'd experienced since before Everitt's death.

'Ever thought to show it?'

'Show it?' she repeated, not certain what he meant.

'At exhibition. Royal Society. All artists able to submit work. Committee decide what to accept. Several female artists accepted.'

'Submit my work for possible inclusion at a Royal Academy exhibition?' she breathed. 'No, of course I've never considered it! Do you really think my work is skilful enough?'

Hal nodded, his expression both serious and enthusiastic. 'Portraits especially good. Natural, unaffected. Capture spirit of subject. Good as Gainsborough.'

'Now you flatter me too much!' she said. 'I do think I'm improving, but never imagine my skill comparable to one of the great portrait painters of our age.'

'Mean it,' Hal insisted. 'Ever think to do portraits on commission?'

'You mean…have clients who would pay me to paint them?' She shook her head. 'No, I've never considered painting anyone but family.'

'Think about it. Don't need income. But work beautiful. Many pay to have portraits. Especially of children.'

By the intent light shining in his eyes and his rapt expression, Elizabeth realised that, incredible as the prospect seemed, Hal was entirely serious. 'You really believe that people outside my own family would pay me to do portraits of their children?'

'Without doubt. Have gift. Should share it.' He gestured to the portrait of David. 'Parents treasure picture like that, long after child grown. Especially after child grown.'

Sipping her wine, Elizabeth considered the possibility. Though the prospect still seemed incredible, a little kernel of excitement began growing within her. Might she actually be, not just a genteel dabbler, but a true artist? Daring to show her paint-ings to the world, submitting them to the Royal Academy exhibit, taking commissions?

The possibilities, the challenges of such a venture, energised her.

It would certainly be a more fulfilling way to spend her day than choosing between twenty different ways of preparing chicken!

'Very well,' she said slowly, almost afraid to voice the words aloud. 'I will think about it.'

Finishing his wine, Hal set down the glass. 'Good.'

For a moment they stared at each other, both seeming reluc-tant to end the evening. Then, with a sigh, Hal stood. 'Will be wanting your dinner. Best go now.'

Reluctantly Elizabeth stood as well. 'I've had a wonderful af-ternoon. A wonderful evening. Thank you so much.' Laughing with a light-hearted glee she'd not felt in a long, long time, she added, 'I shall be forever grateful to your mama and her protégée for desiring you to attend Lady Cowper's ball.'

'I also,' he replied, smiling.

She walked with him to the hallway. 'Goodnight, Mr Waterman,' Elizabeth said softly, catching herself at the last moment from calling him 'Hal'.

'Mrs Lowery.' As he had this afternoon, he took her hand, simply holding it for a long moment before bending down to brush his lips over her knuckles. Spirals of heat, giddy, intoxi-cating, radiated out from the infinitesimal pressure of his lips. Elizabeth had to curl her toes in her slippers to resist the roar of desire that she throw herself at his chest, claim the comforting, exhilarating, intoxicating feel of his arms encircling her.

Finally he released her hand, retrieved his things from a for-tuitously appearing Sands, and, with another bow, walked out.

'Do you wish dinner served in the dining room?' Sands asked, staring with a frown at the door that he had closed behind Mr Waterman.

'No, I promised to tuck David in. Have Cook fix something light for me and I'll take it upstairs.'

Sands bowed. 'I'll have it sent up directly, ma'am.'

As she mounted the stairs, Elizabeth looked thoughtfully after Sands. He was pacing away, his back and shoulders still stiff with disapproval.

Did he frown upon her spending time with Mr Waterman, with Everitt less than two months gone? It was possible, she supposed. Sands had been with her husband for many years and would be very particular about her observing every rule of mourning etiquette.

Which, of course, she had every intention of doing. Just because she'd spent a lovely day in company with a man whom she was coming more and more to like and admire didn't mean she loved her husband any less, or intended to do less than honour to his memory.

No matter how oddly her treacherous body was reacting. After pausing to drop a kiss on the forehead of her sleeping son, Elizabeth returned to her chamber and let her maid help her into a dressing gown. Finally alone, she curled up on the sofa in her sitting room to analyse her unprecedented reaction to Hal Waterman.

Perhaps it was just that her body, after slumbering for months in grief and distress, was suddenly awakening. She'd had no physical intimacy since Everitt's death, of course, and very little in the six months preceding it.

But the prospect of intimacy, the way she felt when near Everitt, had never elicited the strength and violence of the response she'd experienced today. Could it be that, older and more experienced now than the timid virgin she'd been upon her marriage, she felt physical desire more strongly?

How she wished Sarah was here. She'd always been able to ask her wise older sister's advice on everything. Though, to be honest, she wasn't sure she could ask even Sarah about this.

Thinking about Mr Waterman made her feel at once protected, safe, secure, and jittery, impatient…and attracted. She wasn't sure whether it would be wise to see more of him, to discover if these odd, contradictory sensations would abate, or avoid him.

But she didn't want to avoid him. Nor, with him not yet finished the paperwork of Everitt's estate, would that be practical.

Thinking about her attraction no longer made her feel as guilty as it first had. She'd loved Everitt with all her heart, still missed his smile, his wry humour, his gentle touch. He and David had been the entire focus of her world.

But she was beginning to see that in cherishing her, he'd also kept her sheltered from the world, dependent upon him by bonds of affection that were none the less tethers. Handling every worldly detail for her, he'd shielded her from grief and distress, but also from responsibility, excitement and opportunity. Though he'd known her since she was a child, watched the progress of her skill as a painter for many years, never once had he suggested that her talent deserved a broader, more public exposure.

He'd never even taken her to visit the exhibition at the Royal Academy, something Mr Waterman had realised after a mere ten days of acquaintance would thrill her to the very core.

She thought again of the financial tangles in which Everitt had left the estate, his not appointing a solicitor competent to manage his affairs. Of course, he'd not thought having such a solicitor would be so soon a necessity. The fact that he'd apparently borrowed money against David's inheritance to fund his passion for collecting didn't lessen her affection for him, but it did make her realise that he was not the infallible judge of everything she'd long thought him.

It also made her just a bit impatient and more than a little curious to explore the world outside the cocoon in which she'd been living.

After the proper interval, she also wanted to explore more fully the novel feelings Hal Waterman inspired. She knew beyond doubt that, whatever his faults, Everitt had loved her deeply. He would neither expect nor want her to shut herself away in his house, making it a mausoleum to his memory. When the time for mourning was done, he would want her to survive, endure and go on.

With Hal Waterman as her guide into the world beyond grief, she thought, looking up at the framed pastel sketch of her son that hung over her mantel, forging a new life was beginning to seem more and more possible.

Did she have the talent to succeed as an artist? Could she get her work accepted for showing by the Royal Academy? A swell of pride and enthusiasm filled her at the idea of being recognised, even earning money, for doing what she loved. There were women artists in the Academy exhibition, Hal had told her. Could she be one of them?

Despite her excitement, she wasn't at all sure she could. But in the afterglow of this wonderful afternoon, with the reassurance of not having to part yet with David, for the first time in her life, Elizabeth Lowery felt she just might be capable of such a challenge.

Chapter Fifteen

Inspired by her Royal Academy visit, Elizabeth went to her workroom even earlier the next morning, eager to explore in her own study of the swirling mist some of the translucent technique she'd observed in Mr Turner's painting of the storm clouds.

She also hoped by beginning early to have finished her work for the day before nuncheon so she might stop by the library and catch Hal Waterman before he departed. After the closeness and camaraderie of yesterday's excursion, perhaps this time if she pressed him to stay and eat with them, he might accept.

She had just finished mixing her oils when an insistent knocking at the study door pulled her out of her contemplation of the unfinished composition. Annoyed at the interruption, she looked up to see Sands striding in.

'What is it?' she asked, trying to keep the impatience from her voice.

'It's your maid, Gibbons. I discovered her skulking around my quarters. I've not yet done a complete inspection, so cannot be sure if anything is missing.'

The concept of how she would proceed with her brush dissolved as she stared in consternation at the butler. 'You think Gibbons meant to steal something from you?'

'I cannot imagine what other object she might have for lingering by my room. There's no reason for any female servants to be there.' Sands shook his head. 'I warned you when you brought her from the country that it would have been better to let me hire someone from an agency.'

'Gibbons is the younger sister of a maid at Wellingford Manor,' Elizabeth protested. Knowing after her marriage she would live mostly in London, she'd wanted to bring with her someone as fond of her country home as she was, rather than employ a city girl who might scorn Elizabeth's unfashionable rural preferences. 'My sister Meredyth would not tolerate a thief in her employ.'

'Perhaps the sister is more honest. But I would strongly recommend that you dismiss the girl and let me engage someone whose references can be checked.'

Theft in a household was a serious offence. On the other hand, there was as yet no proof a theft had occurred, nor did Elizabeth wish to dismiss someone who had served her for seven years as competently and cheerfully as Gibbons simply on Sands's suspicion. She should at least hear her maid's side of the story.

But, oh, how she hated dealing with disputes! Miss Lowery had always handled disagreements among the staff, Everitt stepping in to make a final decision if necessary.

For an instant Elizabeth considered asking Amelia to assist her. But with her health so fragile, Everitt's cousin did not need to have her still-uncertain recovery disrupted by this, particularly as it might make her feel she must leave her sickbed prematurely to resume management of a household Elizabeth did not wish to handle.

Acutely conscious of her painting time ticking away, Elizabeth said, 'Have you spoken with her about this?'

'To what purpose? She would certainly deny it.'

'That may be true, but I would like to hear what she has to say.'

The butler nodded stiffly. 'I had hoped, ma'am, that you would assume I make the well being of this household my first concern. My late master certainly did. However, if you insist upon speaking with Gibbons, I shall summon her.'

Sighing, Elizabeth watched him walk out. By not immediately following the butler's recommendation, she'd apparently offended him. Since, as the senior servant in the house, his disgruntlement could affect all the others, she would have to find some way to appease him. But surely Gibbons was entitled to speak on her own behalf?

If she dismissed the girl, she would have to tolerate having someone new and unfamiliar inhabiting her private rooms. If she did not dismiss the maid, Sands would clearly be unhappy.

Regardless of what she decided, there was likely to be some lingering perturbation in the household.

While she worried over how to satisfactorily resolve the squabble, a knock at the door announced that the moment to attempt that feat had arrived. Trying to put aside her distaste for dealing with the matter and assume a confident manner she was far from feeling, she bade them enter.

Under Sands's cold glare, Gibbons walked in and curtsied. 'I be so very sorry to disturb you, ma'am. But, Mrs Lowery, you know I would never steal from nobody!'

'I don't think you would. But why were you lingering near Sands's room?'

Her eyes studying Elizabeth's face, Gibbons opened her mouth, then closed it. After casting a glance at Sands, she finally said, 'I never meant no harm. Just wanting to watch out for you and the young master...no matter what someone else might think.'

'And that is all you have to say?' From the girl's manner, Elizabeth suspected there must be more that, for whatever reason, Gibbons seemed reluctant to share.

'Yes, ma'am.'

'Then you may go. I'll speak with you later.'

After bobbing another curtsy, Gibbons walked out, carefully

avoiding the butler's hostile gaze. Once the door had closed behind her, Elizabeth asked Sands, 'Have you determined whether or not anything is missing?'

'Nothing that I could tell…yet,' he conceded.

'Then I cannot see how, in fairness, I can dismiss Gibbons. Perhaps she has her eye on one of the footman and was lingering below stairs hoping to meet him.'

'Immorality is no more acceptable in a female than thievery,' Sands said repressively. 'I still urge you to consider replacing her at once.'

'But in her years with this household, Gibbons has not been proven to possess either fault. Much as I respect your opinion, I cannot feel it proper to take any further action against her now. Of course, I shall watch her closely, as I am sure you will continue to do. I assure you, I do value everything you do for this family.'

Sands's stiff bow of acknowledgement told her he wasn't mollified. 'Very well, madam. I hope nothing untoward comes of your indulgence. By the way, Miss Lowery asked if she might have a word with you.'

For a moment, Elizabeth closed her eyes in frustration. Everything seemed to be conspiring against her accomplishing what she intended at her easel this morning. But despite her eagerness to get to her work, she would never keep the gentle Amelia waiting. 'Tell her I will come up at once.'

Wondering what Everitt's cousin wished to say that could not wait until the tea they normally shared in the afternoon, Elizabeth took off her apron and mounted the stairs to Miss Lowery's room.

She walked in to find Miss Lowery sitting in a chair, her eyes alert and her colour much improved. 'Good morning, dear Amelia. How wonderful to see the roses finally returned to your cheeks!' Elizabeth exclaimed, heartened to see her looking so well. 'You are better, I see.'

'Oh, yes,' the thin, grey-haired lady replied. 'Improving every day. I did miss our tea yesterday. Did you enjoy your outing?'

Was Amelia feeling neglected? Elizabeth wondered with a little pang of guilt. 'Yes, it was wonderful! I'm sorry we returned too late for tea. Oh, I wish you could have seen how David enjoyed himself at Astley's! Afterwards, Mr Waterman suggested we stop by the Royal Academy to view their permanent collection, which was magnificent—and so inspiring. By then David was hungry, so we stopped for meat pies before coming home.'

'David has already visited me this morning, still in raptures over the trip and the wonderful Mr Waterman.' Amelia looked down, fidgeting with the robe covering her lap. 'You may think it's not my place to say so, and you might well be right, but I can't help feeling it isn't wise for you to…to be keeping company with a gentleman so soon after Everitt's passing.'

Anger and a fierce resentment boiled up, surprising in its intensity. Struggling to master it, she said stiffly, 'I am not "keeping company" with Mr Waterman. Neither David nor I have been anywhere since the funeral. David is just a child, and, though he misses his father keenly, he cannot be cooped up indoors for ever, so when Mr Waterman was kind enough to suggest the excursion, I had no reservations about accepting. I hope you are not suggesting—'

'Oh, no!' Amelia said quickly. 'I know how much you loved Everitt.' Her eyes welled up and she dabbed at them with a handkerchief. 'How I still miss him!'

Elizabeth's anger softened. 'I miss him, too,' she said quietly.

Amelia nodded. 'I know, it's silly of me to worry. But when Sands told me you wouldn't be back for tea, and that when you did finally return, Mr Waterman accompanied you into your studio, the two of you lingering there alone for some time, and darkness falling… Well, it did concern me. I wouldn't wish you to place yourself in a situation that might cause talk among the servants.'

Since when was it Sands's business to carry tales? Elizabeth thought, her anger reviving. 'You may remember that Mr Waterman is the dearest friend of Lord Englemere, my sister's husband. Acting in Englemere's stead, he has been of great help in sorting through estate papers, which, I have to say, Everitt had left in some disarray. There is no impropriety in his "lingering", as you put it, or even staying to dine with David and me, though he has declined to do so until you are well enough to accompany us. Thereby, I believe, showing an utmost respect for proper behaviour.'

'I am relieved to hear it.' Anxiously Amelia patted Elizabeth's hand. 'Please don't be displeased with me! But we both have so little experience of the world. I don't want you, in your innocence, to allow Mr Waterman to press you into a closer acquaintance that society at large might take amiss.'

The boot was rather on the other foot, Elizabeth thought. If Miss Lowery had any inkling of the exceedingly *improper* feelings Elizabeth had been entertaining towards Hal Waterman, she would faint dead away.

Guilt scoured her anew, along with a furious resentment. She had grieved and she still mourned. The outing yesterday and, yes, even her turbulent feelings for Mr Waterman had inspired her for the first time since her husband's death with a sense of excitement and anticipation, a hope that the future might offer new opportunities, fulfilment…even love.

Though she would not, until the proper time, explore or act upon the unprecedented sensations that drew her to Hal Waterman, neither did she intend to avoid his company. Regardless of the apparent disapproval of her husband's butler or mutterings among the staff.

'You aren't angry with me for speaking of this, are you?' Amelia asked, recalling Elizabeth's attention.

She forced a smile. As attached as Amelia had been to the cousin who had given her a home and a sense of purpose, Miss

Lowery would probably never look favourably upon any man who seemed to be intruding upon the place Everitt had held in David's life—or her own. In Amelia's situation, she conceded, she would probably react the same.

'No, of course not. I know you speak out of love.' Though that didn't make her advice any more palatable.

'Well, I expect you'll be wanting to get back to your work. You will come by later for tea? I'll look forward to visiting with you then.'

After giving Miss Lowery a hug, Elizabeth proceeded back towards her studio. Though the anticipation and excitement she'd felt earlier had by now dissipated, perhaps she could still accomplish something useful.

She paused by the library door, a little thrill passing through her at the thought that Mr Waterman might even now be seated behind the desk. Before she could succumb to the urge to peep inside and see, a footman trotted up and handed her a message.

Her heart leapt again at the bold, masculine scrawl in which her name had been penned on the outside. She tore open the seal, her anticipation fading as she read the short note in which, begging her pardon for the short notice, Mr Waterman wrote that unexpected business had arisen that would prevent his calling upon them today.

The titillation of holding in her hand something that had been penned by his was offset by the disappointment of knowing she would not see him after all. With a sigh, she refolded the note and proceeded toward her studio.

No need now to rush to her easel. Which was just as well, as the enthusiasm that had energised her when she mixed her paints an hour ago had wholly deserted her.

She'd just reached the studio door when Mrs Graham, the housekeeper, approached at a brisk pace. 'I'm glad I caught you!' she said, dropping a curtsy. 'There's been quite a commotion in the laundry. That…animal of young Master David's got into the back garden and ran after the sheets hanging on the line, tearing several to shreds! Being that we was short on linens anyway, I'll need you to give Sands some coin to purchase more material at once.'

Closing her eyes with a sigh, Elizabeth wondered what else could go wrong. As far as her work was concerned, this day that had begun with such anticipation was looking to become a complete loss.

With resignation, she led Mrs Graham to the bookroom and retrieved Everitt's strongbox, then counted out the staggering sum the housekeeper said would be required to purchase the new linens. Her small remaining stock was nearly exhausted. She knew little about wills beyond the fact that they often took months to probate. In that case, she probably should ask Mr Waterman to begin selling some of Everitt's statues, lest they run out of cash altogether.

She smiled grimly, wondering how Sands would react when the interloping Mr Waterman started disposing of his master's treasures. Well, his master shouldn't have borrowed funds to buy them in the first place! Maybe instead of dismissing Gibbons, she ought to replace Sands, she thought defiantly.

The butler himself entered as she was locking up the strong-box. 'A visitor to see you, Mrs Lowery.' Despite the note informing her it could not be Mr Waterman, none the less her senses jumped in anticipation before he continued, 'I installed Sir Gregory in the blue salon.'

There was no hint on Sands's face of the frown he seemed to direct towards Mr Waterman. Elizabeth also recalled seeing, prominently displayed in Miss Lowery's room this morning, the flowers the baronet had sent her. Apparently the household considered it acceptable for Everitt's long-time friend to visit his widow and son.

By now it was nearly nuncheon. She might well as resign herself to not getting any painting done today and receive Sir Gregory. Though, she thought mutinously, after her wonderful excursion yesterday, if the baronet said a single disparaging word about Hal Waterman, she would show him the door!

'I'll go in directly,' she told Sands, knowing—and not caring—that Sir Gregory's discriminating senses would probably be offended by her receiving him in her shabby painting dress.

She was an artist. A *serious* artist. If her garb offended him, so be it. A decided stomp to her step, she followed Sands to the blue salon.

Chapter Sixteen

'Lizbet, how good of you to receive me!' Sir Gregory exclaimed, coming over to take her hand as she walked in. 'I see you've been painting. I hope I didn't interrupt.'

His acknowledging her work and managing to utter that speech with only the faintest of flinches over her unfashionable attire soothed some of Elizabeth's irritation. 'Thank you, Sir Gregory, for your kindness in calling. And, no, you didn't interrupt. The morning has been such a disaster, I never began.'

'I thought you looked somewhat…perturbed,' he said, watching her with a discriminating eye. 'What's amiss? I would be delighted to assist if I can.'

She had no intention of telling him Miss Lowery had reproved her for being in Mr Waterman's company or that the dog he'd given David had shredded the sheets. Perhaps she could, though, mention the problems among the servants. As master of several diverse households, he might have some useful advice.

'I hesitate to trouble you over such a trifling matter,' she began.

'I could never consider anything that disturbs your tranquillity "trifling",' he responded.

Reassured by that, she continued, 'There was a minor fracas

among the staff, for which Sands believed I should dismiss my maid, although no real wrongdoing was proved against her. After hearing them both, I determined that she should stay, but Sands clearly resented having his opinion disregarded. Did I act rightly? I fear I have little experience in resolving such disputes.'

Sir Gregory frowned. 'It is not the place of the servants to question what their mistress decides.'

Elizabeth sighed. 'That may be true, but I do so hate having the peace of the household disturbed!'

'Of course you do! Nor should you now be troubled by the sort of perturbation that, in the past, I expect Everitt settled before you were even aware of it.'

A pang of sadness resonated through her. Truly, when Everitt lived, she had never heard more than a hint of any problems among the staff. A fierce longing filled her for those lovely, carefree days when he and dear Amelia had so deftly handled all the household concerns, when she had felt cherished and comfortable and always secure.

'Sands is involved, you said?' Sir Gregory continued, his frown deepening. 'As the highest-ranking domestic in the household, he should know better than to dispute whatever resolution you decide upon. Would you like me to speak with him?'

How wonderful it would be to have tranquillity restored—and without her having to be any further involved in the process! Vastly tempted, she said, 'You don't think it would make it worse to have an outsider intervene?'

Sir Gregory smiled. 'I've run tame here since Everitt and I were boys! I hardly think Sands regards me as an "outsider". Besides, knowing how close I was to his late master, he will believe my judgement represents what Everitt himself would have decreed. Having my support would only reinforce your authority.'

Relief welled up in Elizabeth. 'Then, yes, I would be most grateful if you would speak with him.'

'I shall be happy to do so. Men, even servants, can be rather forceful at times, I fear. 'Tis best for Sands to realise that though your husband no longer directs this household, you have not been left completely without a gentleman's advice and support. Shall you send for him?'

Feeling better already, Elizabeth rang the bell pull. A few moments later, Sands bowed himself in. 'Shall I bring wine?' he asked.

'In a moment,' Sir Gregory said. 'First, Mrs Lowery tells me there has been a disagreement among the staff.' Bending a stern look upon the butler, he continued, 'As their senior representative, I would expect you to set the example by upholding her judgement in every particular. Nor should you trouble your mistress, a lady in mourning whose tender sentiments are still so easily disturbed, with resolving petty disagreements that should never have occurred. I trust I need say nothing further?'

To Elizabeth's surprise, rather than seeming resentful of Sir Gregory's unexpected intervention, Sands's face reddened. 'You are right, Sir Gregory,' he said, bowing deeply. 'I beg your pardon.'

The baronet gestured towards Elizabeth. ''Tis Mrs Lowery to whom you should apologise.'

Sands turned and bowed again to Elizabeth. 'I'm sorry if it seemed I was questioning your authority, ma'am. It won't happen again.'

'Indeed, it had better not,' Sir Gregory said sharply. 'We'll have that wine now.'

'At once,' Sands said, making a hasty exit.

Elizabeth stared at the closing door, then looked back at Sir Gregory, both astonished and a little resentful of how quickly he'd cowed the butler. 'How did you do that?'

Sir Gregory laughed. 'Gentlemen wield authority much more convincingly than ladies. 'Tis the way of the world.'

Apparently donning trousers and a waistcoat made it easier

to run a household, Elizabeth thought, still a bit indignant. None the less, she owed Sir Gregory her gratitude for improving Sands's attitude so speedily. 'I am not so sure I approve of the world, then, but I do thank you.'

'You are very welcome. And I cannot agree in disapproving of circumstances that allow a gentleman to be able to render assistance to a fair lady. Speaking of which, had I known you had steeled yourself to begin going about in public, I would have already invited you to go out. And would have chosen a venue more appealing to a lady than the smell of horses and dogs at Astley's.'

Startled, Elizabeth's gaze shot to the baronet's face. 'How did you know I'd been to Astley's?'

'Sands mentioned you'd spent all afternoon and into the evening there when he escorted me in,' Sir Gregory said. 'I hope you didn't fatigue yourself.'

'Sands concerns himself a good deal too much with what I do or don't do,' Elizabeth said with some heat.

'Insomuch as he watches after your well being, I can't fault him,' Sir Gregory said.

''Twas an outing for David as well, and we didn't go just to Astley's. We also stopped by at the Royal Academy. I can't believe Everitt never took me there! The paintings were astounding, awe-inspiring! I could hardly wait to get back to my work today. Though sadly, assorted difficulties this morning prevented me from accomplishing anything.'

'There is always tomorrow,' Sir Gregory said with an indulgent smile.

'Yes, I'm so eager to continue.' Should she mention what Hal Waterman had recommended about her work? On the one hand, she hated to speak aloud of it, so new and fragile was the dream of announcing herself to the world as a serious artist. On the other hand, Sir Gregory was quite familiar with her paintings. If he considered her work as worthy of public viewing as Mr Waterman did, perhaps she ought to be bold enough to exhibit it.

She would ask him, she decided. Summoning all her courage, she said, 'After we returned home, I showed Mr Waterman some of my paintings. He thinks them accomplished enough that he urged me to consider submitting something to the committee for possible inclusion in the Royal Academy's exhibition. Do…do you think I am skilful enough?'

'Your work is charming! Though 'tis naughty of you to tease me by saying you plan to submit it for exhibition.'

Elizabeth stared at him. 'I wasn't teasing. I *am* considering submitting work to the committee.'

Sir Gregory's smile faded. 'You can't be serious.'

Elizabeth raised her chin. 'And why can't I? I remember you saying my oil study of David was exceptional!'

'Heavens, this has nothing to do with your skill! Surely you must know…' He shook his head in disbelief. 'Apparently, living as removed from society as you have, you don't, though even as dreadfully unfashionable as he is, Mr Waterman certainly should! My dear, you couldn't possibly consider submitting your work to the Royal Academy! It's quite acceptable for a maiden of gentle birth to draw and paint for the amusement of her family and friends, but no genteel lady would do something so vulgar as exhibit her work in a public gallery! As if she were some…some Cit trying to attract a patron. 'Tis the purpose for which artists petition to show their work there, you know, hoping that men of wealth and discernment viewing the exhibition will be impressed enough to offer them commissions. Which in your case would be unthinkable!'

'But I am an artist,' Elizabeth said, feeling the bright colour mount her cheeks. 'I would be thrilled to paint on commission.'

'My dear Lizbet, you don't know what you are saying! If Everitt were here, he would tell you as I do that you mustn't think of such a thing. Even if you were willing to face the scandal and reproach that would be directed at you personally, you must consider the effect such an action would have on the welfare of those dear to you. Lord Englemere's family would be humiliated; your youngest sister, who must even now be anticipating her upcoming Season, would have her chances to make a respectable alliance destroyed. And David! Only consider, my dear, the scorn that would be heaped upon him at Eton and Oxford as the son of a lady who so betrayed her birth as to work as a common portrait painter! It would hardly be worse for him were you to proclaim yourself a courtesan.'

Gritting her teeth, Elizabeth listened in silence as each dire pronouncement piled more weight on her fragile new dream, until it shattered into wistful fragments under the onslaught. Sir Gregory knew society well; there was no way she could dispute his arguments. And though she might not worry overmuch about what the *ton* thought of her, she could never do something that would embarrass her family—or ruin the prospects of her little sister or her beloved son.

As the baronet had said, surely Mr Waterman, little as he went about in society, would know these truths too. So why had he cruelly raised hopes he must have known could never be realised?

She stood there mutely, angry with him, with herself, her confidence shredded as effectively as Max had the household linens. Her vision of an exciting, productive future snuffed out before she had barely begun to formulate it, by the time Sir Gregory fell silent, Elizabeth was biting her lip to keep the tears from falling. It needed only this to put a cap on her day.

'Ah, Lizbet, my dear, you mustn't cry,' he said gently, taking on his fingertip one of the tears that, despite her best efforts, had welled up at the corners of her eyes. 'I shouldn't have spoken so harshly. But you can't imagine how surprised and distressed your pronouncement made me. I'm so sorry to have been the one who had to destroy your illusions.'

Still fighting the urge to weep, Elizabeth shook her head. 'It doesn't matter,' she managed after a moment.

'Poor dear, what a morning you have had! First the household imbroglio and now me scolding you. I know just the thing to help lift your spirits. Why not go for a drive with me this afternoon? Let the soothing vistas and fresh air of the park erase from your mind the upsetting circumstances of the day.'

Her mind still roiling with distress and grief for a dream she'd not until this moment realised meant so much to her, Elizabeth had no interest in driving. All she wanted to do was go up to her chamber and weep.

But as she shook her head, Sir Gregory said, 'Now I know you are angry with me. Won't you allow me to make amends? We could stop for ices. I'd even gird myself to escort you past the shops so you might look at bonnets and such. My mama always said there was nothing that raised a lady's spirits faster than the purchase of a smart new bonnet. Come now, say you will go.'

Though Elizabeth had no interest at any time in purchasing finery, at the moment she felt too dispirited to contest his mama's assessment. The baronet was so insistently eager to make amends she simply couldn't summon the energy to resist. 'As long as we are back in time for tea with Miss Lowery,' she agreed. Having been sufficiently abused already today, Elizabeth didn't wish to earn another chiding from that lady.

'Of course. I stopped briefly to pay my compliments to Miss Lowery before Sands announced me. She expressed concern about your health and spirits after having been immured in the house for so long and urged me to see that you get out more. An admonition I am delighted to heed. Shall I call for you at three?'

So Miss Lowery, like Sands, had no objection to her being escorted by Sir Gregory, a gentleman well known to them. Apparently it was just the company of a relative stranger like Mr Waterman that excited their disapproval, Elizabeth thought dully.

It was nice of Sir Gregory to want to make up for upsetting her by telling her what was only the truth. And he had been amazingly efficient in settling the business with Sands. Since there was no chance that driving this afternoon would make her miss a visit from Hal Waterman—and at the moment, she wasn't even sure she wanted to see him again—she might as well go to the park.

'Thank you, you are most kind.'

Sir Gregory bowed. 'Excellent! I'll look forward to seeing you this afternoon, then.'

Nuncheon with David, who required reassurance that Max would not be banished to Lowery Hall for his misdeeds in the laundry yard, distracted her for a while, but the lead weight of discouragement had settled upon her once again by the time Sir Gregory returned for their drive.

Mechanically repeating the deeply ingrained formulas of politeness got her through the greetings and up into his curricle. As they tooled along, she allowed him to carry on the conversation, feeling too lethargic to contribute more than an occasional murmur to his monologue.

What could she say that would be of any interest to a socially polished gentleman like Sir Gregory anyway? The only purpose that had excited her interest since Everitt's death, the tantalising possibility of becoming a working artist, he'd told her to abandon. Nor did she wish to broach the topic of David, whom the baronet felt she should be readying to go off to school, or Hal Waterman, of whom he thoroughly disapproved.

Soon, Miss Lowery would recover enough to resume control of the household, so those tasks would no longer occupy her. Without Everitt to talk to and walk with, her mornings in her workroom would be of no more significance than the time spent by other genteel ladies painting upon china or dabbling in pastels—the only thing she could look forward to was spending time with David. With a tutor joining the household, he would soon have less and less need of his mama's companionship.

What was she to do with herself?

'I see that a turn about the park has not yet managed to raise your spirits.' Sir Gregory's voice broke into her gloomy thoughts. 'Nor have my attempts at conversation managed to penetrate your melancholy reflection.'

It was a measure of her lassitude that this mild reproach, which under other circumstances would have prompted an immediate, guilty demurral, generated no reaction at all. She didn't even bother to apologise for her inattention. My, how unmannerly she was becoming!

'How solemn those lovely lips look,' Sir Gregory said. 'Perhaps something sweet will bring back their smile. Could I tempt you to some ices at Gunter's?'

Elizabeth shook her head. 'Thank you, Sir Gregory, but I don't care for any now.'

'You force me to more desperate measures. It shall have to be a stroll past the shops after all.'

Elizabeth thought about declining, but it seemed too much effort. If it amused him to look at slippers and bonnets, she supposed a walk would do her no harm. She had nothing more important to accomplish, after all.

'If you wish,' she said.

'My wish is to make you happy,' he said, looking at her with concern in his eyes.

At last a niggle of guilt penetrated her depressed spirits. Sir Gregory was doing his best to entertain her. She was being self-indulgent and churlish, acting in this foolishly taciturn, ungrateful manner simply because, like a child whose favourite sweet has been denied him, she would not be able to have what she most desired. Vowing to do better, when he tossed the reins to his tiger and handed her down before one of the *ton*'s leading haberdashers, she managed a smile.

'Ah, that is better!' he exclaimed. 'I knew Mama's bonnets would do the trick!'

Barely refraining from rolling her eyes, Elizabeth forced herself to turn her artist's eye to the colour combinations and designs of the headgear in the shop window. They walked on, lingering next before the shop of the renowned couturière Madame Bissot.

But when Sir Gregory urged her to consider purchasing something, she protested, 'No, I cannot. Apparently Everitt borrowed a large amount to fund his antiquities purchases. Until the estate is settled and those debts repaid, I must economise. Nor do I really require any new garments.'

'If it raises your spirits, a new gown or bonnet is the best of economies,' Sir Gregory countered. 'Although I am shocked to hear Everitt was so careless about finances.'

'I'm sure he thought he had plenty of time to repay the loans and return the estate to a firm footing,' Elizabeth said, compelled to defend her late husband, despite her own misgivings over his poor management.

'I meant no disparagement,' Sir Gregory replied. 'Only…' He paused, pointing out a necklace in the window of the jewellery shop next door. 'How lovely that circlet of diamonds and aquamarines would look about your neck! I never understood why Everitt always sought new items to add to his collection…when he already possessed the finest and most beautiful ornament he could ever hope to acquire.'

He opened his lips, closed them, then shook his head. 'I know it is far too early to speak of this,' he began again. 'But the…the violence of my feelings compels me to say it!'

A little taken aback by the intensity of his voice and gaze, Elizabeth could only stare as he continued, 'Surely you know how much I admire you! How much, though he was my dearest friend, I envied Everitt—because he had you, the most beautiful, gentle, gracious lady I've ever known. Had Everitt lived, I would have kept my feelings hidden, but now… I just want you to know that it would be my dearest wish some day to treat you like the treasure you are. To shower you with beautiful things—gowns, bonnets, jewels, this necklace—to set off your loveliness. To take care of you and smooth—' he stroked a finger over her forehead '—every worry from your brow.'

Though she was too shocked to utter a word, he exclaimed, 'Nay, do not reproach me! I shall speak no more now. I only ask, dear Lizbet, that when your mourning is over, you'll consider what I've said today.'

Still silent, Elizabeth studied him. She'd known he admired her, of course, but never imagined he might cherish any stronger feelings. The idea made her a bit uncomfortable… Yet having a mature, capable gentleman to defend and cherish her, with whom she could recapture the quiet peacefulness of the life she'd led before Everitt's death, seemed suddenly vastly appealing.

Sir Gregory was quite wealthy as well. There would be no worries about school fees or tradesmen or the cost of new linens. No wrangling over domestic disputes.

Or euphoric flights of fancy about a future that turned out to be unattainable.

Though David would not like the idea…

No matter. As the baronet had just assured her, it was far too early to contemplate such an offer. Though, of course, she had to feel gratified that the baronet, whom she'd long assumed to be a confirmed bachelor firmly set against marriage, had abjured wedlock all these years because he'd been pining for *her*.

'I don't know what to say,' she replied haltingly. 'I had no idea.'

He clasped her hand. 'I made sure you did not—and you need say nothing now. Only promise to consider the possibility later.'

She nodded. 'I suppose I can do that.'

'Good.' He gave her fingers a squeeze. 'Now I expect I must get you home, or Miss Lowery will scold me for making you late for tea!'

He gestured to his tiger to bring the carriage, then assisted her in. Taking up the reins, he began a light conversation about the current offerings at the Theatre Royal to which she once again needed to contribute nothing.

Then they were back at Green Street. 'I shall call again soon, dear Lizbet,' Sir Gregory said as he escorted her up the stairs. Kissing her hand once more, he set off.

Elizabeth watched his curricle disappear down the busy London street. If she could not be an artist, would she like to be wife to such a man? He dabbled in politics, attended the best *ton* parties, and knew everyone of importance. She would have to mingle more in society than she ever had. Perhaps such business would fill the sense of emptiness she'd not until today knew existed in the depths of her soul.

He would cherish her, remove all the burdens from her shoulders. And never inspire her to reach for goals that could not be achieved or fill her with the dangerous, stormy gusts of desire and emotion she felt around Hal Waterman.

Chapter Seventeen

The next evening, Hal Waterman sat in his club over a glass of fine burgundy, idly considering finding a congenial gentleman to challenge to a game of whist. Mayhap the game would take his mind off the turbulent emotions still roiling within him—and the image of Elizabeth Lowery that filled his head.

Though he doubted it. Probably he'd just play in a fog of inattention that would enrich some other fortunate friend, as he had Ned Greaves the other night.

He wished Ned hadn't left London before Hal had sorted through all the dramatic revelations of his visit with Sally. He could have sought his friend's thoughts on how to proceed with his suspicions about Sir Gregory. He might even have dared ask Ned his assessment of the likelihood of Hal's inspiring tender emotions in the heart of the lady his observant friend would probably quickly realise had captured Hal's heart.

Ah, Elizabeth, he thought, a wistful tenderness welling up in him. How he missed her after just two days. A hastily called meeting of potential investors had forced him to cancel his plans to work in the Lowery library yesterday. He'd actually felt angry and impatient at having to attend the gathering—an unprecedented reaction for one who normally found the exploration of a potential new venture invigorating and fascinating.

Instead, he'd tapped his fingers on the table while the engineer detailed his plans and the investors debated their merit, wishing for the first time in such a meeting that they might finish the business early enough for him to stop by Green Street after all. He could have justified an unprecedented afternoon call with the excuse of discussing her artistic prospects, since two of the attendees were deep-pocketed bankers with young children. Once shown Elizabeth's sketches of David, Hal felt certain the two would be eager to engage her talents to have their own offspring so vividly immortalised.

However, the meeting had dragged on until dinnertime, frustrating his desire to see her again.

Hal smiled as he remembered their time together at the Royal Academy. Excitement had made her incandescent beauty glow brighter, her avid eyes darting here and there as she took in every detail of the masterworks, her fingers clenched as if she yearned for her brush. The fire did not dim until later, when shyly she showed him her own work.

Until, surprised and inspired by the excellence of her paintings, he suggested she consider showing them in public. Joy and excitement once again illuminating her face, she gazed at him with awe, as if he had just offered her the most precious of gifts.

Simply recalling the moment made happiness surge in his own chest. He'd not witnessed such an expression of gratitude on a lady's face since, after the large return on his first investment project, he'd tried to mollify Mama's dismay over his ungentlemanly foray into finance by giving her a complete new wardrobe.

Elizabeth's joy had cost him not a penny.

He hoped, after considering the possibility, she would decide to make her work publicly available. There would be social repercussions to such a move, of course, of which she might not be aware. Nothing that could not be circumvented or overcome, he felt confident, but if she did favour embarking upon an artistic career, he meant to spell out all the drawbacks plainly before she made any move.

His smile lingered as he recalled the camaraderie that had linked them as they talked about art in her studio. She saw him as a friend now, he believed, one who admired her for more than just her beauty, one who was genuinely concerned about the welfare of both her and her son. Which made it more important than ever to ascertain Sir Gregory's intentions, so that he might protect her from them…if she wanted protection.

That lowering thought banished his smile and revived the vague sense of unease remaining after his visit to the Lowery house today. Brimming with ideas and plans, desperately impatient to see Elizabeth, he'd arrived early. He'd spent some time with David, heard about Max's iniquity in destroying sheets in the laundry yard and had a word with the groom, whose inattention had allowed the dog to escape his quarters in the stable. Then he'd worked in the library, every minute straining his ears to catch the soft tread of Elizabeth's step in the hall.

A step that never sounded. After lingering as long as he could over his work, he'd summoned Sands and asked to consult her on some non-existent matter of paperwork. Sands frostily replied that the mistress was in her studio and had instructed that she was not to be disturbed.

He'd been severely disappointed…and a bit worried. Was it merely that, buoyed by the prospect of beginning her career and alight with inspiration, she wished to work uninterrupted on her current project? Or might she be angry with him over Max's disruption of the household?

Then Sands, always distant, had seemed particularly cool today. It was more, Hal suspected, bending all his intuitive powers on analysing the butler, than the man's probable upset over Max's transgressions. Sands seemed to resent Hal's very presence in the house.

Did the butler suspect Hal of wanting to fill his late master's shoes? Though he was nearly certain he had not yet betrayed by speech or manner how much he longed to do just that, Hal felt his face redden.

Not that Sands's disapproval meant he would give up his visits. See Elizabeth he must, but he was prepared to wait patiently, his love unspoken, and be no more than a concerned friend to her for as long as it took her to recover from her grief.

Despite the growl of protest from his frustrated body, the notion of remaining just a friend was comforting, even. It allowed him to put off the terrifying moment when he must reveal his true feelings and put himself in contention with all the others who would doubtless wish to lay claim to the lovely Elizabeth Lowery.

Unless she chose the artist's path. That decision would severely restrict her chances of remarriage to a *ton* gentleman, unless her prospective spouse was as supportive of her talent— and as indifferent to the opinion of fashionable society—as Hal was himself. It was a measure of idiocy of the *ton*, he thought with disgust, that a lady who embraced such an occupation would be damned as a disgrace to her birth while Society leaders like his mama, who did little more than plan soirées and destroy reputations, were said to embody feminine gentility.

No wonder he eschewed society as much as possible!

As he finished his glass, a party of gentlemen entered. Having nothing in common with Montclare, Fitzhugh and Carleton— Corinthians of the first stare primarily interested in drinking, enriching their tailors and pursuing loose women—Hal merely nodded as they passed.

They were also boisterous, Hal thought with annoyance. He was trying to shut out their overloud conversation when the mention of Sir Gregory's name seized his attention.

'What interesting news about Holburn?' Montclare was asking.

'Saw him strolling down Bond Street yesterday with a striking blonde beauty,' Fitzhugh replied. 'Has he given up his last ladybird, do you know?'

Blonde beauty? Hal's heart slammed into his chest. Could it be Elizabeth?

'Heard Lord Wentworth finally returned from country,' Carleton said. 'Perhaps Lady Wentworth decided 'twas time to terminate their little affair before her husband caught wind of it. Or perhaps the spark died. You know Holburn. Never stays with the same woman overlong.'

'As easily as he seems to charm them, why not sample some new delight? Lady Wentworth, Mrs Simmons, Lady Carlisle, plus that lush little actress from the Theatre Royal…and that's just this year!' Fitzhugh said.

Uninterested in Sir Gregory's past conquests, Hal nearly came out of his chair with impatience to learn the newest lady's name. Identify the lady! he urged silently.

'So who was this new beauty?' Montclare asked.

'Didn't recognise her,' Fitzhugh replied. 'Maybe a demi-rep fresh from the provinces. Had the appearance of an angel, though. Hair of deepest gold, the face of a goddess, eyes blue as a summer sky. As for her figure, 'twas impossible to tell, bundled up as she was in a shapeless black pelisse.'

'If she was in black, she's probably a widow,' Carleton observed. 'He does favour widows. But whose?'

Golden hair. Face of a goddess. Blue eyes like summer sky…and dressed all in black. It must have been Elizabeth, Hal thought, chest so constricted by anxiety and rage he could barely breathe.

'She looked genteel enough,' Fitzhugh said. 'Though she could be the relict of some Cit, I suppose.'

'I expect we'll sniff out her identity soon enough,' Carleton said. 'On Bond Street, you say?'

'Yes. It appeared they'd just come from Madame Bissot's, which is where Holburn dresses most of his mistresses. He was pointing out a fine necklace in the window at Rundell & Bridge, probably telling her how the aquamarines would echo the blue of her eyes.'

The gentlemen all laughed before Carleton said, 'He must be well along the way to seduction if he's dangling jewels before her. I bet she succumbs before her mourning period ends. And I wager I can discover her name before the deal is concluded.'

Hal found himself recalling Sally's words. If the unknown beauty was Elizabeth, her appearance on Bond Street with Sir Gregory could have her walking into scandal. The question was—did she do so willingly or totally unaware?

After arguing for several moments over the speed with which Carleton could uncover the beauty's name, the men signalled a waiter to bring the betting book. 'Fifty guineas says I learn the lady's name before that sly dog finishes setting up his love nest,' Carleton said.

'You're on,' Fitzhugh replied.

'I'll back Carleton,' Montclare said. 'His sources are impeccable.'

As Hal watched covertly, appalled, the men recorded the wager. A furious desire seized him to find Sir Gregory, grab him by the throat and choke the life out of him. He might not press Elizabeth to accept a *carte blanche*, but he was too experienced not to know that in strolling her down the merchandise row that was Bond Street, as Sally had warned, he was creating among gossipmongers like Fitzhugh and Montclare the perception that she was, or soon would be, his mistress.

He recalled how she'd confessed her shyness had led her to avoid a Season. She would loathe becoming the object of some lewd wager in a gentleman's club.

He must do something quickly. But what…and when?

If he delayed too long and the lady was identified to be Elizabeth, rumour would spread swiftly. Her name would be bandied about in every gentleman's club in London; curious men with only the slimmest of ties to her late husband would use them as an excuse to call upon and ogle her, wondering if they should try their own luck. Sooner or later, she would discover the reason behind this sudden influx of visitors. Hal could only imagine how devastated and angry she would be.

Of course, there was the possibility that they were all misjudging Sir Gregory. The baronet's goal might well be marriage. He, like Hal, had known her for years and could not help but admire her. Now that she was free, perhaps the baronet saw a chance to claim as his own a lady for whom he'd long pined.

'Twas too late for Hal to approach the Lowery groom and see about setting him to spy on Sir Gregory's activities, as Sally had suggested. Elizabeth or unknown beauty, *carte blanche* or wedlock—he had to find the answers before the industrious Carleton ferreted out the lady's identity.

A sense of doom settled heavy in his chest. Unless by some miracle he thought of a better plan, despite the ineptness of speech this delicate situation would render even more acute, Hal feared he was going to have to speak about this to Elizabeth herself.

The next morning, after dressing with care, Hal arrived in Green Street somewhat earlier than his normal hour. He went on to earn a raised brow from Sands by requesting that, rather than be conveyed to the schoolroom to see Master David, Sands request his mistress to receive Hal in her studio to discuss a matter of some urgency.

Having not come up with a swifter means of resolving the situation than speaking directly with Elizabeth, Hal had decided to seek her out immediately. Knowing he couldn't endure waiting even three more hours to find the answer to the question plaguing him, while he looked for an opening to broach the subject of Sir Gregory, he could resume their discussion about her work.

If a casual question about her whereabouts yesterday confirmed she'd not been strolling Bond Street with Sir Gregory, Hal need say nothing further.

Oh, how he hoped it had been some other blonde lady!

Sands returned to inform him that, though his mistress did not appreciate having her morning's work disrupted, if the matter was truly urgent, she supposed she could receive him.

The butler delivered that less-than-courteous response so smugly, Hal had to bite back a blighting retort before following Sands to her studio.

Pausing on the studio's threshold, Hal took a deep breath. He must bottle up all his anxious, angry, explosive emotions and speak with the dispassionate concern of a true friend, and not rant like a wildly jealous lover whom the wrong reply could cast into despair. For if it appeared that Elizabeth actually favoured the baronet, he must follow Sally's advice, say nothing and walk away.

Realising that, the tension inside him coiled tighter. Could he return to the dull stability of his existence before he'd recognised the life-altering truth of his love for Elizabeth? Hal wasn't at all sure he could.

Somehow, he would have to. The choice was all Elizabeth's, not his. If she elected to accept Sir Gregory's offer—be it *carte blanche* or marriage—he would have to hie himself north, bury himself in work on the new project, and try to forget he'd ever conceived of a different future for himself.

The only saving grace in that dismal prospect was the fact that, since he'd never declared himself, he would be spared her pity.

He'd never allowed himself to truly believe he could win Elizabeth. Surely it wouldn't take too many months of hard labour and grim determination to stamp out the tiny flare of hope that had been ignited by Sally's encouragement and one after-noon at the Royal Academy.

Then Sands was announcing him. Resolutely he walked into her studio.

'So, Mr Waterman, what is this urgent matter that cannot wait?' she asked coolly.

His pulse leapt as always at the sound of her voice, even though its tone seemed remote rather than as warmly welcom-ing as it had been of late. He hadn't been mistaken; she was dis-pleased with him.

But not because he'd interrupted her at work. To his surprise, she was seated at her desk staring at her oil study of David, not even wearing her painting smock. The palette on the stool beside her easel held only the dry, crusted remains of a previous work session, nor did the scent of oil and fresh paint hang in the air.

'Sorry to disturb,' he said, bowing. 'See not yet begun.'

'No,' she said shortly. 'What did you want?'

She looked tense and…unhappy, Hal thought, studying her closely. Something had obviously occurred to upset her since he'd last seen her. But what—and how could he make it better?

Might as well broach the easiest topic first. 'Have you con-sidered idea of painting?'

She straightened with a jerk and turned on him a look filled with so much pain and anger that he recoiled. 'Yes, I have. Rather too much, I expect. Did you enjoy a good joke at my expense? Laughing at how easily you gulled me, how disappointed I'd be when I learned the truth?'

Hal stared at her blankly, his usual perceptiveness deserting him. 'Joke? Gulled? Don't understand.'

'Are you truly are as blockish as your mama says, then?' she lashed out at him. 'Too oblivious not to have realised the…the drastic social consequences for me and my family were I to pursue the course you were recommending?'

Before he could attempt a reply, she jumped up and took an agitated turn about the room. 'How could you?' she demanded, looking back at him. 'How could you inflame my hopes and encourage my dreams, knowing that if I had any sense of responsibility for family at all, they must be immediately crushed. As infrequently as you go about in society, surely you must have known!' She halted before him, accusation and misery on her face.

'Eliz—' Horrified by the conclusions she'd drawn, Hal blurted out half her given name before choking off his reply. 'Mrs Lowery, please!' he began again. 'Never intended to lead on! Of course, repercussions. But late when spoke. Protect reputation, needed to leave. Thought to talk more later. If think about, not interested, no need to discuss further. Came this morning to find out.'

Bosom heaving with emotion, tears glittering on the ends of her lashes, she studied him. 'So you didn't intend to mislead or deceive me?' she asked slowly.

Hal shook his head vehemently. 'No! Never do that. How could you think it?'

For a few moments longer she gazed at him, apparently assessing his sincerity. Finally, she gave him a small nod. 'All right. What do you judge to be the repercussions, then, if I were to exhibit my work?'

Anxious to explain himself, to redeem himself—and erase the reproach in her eyes—he found the words almost tumbling out. 'Lady of quality not have profession. Scandalous. Artist considered like singer, dancer. Reputation little better than courtesan. Close doors of society if known openly. Affect family, too. Need to consult Sarah, Nicky. But don't think they'd counsel you to hide gift.'

She raised her eyebrows sceptically. 'You think they would advise me to do something that could embarrass them, perhaps ruin my sister Faith's début? Or David's future?'

'No. But if careful, could pursue gift, avoid scandal. Delay public exhibition until Faith married. Also thought of David. Know what it is to be object of scorn. If keep at home with tutor, avoid that. Once older, at Oxford, much forgiven young man of birth and fortune, despite unfashionable connections.' He gave her a deprecating smile. 'Consider me. Despite reputation, Mama still finds willing marriage candidates. If prefer, work through intermediary. You remain anonymous. But work still exhibited. Gift still shared with world. Wonderful gift. Shame to hide it.'

She stared away, obviously considering his words. 'So, it might yet be possible. Without harming my family?'

'Yes, if want it. Do you want it?'

She nodded absently, pacing once more. 'I wouldn't submit anything to the exhibition committee until after Faith is settled. As lovely and charming as she is, she may well be affianced in her first Season. I'd much prefer to have David remain with me until university anyway! I shall talk with Sarah and Nicky, but you are right—I do not believe they would urge me to abandon work that means so much to me, as long as pursuing it quietly would not injure the family. As for myself, I care little about Society's disapproval, but, to protect them, I would be content that my paintings remain anonymous.'

Immensely relieved, Hal watched as the hurt and unhappiness of her expression changed first to pensiveness and then to a growing excitement. 'Could delay public showing longer, if wanted,' he encouraged. 'Until David out of university. Build up body of work, exhibit later. Take private commissions now. Have agent show sketches to select individuals, secure commissions. Continue to paint, develop skill.'

'Yes! Oh, yes! How strange that before you mentioned the possibility to me, I'd never once even considered exhibiting my work or painting on commission. Now I find that the idea of pursuing my craft is dearer to me than almost anything except the welfare of my family.'

Hal gestured around the room. 'Skill gift from God. Wrong to hide it away. Some businessmen at meeting yesterday, if see sketch of David, want one of own children. Gift not vanish if not begin today. Can wait.'

She smiled tremulously. 'Would you act as my agent?'

Hal nodded. 'Be proud to. Conceal identity indefinitely, unless wished me to reveal it.'

She nodded back. 'I shall have to think more about it. And consult Nicky and Sarah, of course. For now, I must get back to work!' Grabbing the smock hanging on her chair, she shrugged it on and came over to stand before him.

'I apologise for misjudging you. I should have known you would never advise anything that would harm me or my family. Thank you...for giving me back my dream.'

Her intense gaze fixed on his face, for one heart-stopping moment Hal thought she meant to rise up on tiptoe and kiss him.

Dizzy from her rose scent, the warmth and nearness of her, it took every bit of self-control he could muster not to reach out, draw her against his chest and take the lips she seemed to be offering while he tangled his fingers in the golden silk of her hair.

Though the effort nearly killed him, he was glad he managed to restrain himself, for at the last moment, she stepped away. 'Thank you,' she whispered again.

Clearly she meant to dismiss him. With a blessed harmony restored between them, Hal wished more than anything that he could ignore his conscience and walk away.

But the matter of Sir Gregory and his intentions remained unsettled. Hal had little doubt who had been filling her head with dire pronouncements on the disasters that would befall her becoming an artist. Which meant that some time between their excursion to the Royal Academy and this morning, she must have seen the baronet. When and where, he had to ascertain.

Girding himself, he said, 'Ride with Sir Gregory, day I did not work here?'

Already heading toward her easel, she glanced over her shoulder, an almost coquettish smile on her lips. 'And if I did?'

Dreading what must come next, hoping without much conviction that she'd answer in the negative, he continued, 'Stroll with him on Bond Street?'

Her smile was definitely coquettish now. 'I did indeed. Have you been spying on me, Mr Waterman?'

Having confirmed that she was the mysterious blonde beauty, he now had no choice but to warn her. Trying to resurrect bits of the speech he'd prepared before the misunderstanding over her artistic career had blown those thoughts from his head, he began, his face already flushing. 'Sorry, must speak. What Nicky would say. May favour baronet. If so, not my place to object. Maybe in speaking, do disservice to Sir Gregory. But must know. Baronet not marrying man. Long series of mistresses. Most well-born matrons or widows. Prefers widows.'

Hal saw her struggle for comprehension, knew with anguish that his explanation had been even more tangled than usual. Finally understanding dawned.

Her eyes widening in indignation, she exclaimed, 'What a…a tawdry thing to infer! It so happens that Sir Gregory has spoken to me of his affection and admiration. He indicated quite clearly that later, when the time is right, he intends to make me an offer.'

His worst suspicions confirmed, Hal nodded miserably. If only he'd followed his instincts and strangled Sir Gregory when he first suspected the baronet's unsuitable interest! 'Sure he will. But probably *carte blanche*.'

Elizabeth gasped and drew herself up. In the fury of her eyes, the rigid angle of her arm, Hal saw the blow coming and braced himself.

Her slap caught him full on the cheek, the crack of it resounding in the silence. After staring at her hand as if shocked by what she'd just done, she looked back up at him, lips trembling. 'I think you'd better leave.'

Hal bowed deeply. 'As you wish. But felt must warn. Seen by gentlemen on Bond Street, stopping at modiste, looking at jewels. Places Holburn usually outfits mistresses. Gentlemen didn't recognise you. But already in betting book that Bond Street lady to be baronet's next *chère-amie*. Before mourning period even over.'

She'd walked away from him, but at this she turned back. 'Are you telling me there is already a wager at White's that I will become Sir Gregory's…mistress?' she asked, uttering the last word with revulsion.

'Don't yet know beauty with baronet was you. Find out soon, though. Then be in betting book by name.'

'They would put such a shameful assumption in writing, when I have done no more than stroll with Sir Gregory?'

Hal nodded regretfully. 'Bet always speculative.'

'But to impugn my reputation on so slender a grounds? Why, that's—that's *vile*!' Her face flushing with anger, she looked as if she'd like to take another swipe at him.

Grimly Hal stood his ground. 'Vile,' he agreed. 'But fact. Thought you should know. Protect yourself…unless wish to be mistress?'

'Of course I do not!' she declaimed furiously. 'How dare you say such a thing! Still, I cannot believe Sir Gregory would use me so shabbily. Why, he was Everitt's greatest friend! Surely these—I hesitate to call them "gentlemen"—are mistaken, attributing to a man of honour their own wicked thoughts.'

'Might be,' Hal admitted. 'But might not. You innocent of men's ways. Must avoid actions that support conclusions of evil-minded. Like walking with gentleman on Bond Street, where men outfit mistresses. Deserve only gentleman of pure intentions.'

Which he'd hoped one day to prove himself…before necessity compelled him to ruin everything by speaking to her in a manner she obviously saw as insulting her character and honour.

'I suppose I am ignorant if a stroll down Bond Street could be so damning!' she retorted, still clearly incensed. 'If that simple a misdeed can cast a shadow upon my reputation, there are probably other equally innocuous actions that might endanger it. How do I protect myself? I cannot baldly ask Sir Gregory his intentions!'

'No, but lady. Feminine mind. Clever at questions, hints.' He was certain his mama could sniff out the truth of the situation in a moment. Unfortunately in this instance, Elizabeth wasn't as devious as his mother. 'Think of something,' he urged.

Clasping her arms protectively around her, she stared accusingly at him, doubtless consigning him to the outer reaches of hell along with the rest of his lecherous brethren. 'Now I understand why ladies went so willingly to nunneries. I suppose I must thank you for the warning. But I'd prefer that you leave now.'

Trying—and failing—to think of something that might comfort or mollify her, Hal bowed again. 'As you wish. Sorry. So very sorry to trouble you.'

His cheek still stinging where she'd slapped him, his heart heavy, Hal left her, weighed down by knowing that, in trying to protect Elizabeth from Sir Gregory, he'd probably just alienated her from himself for ever.

Chapter Eighteen

For a long time after Mr Waterman walked out, Elizabeth paced her studio. Just two days ago, she'd been so full of hope and energy, excited by thoughts of the future, believing that her life at last had taken a turn for the better. What false illusion that had been!

She closed her eyes tightly, willing back the tears. When she opened them again, her gaze fell upon the portrait of Everitt over her desk. A wave of grief and longing swamped her, so intense she nearly staggered.

How she craved the sweet peace of her life with him! A tranquillity and comfort that, just yesterday, she had contemplated recapturing by wedding Sir Gregory. Who might instead be thinking of taking advantage of her loneliness and grief by setting her up as his mistress.

She still could not believe him capable of such perfidy. But according to Mr Waterman, her person, if not yet her identity, had already been entered in the famous betting book at White's, to be perused by every gentleman of the *ton*. And once that identity was discovered, as it most certainly would be, her name would be added to the wager for men to lust over and speculate about, as if she were the newest doxy on the

London stage. The idea made her feel faint and dizzy with humiliation, as if she'd been thrust on to a London street in nothing but her chemise.

What was she to do about it?

How she longed for Sarah, that she might ask her advice. Or Nicky. If he were here, surely he'd be able to squelch those horrid rumours.

Suddenly furious, she ceased pacing and turned to slam her fist on the desk. Why, just when it seemed simply surviving had grown easier, must she deal with problem after problem, each one more distressing than the last?

The blaze of indignation spent, she sighed and seated herself behind the desk. Unfair or not, equipped to deal with it or not, somehow she must cope.

First she had to ascertain Sir Gregory's true intentions. Focusing her mind on their outing two days ago, she scoured her memory to recall exactly what Sir Gregory had said as they strolled down Bond Street.

He wished to treat her like the treasure she was, shower her with beautiful things, she remembered. Men were known to lavish money on their doxies…but a husband might also wish to bedeck his wife in splendour, mightn't he? A niggle of doubt shook her.

He'd also said he wished to take care of her and smooth every trouble from her brow. She recalled the touch of his finger against her forehead, the warmth in his gaze both shocking and disconcerting. Surely he knew her well enough to guess that she could never feel 'untroubled' if all society assumed her to be his mistress!

At the time he spoke those words, she had immediately thought he meant marriage. But, her face burning with shame at the realisation, she supposed his vows could just as easily support an intention to offer her *carte blanche*.

He couldn't truly believe she would accept so shabby an offer, did he? she wondered, her anger rekindling. If he dared offer her such an insult, she would toss him out on his ear and never speak to him again!

But perhaps she was maligning him. Perhaps he'd meant exactly what she'd first assumed. How was she to tell?

Use her feminine mind, Hal had advised her.

Leaning her chin on her hand, she stared into the distance, pondering. Then she took up her quill and wrote Sir Gregory a note.

As Elizabeth had hoped, at mid-afternoon Sir Gregory came in answer to her summons. Receiving him in the blue salon, already garbed in her carriage dress, she had to make herself smile in response to his greeting.

Suspend your suspicions, she told herself as he bent over her hand. You may yet discover that his intentions are entirely honourable. Though the enormity of the wrong he was doing her if they were not made it difficult for her to act naturally around him.

'The fresh air of our last ride must have had a beneficial effect, else you'd not have requested my escort again so soon,' Sir Gregory said as he escorted her down the stairs. 'How delighted I was to find myself free this afternoon and able to accept your invitation!'

'I, too, am delighted,' Elizabeth replied after he'd helped her up and assumed his own seat. 'When one must contemplate a weighty matter, 'tis a relief to move closer to a decision.'

Occupied in setting the horses in motion, Sir Gregory slid her a glance. 'And what weighty matter is it about which you must decide?'

'I shall tell you once we reach the park, when I may claim your full attention.'

'I am ever happy to devote my complete attention to you, dear Lizbet,' Sir Gregory said with a fond look.

After a brisk drive through the busy Mayfair streets into Hyde Park, they at last reached the carriageway, not yet crowded at this relatively early hour. Pulling up the horses, Sir Gregory looked down at her.

'You intrigue me, my dear. Pray, what is this serious matter you would discuss?'

'Surely you haven't forgotten already,' Elizabeth said, giving him a little pout. 'You spoke to me of it just two days ago, while we were walking on Bond Street.'

Sir Gregory's eyes lit. 'Ah, that matter. You don't mean to chastise me now for speaking hastily, I hope! I assured you I was willing to wait.'

'Perhaps I am not,' Elizabeth said, peeping up through her lashes at him in what she hoped was a flirtatious manner. 'Though I would not have you believe that I didn't truly love Everitt nor that I do not still grieve for him, I somehow find myself anxious to contemplate the future.'

An ardent look came over Sir Gregory's face. 'And you are considering allowing me a place in it? Dear Lizbet, 'twould be my fondest dream!'

'Of course, nothing could be settled yet. I intend to observe the full mourning period,' she cautioned.

'I would expect no less.'

'Still, I understand an estate can take a very long time to settle, and I must anticipate what I might need.'

'Only give me the right to cherish you, my dear, and you need worry about nothing.'

'You are so gallant, Sir Gregory! But it wouldn't be fitting for you to supply my bride clothes.'

Sir Gregory's smile faltered. 'Bride clothes?'

'Indeed, for I could not contemplate being married in my blacks! Then there is the matter of which residence we would occupy. I would need time to secure new positions for Everitt's servants before I closed up the house, as I assume you would wish your wife to preside over one of your own properties?'

She gazed up at him, trying to keep a look of innocent inquiry on her face.

An attempt that grew ever more difficult as Sir Gregory looked away, obviously uncomfortable. 'Well…with more than six months of mourning left, it's far too early to concern yourself with such matters now.'

She had no need to feign the blush of embarrassment—and rage—that mounted her cheeks. 'Why, Sir Gregory!' she exclaimed, trying to look confused. 'Did I misunderstand? I thought you said you wished to cherish and—'

'Yes, yes, I did,' he cut her off. 'You must know how much I treasure you.' He attempted a reassuring smile, which did not quite succeed.

'You wanted to shower me with beautiful things,' she pressed on, ignoring his obvious desire to terminate the conversation. 'Remove the frown from my—'

'So I did!' he snapped. Catching himself, he smiled again and patted her hand. 'But your cheeks are so flushed, I can see it distresses you to speak of this, while you are still so overset by Everitt's passing. Let me take you to Gunter's for some cooling ices.'

It would take more than ices to cool the rage building in her chest. Determined to push him into the denial she was now certain he meant, she said, 'I am only distressed that you no longer seem willing to discuss what you were so anxious to broach to me only two days ago. You were speaking of marriage, were you not? As Everitt's dearest friend, surely you could mean nothing else.'

'Remarriage before the end of your mourning period would be most improper,' he said primly, as if he could slough the perfidy of his desires off on her. 'You must be feeling out of sorts, to persist so in these thoughts. I think I'd best return you home.'

Though she'd not managed to manoeuvre him into denying he'd meant to offer marriage, his failure to reassure her that he did during the several opportunities she'd given him was telling enough.

'Yes, perhaps you'd better take me home,' she said, suddenly finding it required all her self-control not to seize him by the lapels and scream at him like a fishwife.

Silence reigned during the short drive back to Green Street. Once they arrived, she stayed his hand when he would have dismounted to help her down. 'James the footman can assist me to alight,' she told him. 'You'd do better to return to your club and assuage your disappointment over losing that wager.'

Sir Gregory's eyes widened. 'Wager?'

'Since I now have a clearer idea of just how you meant to "cherish" me, you needn't call here again. Ever.'

Comprehension flashed in his eyes. 'How did you know— Waterman! It must have been him. I can't believe he repeated such salacious nonsense to you—or that you believed him. How despicable to sully the ears of a gently born lady with such a thing!'

'Do you deny that there is such a wager?'

He remained silent for a moment, obviously casting about for an answer that would mollify her.

'No matter.' She cut him off before he could begin. 'So it's not despicable for someone to wager on the probability of my becoming your mistress? For you to allow men I don't even know to sully my reputation? 'Tis only despicable for Mr Waterman to warn me of it? What a twisted code of honour you embrace!'

'Lizbet, you misunderstand,' he protested. 'I'll come back later, when you're calmer. We'll discuss this…'

She stared him back into silence, her hard blue gaze cutting off his attempts to explain. For a moment, beyond the furious beating of her heart, Elizabeth heard only the jingle of harness as his restive horses shifted their feet.

'My name is "Elizabeth",' she said coldly. 'And I do not recall giving you leave to use it.'

Nodding to the footman standing beside the curricle, she let him hand her down, then mounted the stairs to the front door without a backward glance.

Late that night, Hal returned to his club. He'd spent the afternoon and evening in another meeting of investors. Their agreement on funding complete, the engineer on the new project would be leaving for the north to begin the initial phases. Hal had promised to travel there shortly to oversee the initial construction and bring back a report of its progress to the other investors.

He might as well leave London. He'd done all he could to put the Lowery finances in order, save file the still-missing will for probate. Everything else could wait until Nicky returned to take up the reins. Having alienated Elizabeth Lowery, there was no need for him to call again. A dull ache throbbed in his chest at the thought.

David would miss him if he just took himself off with no warning. He'd have to arrange a time—early in the morning, when Elizabeth was working—to visit the boy and explain the obligations that required him to leave London.

Then there was the pending matter of Elizabeth's artistic work. He supposed he could pen her a note asking if she wished him to begin a list of potential clients from among his industrialist contacts in the north.

Sending a note would be far better than seeing her in person, standing before her while she stared accusingly at him, her eyes brimming with tears of hurt and outrage. It felt like someone drew a knife across his chest, just remembering it.

He only wished his speech had been clever enough to warn her while somehow sparing her feelings. Having been warned, he felt confident she was intelligent enough to somehow ferret out Sir Gregory's true intentions. In any event, having made it quite clear she had no desire to become the baronet's mistress, she would know to avoid appearing with him in places that might cause the idle and evil-minded to draw wicked conclusions.

A sudden idea sent a surge of new purpose through him. Perhaps there was one more thing he could do to help her.

Glancing around, he noted most of the denizens of White's, having dined some hours earlier, were now occupied in gaming or deep in their cups. Those who chanced to walk by gave him no more than a nod in passing.

Quietly rising from his seat, Hal strolled unhurriedly to where the betting book was kept, waiting until the waiters were all occupied serving the crowd that had assembled around a table where four members were finishing a hard-fought game. Seizing the book, he slipped it beneath his coat and walked to the hearth.

A few moments later, a great shout went up as one of the players won—or lost—a hand. While the outcry continued, Hal flipped to the page on which Carleton's wager had been recorded, tore it out and tossed the page into the flames, then ambled back to replace the book.

Every day some new scandal became the most talked-about happening at the club. As long as Elizabeth avoided being seen with Sir Gregory—and Hal felt sure she now would—the idle gentlemen who'd made the bet, finding it impossible to determine her identity, would turn their attention to the next salacious story. Should they ever pick up the book to review the wager, Hal thought it unlikely they'd care enough about so minor an event to protest much over the missing page.

Elizabeth might escape with her name and reputation unsullied after all.

He was watching the last bits of the page blacken into cinder when a voice taut with anger assaulted his ear. 'My, Mr Waterman, how busy you've been.'

Chapter Nineteen

Hal's mood rocketed to simmering anger in the instant it took him to recognise Sir Gregory's voice. He turned to stare at the baronet who'd walked up behind him, several friends loitering in his wake.

'Not as busy as some,' he responded tightly.

'Have you no tact or discretion at all?' Sir Gregory demanded. 'To have broached such a topic to…a certain lady now, while she is still so vulnerable to upset and alarm! 'Twas as unpardonably cruel as it was unnecessary.'

Hal looked down at Sir Gregory. 'Crueller than making her object of wager? Crueller than what you intended?'

Sir Gregory made a deprecating noise. 'You can't claim to know how she would have reacted to the…prospect, had you not ambushed her with it now, all unprepared and her emotions so unsettled. Once a widow recovers her spirits, she often finds she enjoys her independence and has little desire to remarry. For a widow in…this lady's position, virtually unknown and with limited means and standing, a discreet liaison with a well-respected *ton* gentleman could have many advan—'

Unable to tolerate another word of the baronet's self-serving justification, Hal grabbed Sir Gregory by his fashionable lapels, cutting him off. 'Ruin reputation an advantage?' he asked savagely.

Pulling himself free, Sir Gregory smoothed his coat. 'I marvel you have the effrontery to make such an accusation to me! *I* am not the one urging her to pursue something that would damage her position in society much more thoroughly and permanently.' He wrinkled his nose in distaste. 'To become a common artist! Have you run mad?'

'She *un*common,' Hal countered. 'Has rare gift. Could employ it discreetly.'

'Is that what you've been telling her?' Sir Gregory laughed scornfully. 'You think by inspiring false hopes, she'll look kindly on you? If so, you're more bacon-brained even than I suspected! Very well, go advertise her wares to all your low-bred banker friends like some itinerant pedlar. Perhaps the lady will smile on you—for a time, until she comes to her senses, which, as a lady of breeding, she surely must. An ungainly, incoherent lump like you could never be more to such a beauty than a convenience. Like the horse that draws her carriage or the maid who kindles the fire in her room.'

The baronet's words cut deep, touching Hal's innermost fears. All the anger, uncertainty, regret and pain that had made his last days a torment expanded until he thought he must explode. That volatile tempest of emotion focused on the man before him, Hal forgot that he avoided fisticuffs, no longer cared how severely a man of his size and power could punish his opponent in the ring.

'May be right,' he replied. 'But never be what you intended. Someone to use her, cast her away.'

Hal exulted as Sir Gregory's face flamed. *Just say it*, he urged silently, every fibre of him raging to expand their confrontation beyond words into the physical. *Utter an insult that will justify a challenge.*

Before Sir Gregory could speak, though, one of the baronet's friends interposed himself between Hal and Sir Gregory. 'Think you've said enough, Holburn,' the man said. 'You, too, Waterman. White's is a haven for gentleman, not a tavern for brawlers.'

Reaching over the shoulder of the baronet's protector, Hal grabbed Sir Gregory's neckcloth and jerked the man to face him. 'Leave her alone. Or find you later, when watchdogs not on guard.' He shoved the baronet away.

His hands trembling as he attempted to repair his neckcloth, a shaken Sir Gregory ducked back behind the protective circle of his friends. Cautiously the group edged away from Hal.

Once the red haze of rage in his brain faded, he realised his own body was shaking, his hands curled into rigid fists. Only gradually, as his blood cooled, did Hal realise he should thank the level-headed man who had prevented him from assaulting the baronet. In his fury, he might easily have killed Sir Gregory and now be facing a flight to the Continent rather than a trip north.

Sadness and fatigue seeped in to take the place of the strong emotion leaching out of him. He'd return home, drink enough of the excellent brandy Nicky had sent him from France to capture sleep. Then tomorrow he'd begin finalising his plans to leave London.

Late the next morning, his head throbbing from the prodigious quantity of brandy that had been required to finally lull him into sleep, Hal sat at his desk, trying to force his aching head to concentrate on the figures the engineer had left. A sharp rap at the door made him wince.

Jeffers entered, holding out a note. 'Ah, roses!' the valet said, sniffing the cream velum before handing over the missive. 'Perhaps the fragrance will ease your headache better than my infallible morning-after brew!'

'Not infallible,' Hal said acidly. 'After two cups, still have headache.' Even so, the scent of roses made his pulse accelerate while hope, that treacherous, unruly brat, began to jump up and down in his gut.

For a moment he simply held the note in his hands, breathing in the scent that was Elizabeth, knowing without even glancing at the handwriting it must come from her. After their acrimonious parting, would it bring him good news or bad? Taking a deep breath, he broke the seal.

'Dear Mr Waterman,' she began, 'I sincerely beg your pardon! I now recognise that only a deep concern for my welfare prompted you to broach a matter you must have found distasteful and embarrassing. In this, as in all things, you braved censure to do what you felt necessary to protect me, just as Nicky would have. Your generosity of spirit leaves me ashamed of my own abominable behaviour.

'Will you not let me make amends? I should be most grateful if you could call and take tea today. Sincerely yours, Elizabeth Lowery.'

Intense relief washed through him, followed by a wave of euphoria. Perhaps he'd not ruined his chances after all. It seemed she now understood that he'd been forced to speak in order to safeguard her.

In the midst of his gladness, one small voice warned that perhaps, having begun yesterday the process of distancing himself from her, it would be wiser to remain so. Savagely he stifled it.

Mayhap he would never become more to Elizabeth Lowery than a friend who'd stepped in to assist her when she'd most needed it. Just a convenience, as the baronet had taunted. At some point, longing for her, desiring her, mere friendship might become too painful to bear.

But for now, friendship meant hope. Which was a thousand times better than exile.

He realised Jeffers was still standing beside the desk, smiling.

'Wipe smirk off face, bring another mug,' Hal said, gesturing his valet towards the door. 'Must get through figures before head explodes. Then brush best coat. Have appointment later.'

Jeffers's grin widened. 'Very well, sir,' he replied, backing toward the door. As the portal closed behind the valet, for the first time since he'd steeled himself to warn Elizabeth about Sir Gregory, Hal smiled.

Jittery and uncertain as he was, Hal was relieved to discover when he arrived at the Green Street town house that afternoon that David sat with his mother in the parlour, reading from a primer. The boy broke off as Sands opened the door and announced him, his face lighting up.

'Uncle Hal! Mama's letting me drink tea with you!'

'As long as you can behave like a young gentleman,' Elizabeth admonished.

'Oh, I can!' he assured her as he hopped to his feet. Making Hal a creditable bow, he said, 'We're so pleased you could join us this afternoon, Mr Waterman.'

Solemnly Hal returned his bow. 'Delighted, sir.'

'Good,' David said, grabbing Hal's hand and tugging him to a place on the sofa. 'Cook made her special macaroons just for today. Have one, they're 'licious!'

Elizabeth motioned for Sands to pour the tea. After the butler bowed himself out, she handed Hal a cup, then listened, faintly smiling, as David chattered on about how much he liked macaroons, how well he was learning the stories in his new reader and Max's latest exploits.

Once or twice while her son talked, Elizabeth looked up to meet his gaze. Her cheeks pinking, her smile deepening, she held his eyes for a moment before modestly dropping her gaze back to her son.

Restored now to Elizabeth's presence after fearing she might never receive him again, it seemed as if the very air he breathed was purer, the tea more flavourful, the colours of the fire playing on the hearth more vivid. All of existence, every thought and feeling, seemed sharper, brighter, more intense because he was with her.

So grateful was he to be here with Elizabeth smiling at him, her demeanour warmly welcoming, Hal could have remained for ever on the couch while the tea grew cold and David talked himself hoarse. His senses hummed, his heart swelled in his chest like a hot air balloon being readied for ascent, merely at the pleasure of watching her.

After David had finished his cup and devoured every crumb of the macaroons, in response to a nod from his mother, he stood up. 'Mama says I can go and play with Max now, since the grown people need to talk. Thank you, Mama, for letting me have tea with you. G'bye, Uncle Hal!'

Giving his mother a kiss and Hal another bow, with a mischievous smile, David bounded out.

The room seemed still and silent after his departure. Suddenly nervous again, Hal felt his face flush. He wanted badly to say the right thing, something that would preserve the smile on her face and the warm glow in her eyes.

'Wanted to say—' he began.

'I wished to tell you—' she said at the same instant before they both fell silent.

'You first,' Hal invited.

'Well,' she began, her cheeks colouring as she took a deep breath, 'first let me tender you an apology. I'm afraid your suspicions about…about a certain delicate matter were entirely correct. Your courageous intervention prevented me from making a disastrous and potentially humiliating mistake.'

'Sorry suspicions correct,' he replied, anger flaring again at the memory of Sir Gregory's duplicity. 'Deserve better.'

'Thank you, although you would have every right to despise me after how shabbily I treated you!'

'Upset. Understandable.'

'I don't know about that. I do know I shall never again doubt or question your advice.'

Gratification warm and sweet as melting butter filled him. 'Hope advice good. Finances stabilised, anyway. Ledgers in order. Repayment begun on debt. Coin available at bank. Should do until Nicky returns.'

'Do you mean to abandon us, then?' she asked, looking alarmed. 'What of our discussions about my work?'

Hal wanted to tell her he'd never abandon her, that it was his greatest pleasure to listen to her voice, bask in her smile, that he'd love to advise, counsel and cherish her with all the strength he possessed for the rest of his days. But now—especially now, after she'd just gone through that unpleasantness with Sir Gregory— was not the time for a declaration.

'Still stop by, consult. Have to train Max. And pony soon to come. What wish to do about art? Can speak with potential clients, assess interest.'

She nodded. 'I think that would be wise. Despite your assurances, having viewed the work at the Royal Academy, I hardly feel qualified to proceed.' She sighed. 'How I wish I might study there!'

'Could visit rooms, sketch. Perhaps one of members give private lessons. Look into it, if like.'

'If it would not be an imposition, I should like that very much!' Her smile turned tender. 'You are so very kind. I can't believe I struck you! I don't know what came over me. Never would I wish to hurt you.'

To Hal's surprise, she reached over and stroked the cheek she'd slapped, as if to erase some invisible mark.

Instinctively he laid his own hand over hers, cradling it against his cheek. 'Not hurt me. Never hurt me.'

'Twas a lie, he thought even as he spoke the words. An outrageous lie, for she'd long ago skewered his heart on the lance of her goodness and beauty. No one living had more power than she to hurt him, shrivel his soul and leave him utterly desolate.

But the ability to form thoughts slipped away as his body began to pulse from the heat of her hand against his face. As if each slender finger triggered a whaler's dart, sensation fired at their gentle touch from his cheek through his body to his loins, his chest, his toes, trailing everywhere a stinging, scalding flame.

He couldn't speak, couldn't breathe. His mind, his soul, his whole being smouldered and burned for her.

Under his avid gaze her face flushed. Her chest commenced to rise and fall rapidly, her breathing growing as shallow and frantic as his own.

He stifled a groan as the image seized him…the full breasts outlined by the bodice of her gown naked, free of their stays, rubbing against his bare chest, the pink-kissed nipples pebbled with desire. Passion and adoration intertwined, each inflaming the other, expanded to fill him until he felt he must turn molten on the spot.

Hal had no idea how long they stood, he as incapable of motion as he was of speech. Finally, she gently pulled at her hand. Releasing the slight pressure he'd used to hold it against him, he caught her fingers and brought them to lips, kissing them reverently before letting go.

'Never hurt you either,' he murmured.

Her heart pounding ferociously, Elizabeth gave him a minute nod, afraid if she moved too quickly the dizziness in her head and the scintillating vortex of sensation in her body might make her fall right off the couch.

Once again, every tingling nerve had urged her to lean into the arms Hal looked as if he would have willingly wrapped around her.

Except this time, that desire was even more intense. Only

terror over what she might have done next, with David no longer present to forestall her madness, had given her the strength to pull her hand back and move away.

Her nerves still afire and her mind fogged by the battle between desire and sanity, she struggled to focus on what Hal was saying.

'Borrow sketches. Show to select gentlemen? When ready to begin, demand for your work.'

Sketches. Work. They'd been talking about her painting. Perhaps beginning art lessons or even discreetly exploring commissions.

'Yes, I'll…I'll gather some to send you.'

'Good.'

The mantel clock struck the hour and—as disorientated and befuddled as she?—Hal jumped. With a regretful glance toward the clock, he drained his cup and rose. 'Another meeting. Must go. Thanks for tea. And forgiving me.'

He was grateful for her forgiveness, when the fault was all hers? What a truly noble gentleman he was!

'You did nothing for which you need ask pardon. 'Twas I who was hasty, quick tempered and in error. Thank you for your forbearance with my foolishness. And again, for watching out for both David and me.'

He bowed. 'Pleasure.'

She rose to escort him to the door. Now that she'd become so attuned to him physically, she didn't seem to be able to turn off the awareness. As she followed him, her eyes drifted to the crisp curl of red-gold hair at his collar, the broad width of his back, the muscles of his arms and shoulders under the snug-fitting jacket.

And when he turned back to face her…oh, my, how wicked was the knitted cloth of his breeches, moulding as it did so closely over his thighs, against the flatness of his belly, the impressive ridge at the junction of his legs…

Her cheeks flaming anew, she jerked her gaze back up to his

face, hoping the disjointed farewell she uttered made some sense. As he bowed and walked away, she watched him stride out, trying to get a peek at the contour of his derrière beneath the tails of his coat.

She plopped back on the sofa, reached for her cup and gulped down some tea. Maybe the tepid brew would help cool her over-heated thoughts.

What had come over her? She'd surmised the first time she experienced a strong physical reaction to Hal Waterman, before and during their trip to Astley's, that her long-dormant physical urges must be awakening. But the power of the desire that consumed her for Hal far exceeded what she'd ever experienced before.

If maturity increased one's passion, she had best not grow much older! She wasn't sure she could survive a greater intensity without fainting dead away.

A danger that might well concern her, for she had best acknowledge the truth. Unless distracted by some crisis, whenever she looked at Hal Waterman…she desired him.

What would it be like to strip the coat from that powerful frame, run her fingers along the muscles of his arms and shoulders? Nuzzle the red-gold hair adorning his chest down to the waistband of his breeches, licking and stroking…

What would it be like to pleasure him, to let him pleasure her?

Her skin grew hot and damp while a heated sensation surged in her belly.

Elizabeth brought unsteady hands up to fan her fevered cheeks. Goodness! If Hal could affect her thoughts this strongly, she couldn't imagine how intense the reaction would be if he were to actually caress her.

Dizzy at the thought, she tried to steady herself. She must stop this! Transfer the passion Hal seemed to rouse in her to her painting. Perhaps resume the walks in the park she used to take with David and Everitt, which might dissipate some of the nervous energy sparking within her.

Much as she wished she had someone to ask about the frightening, exhilarating sensations her body had suddenly begun producing, even were Sarah in London, Elizabeth wasn't sure she'd be able to talk to her about them. Somehow, she was going to have to manage on her own to bottle up her desire and behave in a proper, genteel manner around Mr Waterman.

At least for the present. Once her period of mourning was over, once she was freed from constraint and convention, if Hal Waterman were willing, Elizabeth meant to give herself free rein to follow her emotions and desires wherever they might lead.

Chapter Twenty

His heart and body still aflame after his meeting with Elizabeth the previous afternoon, Hal turned his curricle once again toward Green Street. He'd driven halfway to his meeting with the investors yesterday before he realised he'd forgotten to inform her about his imminent journey north. Now that a warm rapport—oh, my, how warm!—had been re-established between them, he wished mightily that he hadn't agreed to go. But he always supervised a project's beginning, the engineer and foreman were expecting him, so there was no question of cancelling.

Go he must. But in the time remaining before he must depart, he intended to visit Elizabeth as often as possible. So before meeting this morning with the bankers to arrange for the last of the drafts, he'd sent her a note telling her he'd call in the afternoon.

He even had a special treat to propose. After his investment meeting yesterday, he'd visited several dealers, investigating the possibility of selling some of Lowery's art collection. At one of them, he'd discovered something he thought she'd like very much. Hoping she might be free to accompany him, he'd arranged with the proprietor for them to meet in a private showroom where no one in the *ton* in pursuit of new art acquisitions might chance to see them and generate gossip that could reach the ears of the gamesters at White's—or his mother.

He pulled up his carriage before her door, the now-familiar surge of excitement and anticipation filling him. Tossing his reins to a waiting groom, he leapt down, almost running up the front steps in his eagerness, too expansive of spirit to be bothered by the chill greeting Sands extended before escorting Hal to the parlor.

He found Elizabeth already seated on the sofa when he entered. Joy fizzled in his veins at the brilliance of the smile she gave him as she rose to curtsy to his bow.

'Good day, Mr Waterman! I hope the important business that brings you here today is more pleasant than the last.'

At her oblique reference to his warning about Sir Gregory, Hal grimaced. 'Much more pleasant. Would like you to ride out, visit dealer. Interested in purchasing some of husband's collection. Brief visit, not take long.'

'If you think it useful. I don't know enough of prices to ascertain its value, but I could describe the individual pieces,' she replied. 'Let me collect my pelisse and cloak and I'll rejoin you shortly.'

'Could bring sketchbook also?'

She halted in mid-step, her face colouring. 'You…you would have a dealer look at my sketches?'

'Give him idea of talent. Good appraisal of potential clients too.'

She stood irresolute for a moment, nervously clasping her hands. 'I'm not sure I'm ready for this.'

'Won't commit you to anything,' he assured her. 'Dealer not know it's your work. Describe sketches as part of husband's collection.'

'I suppose that would be a rather painless way to receive an impartial expert's evaluation,' she said thoughtfully. 'Very well, I shall do it.'

A few moments later, after ordering a hackney which Hal thought would prove more discreet than driving her through

Mayfair in his open curricle, they set out, Elizabeth clasping her sketchbook nervously.

'If possible, like to take some sketches with me,' Hal said, pointing to the book. 'See prospective clients while in north.'

Did he only imagine the flash of dismay that passed over her countenance? 'You are going away?' she asked.

'Soon,' he confirmed, certain, to his immense gratification, that he had indeed detected a note of concern in her voice. 'New canal project beginning. Must oversee.'

'David and I will certainly miss you. But with your work on Everitt's papers complete, I suppose we could not hope to monopolise your attention for ever. Will you be gone…long?'

Did she sound wistful? Hal wondered. 'Fortnight or less.'

'I hope you won't desert us completely upon your return. After all, thanks to your kind offices, some of David's inheritance will be invested in this new project and I shall wish an accounting of it!' she said, waving a finger at him with mock severity.

She would miss him. She wanted to see him upon his return. Hal felt his spirit soar as if the hackney were rolling on clouds rather than cobblestones. 'Give proper accounting upon return,' he agreed. 'May have new venture to propose.'

'And what would that be?'

Too effervescent with happiness to be sure he could read her level of interest accurately, Hal asked, 'Truly wish to know?'

'Yes. If it intrigues you, it must be both innovative and lucrative. For too long, I've been painfully ignorant about management and finance. If I am to be a good guide to David—and to myself—I need to know more. Besides, the new machines that have driven the building of canals, the draining of marshes, the mining of coal—you see, I have begun reading about it—sound so intricate and fascinating. Rather like a painting, begun with a sketch and built up with layer upon layer of pigment until a whole emerges that is both unique from, yet part of, the many individual brush strokes which make it up.'

Though Hal's mathematical mind had never conceived of the construction of a coal engine or mechanical loom as similar to the creation of artwork, he was struck by her observation. 'Suppose it is similar! Latest possibility intriguing—might replace canals in moving goods. Been using engines on rails to move coal from mines. Now George Stephenson invented better engine. Can move itself, pull cars anywhere iron track is laid. Cheaper than digging canals.'

'This new system could supplement canals, then?'

Hal nodded. 'Go over uneven ground where canals impractical. From port landing cotton right to mill, then carry finished cloth to market. Coal, too. Stockton and Darlington Railway preparing bill for Parliament to convey coal from collieries to port. Maybe passengers later.'

'So one might ride upon an engine of steel rather than gallop upon a fiery steed? Wouldn't David just love that! What bold vision you possess, Mr Waterman! If you judge that investing our money in such a venture is sound, by all means do so.'

She thought him bold and forward-thinking. No longer questioning her sincerity, he simply revelled in the unaccustomed praise, giddy bubbles of delight rising to his head as if he'd been drinking fine champagne. She'd also referred to 'our' money…how Hal loved the sound of that!

Of course, she meant capital belonging to herself and her son. But the idea of her wanting to invest in the emerging enterprises that so fascinated him created a new sense of camaraderie between them, reinforcing the connection he'd always felt to her.

Having learned years ago not to expose himself to his mother's scorn by discussing technological developments in her presence, Hal seldom introduced the topic to anyone beyond a small circle of similarly committed investors. Not even with Sally had he thought to find someone with real curiosity about the vast changes in commerce and technology he believed would soon overtake English society. Imagine discovering such an interest in a sheltered society beauty like Elizabeth Lowery! Her unexpected enthusiasm about the ventures in which he was so deeply embroiled both surprised and delighted him.

Still, he'd better curb his exuberance before he started nattering on like Ned with his farming. In any event, the hackney was pulling up before the art dealer's establishment. Time to shift the focus of conversation from his great passion to hers.

Mister Christie, the proprietor, quickly ushered them into a showroom out of view of the main display area. For several minutes, the dealer listened with rapt interest as Elizabeth described her husband's extensive collection of Roman sculpture and Italian Renaissance paintings, occasionally mentioning connoisseurs whom he would contact concerning specific works. Finally he looked inquiringly at the sketchbook Elizabeth kept tucked under her arm.

'Do you have unframed works you wished me to see?' Mr Christie asked.

Panic flaring in her eyes, hands clenched on her sketchbook, Elizabeth hesitated. Possessing no doubt whatsoever about the exceptional skill of her drawings, Hal sent her a reassuring look before turning to the dealer. 'Yes. Also some works in oil based on sketches.'

'I don't normally handle sketches, but if some represent finished works, I should be happy to look over them.'

'View other items while you do?' Hal asked.

'Of course. I've hung the watercolours you requested on the far wall. Please enjoy them while I review these in my office.'

'Don't worry,' Hal reassured her as she stared after the retreating figure of the dealer, her expression as dismayed as if she'd sent her child off with a stranger. 'Will love work. But now—best for last.'

Nerves humming with anticipation at offering her what he hoped would be a welcome surprise, he led her away.

'You wanted me to see some—ooh!' Elizabeth stopped short, her query ending in a gasp as she caught sight of the grouping of watercolours Hal had ordered.

'More works by Mr Turner, artist admired at Royal Academy,' Hal explained. 'Does oils, but especially noted for watercolours like these. Rivers, cities, castles, landscapes, ships at sea.'

As she had at the Royal Academy, for several long moments Elizabeth said nothing. Standing in rapt contemplation, her eyes darted from one to another as she took in composition, colour, theme. 'They are magnificent!' she pronounced at last.

Hal had hoped she would enjoy seeing more examples of the artist's work. Gratified to have been proven correct, he focused his gaze not on the extraordinary paintings of Mr Turner, but on the lady examining them.

How he loved seeing that joyous smile on her face, the glow of enthusiasm that made her already striking beauty even more luminous. 'Glad you admire them,' he said.

'How could anyone with a shred of sensibility not admire them?' she demanded. 'See this one—the calm water, boats bobbing at anchor beneath the gold of the mountains and the soaring, swirling clouds of the sky! One almost expects the vapour to float off the image on to one's hand! And this—the town, glowing with light, towering over the placid river, all of it overlooked by a restless, wind-driven sky. And the last—the group of workmen carrying their burdens in the foreground, the city in the distance so mysterious, veiled in mist and smoke. Extraordinary!'

No, you are extraordinary, Hal thought, smiling at her enthusiasm.

'Thank you so much for bringing me! I've never been tempted by gowns or bonnets, but I must admit I'm regretting that we came here to sell rather than buy art. For the first time I can appreciate the fervour that drove Everitt to collect.'

'You like the Turners, Mrs Lowery?' Mr Christie's voice interrupted them. So intent had she been on studying the art and Hal on studying her, they'd not noticed the dealer's return.

'Very much.'

'Your late husband was a most astute investor. I shall have no trouble placing those pieces with which you are willing to part. Or if you would care to arrange a trade…' He gestured to the Turner watercolours.

Elizabeth sighed. 'Regretfully, no.'

The dealer nodded. 'Though he has acquired several patrons, Lord Egremont among them, Mr Turner is a prolific artist. Perhaps another time.'

She nodded. 'Perhaps.'

'By the way, the sketches you brought were quite well done, particularly the portraits and the delightful drawings of dogs. If the paintings based on them are of similar quality, I shall have no trouble finding purchasers.'

Hal looked at her and raised his eyebrows, an 'I-told-you-so' expression on his face. 'Appreciate your time,' Hal told Mr Christie. 'Contact you soon.'

The art dealer bowed. 'I shall be at your disposal. Mrs Lowery, a pleasure.'

A few minutes later they re-entered the waiting hackney. After they seated themselves, Elizabeth turned to Hal, her face glowing with a look of such happiness and affection that his heart expanded in his chest. 'Thank you again for today,' she said softly. 'Even if I can't purchase a Turner landscape, I now have hope I might some day sell my own work.'

'Told you would recognise your talent.'

'Well, he hasn't actually seen the oils, so I shall not count my commissions yet,' she replied with a twinkle.

'Value them when sees them. Possess great talent. Expert confirm it. Have only to decide how wish to utilise it. Still need not show work publicly if choose not to. But now know for sure you have choice.'

Her eyes lit, as if she were realising that fact for the first time. 'I…I suppose I do. Elizabeth Lowery, artist.' Hugging the sketch-book close, she threw back her head and laughed, the sound joyous and free.

He could almost see a sense of confidence and excitement growing in her as he watched. Tenderness curled in his chest—and pride, that he had been the one who'd led her to discover this new power within.

'Can keep sketches of David, Max?' he asked. 'Show investors when travel north. Some hold dogs as dear as children.'

'What unnatural beings,' she replied, her quick smile fading as she asked, 'Must you leave…soon?'

'Within day or so.'

'You will stop to say goodbye before you go?'

Had nodded, wishing once again he didn't have to leave. He could sit here for ever in this hackney, watching Elizabeth Lowery smile at him. 'Couldn't go without seeing you.'

'I shall miss you,' she said softly, gazing up at him with a tenderness that made Hal's heart thump in his chest. 'You won't…stay away too long, will you?'

'Come back as soon as I can,' he confirmed.

'Good,' she said, her eyes drifting shut on a sigh as she inclined her head toward him.

With her chin tilted up, her lips were so close that in the space of a heartbeat he could have bent down to capture them. Kissing her, tasting her, wrapping her in his arms was a vision that had possessed and tortured him for so long, he could scarcely imagine not living under her spell. But badly as he wanted to kiss her—and much as his no doubt fevered imagination tried to whisper that with her leaning toward him, her face upraised, she *wanted* him to kiss her—he didn't dare believe the time was yet right.

He would rather die of frustrated desire than spoil the golden harmony of shared interest and affection that had bound them together so strongly all afternoon.

It was then he realised he could do it. He could wait for her. Though he wanted so much more, to laugh with her, to share moments like these with her, to have her gaze at him with trust and affection would be enough to hold him until she was ready to leave the past behind and embrace her future.

Whether or not that future would realise all his dreams for them, he refused to spoil the wonder of today worrying about.

In a sudden squeal of harness, the hackney braked to a halt. Elizabeth started, her eyes flying open, her cheeks pinking as she sat back, moving her tempting lips out of reach.

Hal sighed, not completely sure he'd done the right thing by refraining from kissing her. Before he could sort the matter out, her footman threw open the hackney door and helped her alight.

She turned to him after he'd followed her out. 'Can you stay for tea?'

Regretfully he shook his head. 'Sorry, must collect carriage and go. Appointment.' One of the last in the series of consultations that preceded his departure to begin the project. A project he now intended to expedite so he might return with all speed.

She nodded. 'Then I suppose nothing remains but for me to thank you again. And give you this.' She offered him the sketchbook.

'Will take good care of it,' he assured her.

'Good day, Mr Waterman. I hope I shall see you again soon.'

'Count on it,' he promised, savouring her rose scent as he bowed over her fingers.

He watched as she ascended the stairs, stopping as the front door opened to give him a little wave before disappearing into the house. Smiling to himself as he played over in his mind the events of the afternoon, he waited on the kerb while the groom brought his curricle.

A short time later, he whipped up his team and headed off to his meeting. Yes, he would have to leave London. But, he thought, excitement licking up his veins, when he'd completed what must be done, he would have Elizabeth to call on when he returned, Elizabeth with whom to discuss the new investment ventures he contemplated, Elizabeth—he glanced down at the sketchbook beside him—to consult about potential portrait commissions.

Elizabeth. His shout of exultation at that glorious fact caused his leader to shy. Laughing at himself, he brought the horse back under control and steered the vehicle toward Hyde Park. His meeting occurring at the town house of an investor on the opposite side of the park, since it was nearly past the fashionable hour, driving down the carriageways here would probably be faster than navigating through the busy London streets.

Some of that euphoria dimmed, however, when he reached the park and noticed a lady in a carriage approaching him, waving wilding, obviously trying to catch his attention. His delight died altogether when he recognised his mother.

Damn and blast. The last thing he wished was to have to stop and chat with her—and Lady Tryphena, whom he recognised beside her as the two vehicles converged.

But there was no way now he could pretend he'd not seen her. He would have to pull up and greet them.

Stifling a curse, as he halted his team and threw the reins to his tiger, he tried to tell himself it wasn't such a bad thing. He would have to pay a call on his mother before leaving London to inform her of his plans anyway, at which time she would undoubtedly abuse him for deserting her, not honouring his promise to escort Lady Tryphena, and being generally the most unsatisfactory of sons. Here in the park, with Lady Tryphena at her side and perhaps some other friends as well, he might escape with a shorter version of the rebuke.

He paced to the carriage and leaned up to kiss the hand she offered. 'Hello, Mama, Lady Tryphena.'

'Well, if it isn't my long-absent son! Having done your duty by Englemere's widow, I trust you are now ready to assist your own mama. Lady Tryphena has also been awaiting your return with impatience, haven't you, my dear?' Mrs. Waterman asked, smiling at her protégée.

Brown curls bobbing, the young lady shook her head. 'With the greatest impatience, I assure you, ma'am.' Turning a brilliant smile on Hal, she said, 'I do so hope we will now be privileged to share your company.'

Somewhat taken aback, Hal blinked at her. She continued to smile ardently at him, as if he were the answer to her maiden's prayers.

Hal found himself wondering if for some reason she needed his mama's approval—or the Waterford wealth—more than he'd thought.

At least she'd not begun by correcting his speech.

His mama patted the carriage seat beside her. 'Take a turn around the park with us, my dear, and let us catch up on all your news. So much has happened! Why, just last night, the Layton chit—Lord Sidney's youngest, and a paler, more tongue-tied girl you can hardly imagine—was caught tête-à-tête behind the potted plants at Lady Mansfield's gala with that naughty Lord Montclare! Rogue that he is, I imagine he'll manage to slither out of having to offer for her. Shall you dine with us tonight?'

'Can't dine. No turn about park either. On my way to meeting. Just say hello.'

'Another one of your dreary finance meetings, I suppose!' she said with a moue of distaste. 'Surely you can make time tomorrow, after so sadly neglecting us!'

'Was going to call. Leaving London soon. More business in north.'

'Again?' she protested. 'Why, you've only just returned! I declare, you use me monstrously. Lady Tryphena, tell my son what an unfeeling monster he is to his mama.'

'We will both sorely miss you, Mr. Waterman,' Lady Tryphena said. 'How long do you expect to be gone?'

'Not sure. A fortnight, perhaps longer.' In truth, he now hoped to return within ten days. But with luck, if his Mama thought him still out of town, he might escape a summons from her for at least that long.

'A fortnight!' his mama echoed. 'But the Season is already begun! There are any number of important events in the next two weeks. You cannot be so cruel to me—and Lady Tryphena—as to deny us your escort for all of them!'

'Indeed, Mr Waterman, I shall be quite desperately disappointed if you abandon us for two whole weeks,' Lady Tryphena cried.

She actually looked a bit desperate, gazing so earnestly at him. She really must be eager to start spending his blunt.

Maybe he should tell them he meant to be gone a month.

Not quite able to reconcile it with his conscience to tell that great a fib, Hal said, 'Sorry to disappoint. Must go now. Send you note, call when return, Mama.'

'Oh, please do, Mr Waterman! We shall be quite devastated until your return,' Lady Tryphena declared.

'Indeed we shall,' his mother agreed, pouting as she offered him her fingers to kiss. 'I should have expected you to display a stronger sense of duty towards your mama—but I shall say no more now. I'll anticipate seeing you again in no longer than a fortnight!'

'Perhaps even sooner,' Lady Tryphena added.

Declining to comment on that, Hal bowed to them both.

'Good day, ladies.' With a huge sense of relief, he turned and moved off to catch up with his carriage…acutely aware of Lady Tryphena's sharp gaze following him.

Daylight was fading by the time Hal returned to his lodgings. Striding into his study, he began packing up the rolls of engineering drawings, expense ledgers and letters of introduction he'd obtained to other potential investors.

With the consultation he'd just completed, he had now enough investors pledged to the project that he could, if he wished, begin his journey tomorrow. Loathe as he was to leave London and Elizabeth Lowery, the sooner he got the project underway, the sooner he would be able to return.

He would delay his departure only long enough to call in Green Street and inform Elizabeth of his plans.

A wistful smile touched his lips. Would Elizabeth protest his leaving as vociferously as Mama had? He thought she'd looked kindly at him today…even ardently, though he must be careful not to project his sensual desires on to her. Indeed, newly widowed as she was, he'd most certainly been mistaken in thinking she'd deliberately leaned toward him in the carriage, as if offering up her lips for his kiss.

Would she ever offer them? Could he bear it if she did not?

Dimly he became aware of a murmur of agitated voices in the hallway beyond the heavy mahogany door. When, after several moments, the noise continued, accented by the sounds of scuffling, with a frown he rose from his desk.

About to ask Jeffers what the devil was going on, Hal opened the door to the hallway and stopped short. To his consternation, straining against Jeffers, who was apparently trying to drag her toward the front door that stood wide open behind them, her cheeks flushed pink with effort and her face determined, there in his entryway stood Lady Tryphena Upton.

Chapter Twenty-One

To the murderous glare Hal turned on him, Jeffers protested, 'It wasn't my fault! I told her she mustn't come in, but she—she wrestled her way past me!'

Aghast, Hal hastened to close the front door, praying that old Lady Worthington, who resided across the street and lived for gossip about the *ton*, hadn't chanced to look out of her front windows. He added another prayer that in the few moments Lady Tryphena had stood on his doorstep, no *ton* carriage had passed by bearing someone who recognised her.

'Insist on entering, go in,' he told Lady Tryphena grimly, gesturing to the study. 'Stay here!' he snapped at Jeffers before he followed her in, leaving the door to the hallway ajar and wondering what in heaven had possessed the girl to do something as unforgivably scandalous as pay a visit upon a single gentleman in his rooms—without even the vestige of a maid to lend her respectability.

Indicating she should take the chair behind the desk, he strode over to the hearth, his mind already reeling at the possible calamities that might result from this unprecedented invasion of his privacy.

Voicing his first suspicion, he demanded, 'Mama put you up to this?'

Now that she'd achieved her object, Lady Tryphena looked less sure of herself. 'Well, not precisely,' she replied, perching on the edge of Hal's oversized desk chair and rubbing her hands together nervously. 'She did hint that perhaps I might speed things along by inducing you to linger alone with me in some drawing room, where we might be discovered so society would decide I'd been compromised. But how am I to do that, if you never escort us anywhere?'

'Want to marry me?' he asked bluntly.

Her face coloured. 'No! I mean, yes! Oh, it's so complicated!' To his disgust and dismay, Lady Tryphena burst into tears.

Of all feminine stratagems, Hal most disliked waterworks. Biting back a curse, he stomped to the side table, poured a generous glass of wine and carried it to the sobbing girl. Shaking her shoulder none too gently, he held out the glass. 'Drink,' he ordered.

With a little hiccup of surprise, she ceased weeping and stared at him, then accepted the glass.

After waiting for her to take a sip, Hal said, 'Better tell the whole.'

'Well, everything was going splendidly until this Season. Though Mama was upset that I'd rebuffed all my suitors, since Papa and Reginald—my eldest brother—never pay any attention to me, I was left alone. But then, at the race meetings last fall, Reginald lost an enormous sum gaming. Papa's losses were almost as great, plus he invested a huge amount in some ships that got lost in a storm off India. So now he's demanding that I help the family by marrying a man of wealth, and soon.'

If it weren't his neck she was trying to stick in a noose, Hal might almost have felt sorry for her. 'Chose me for honour?' he asked drily.

She nodded. 'When your mama approached me, it suddenly occurred to me that you were perfect! If I could please Mrs

Waterman and remain near you, I could figure out a way to get us engaged. I have to become engaged to some gentleman of means, you see, or Papa threatened he would send me to live with Great-Aunt Serephina in Northumberland, and I should never have pretty dresses or go to the theatre or see my darling Charles again!'

Hal blinked. 'Charles?'

Her teary visage grew rapturous. 'He is the dearest, most wonderful man! And I shall never, ever love anyone else, no matter what Papa threatens to do to me!'

'Why marry me, then?'

'Charles is just a younger son and dreadfully poor, so Papa wouldn't hear of us marrying, nor Charles's family either, once they discovered Papa and Reginald had lost so much money that I no longer had a large dowry.'

'Marry me, lose Charles,' Hal pointed out, trying to hang on to his patience.

'But that's just it! Everyone knows your mama has been trying to marry you off for ages, yet you've managed to resist all her attempts. I thought if I could just compromise you enough that you had to offer for me, you'd be in no hurry to wed. As long as I was affianced to a man of great wealth, Papa's creditors would leave him alone and Charles would have time to figure out how we could be together.'

'Asinine scheme!' Hal said curtly. 'What if went ahead and married you?'

Shock and distress coloured her face. 'You—you wouldn't do that, would you?'

'No wish to marry you,' he assured her, brain racing as he tried to think a way out of this tangle. Coming up with a possible solution, he asked, 'Willing to elope?'

'Elope—with Charles?' she gasped. 'How scandalous!'

Before Hal could compromise his integrity by urging on her a solution that would ruin her reputation as thoroughly as leaving his house unaffianced, her eyes brightened and she cried, 'But how exciting! That would be perfect! You're not as slow-witted as your mama claims after all.'

'Not bacon-brained enough to compromise someone don't want to marry,' Hal retorted.

'I am not bacon-brained!' she flashed back. 'I think my delaying action was brilliant. It's all well for you to sniff. You're a man; you can inherit or earn the money you need. Or borrow it. Or flee the country and start over. A girl has only herself in marriage to bargain with.'

She had a point there, Hal conceded reluctantly. 'This Charles willing to elope too?'

She straightened, looking affronted. 'Of course! He would face any danger or scandal to claim me for his own!'

Still thinking rapidly, he asked, 'Charles have profession? Skills to support wife?'

Lady Tryphena frowned. 'He's a gentleman.'

Hal sighed. 'No skills. Could live outside London?'

'If we are together, we could be happy in a hovel!'

Hal doubted that, as hovels seldom came equipped with theatre seats and pretty dresses, but if the couple were prepared to eschew London, he might arrange something. He had a large estate in the Marches that could provide its manager enough income to support a wife, and the property was in good enough order that even if the unknown Charles were as great an idiot as Lady Tryphena, he probably couldn't ruin it.

'Who knows you here?'

She lifted her chin, eyeing him warily. 'I told my dear friend Olivia Compton that I might have to Do Something Desperate. And Lady Worthington saw me from her window. I waved at her just before I came in.'

Groaning, Hal poured himself a generous glass of wine, downed it in two gulps and began pacing the room.

He'd hoped to delay his departure and take several days to sort this out, but with Lady Worthington doubtless glued to her front window, waiting for Lady Tryphena to emerge from his house, there wasn't a second to lose, lest he find the parson's mouse-trap closing around him.

He only hoped Lady Tryphena's Charles was as ready to flee to Gretna as she was to go there with him. If not, Hal would find himself in a difficult situation indeed.

Regardless, though, he thought, setting his jaw, he would not be bullied into wedding the girl just to save her reputation—or his own. Would Elizabeth ever speak to him again, he wondered, an ache in his heart, if she thought he'd ruined and abandoned a young lady of quality?

He'd have to see that it didn't come to that. Which meant Charles was going to find himself married over the anvil, if Hal had to use half a fortune to bribe him to it.

Just figuring out how to justify to Elizabeth how he got into this coil to begin with would be difficult enough.

Telling himself he'd deal with that problem when the time came, he turned to Lady Tryphena, who'd been watching him pace, a hopeful expression on her face.

'Can get private message to Charles?' Hal asked, not at all surprised when she nodded enthusiastically.

Hal pulled out paper and a quill. 'Tell him come here tonight.' Beckoning to Jeffers, he said, 'When finished writing, take lady out to mews through kitchen. Summon hackney. See home. Then deliver note where tells you.'

Turning back to Lady Tryphena, he said, 'Pack bag. Unless Charles fails, leave tonight.'

'Charles will not fail! You're going to help us elope, aren't you?' she asked eagerly. 'Oh, that is a million times better than getting engaged to you!'

'Indeed,' Hal agreed drily. Deciding he'd better remove

himself before he strangled a girl who was more self-absorbed and oblivious even than his mother, he gave her a short bow and trotted up the stairs to his bedroom. With an elopement to arrange and the project papers to pack, he had a thousand details to settle before they left this evening.

And neither the time nor the eloquence necessary to explain in person his abrupt departure to Elizabeth Lowery.

Chapter Twenty-Two

Late the next morning, after a flurry of painting, Elizabeth put down her brush. Wiping azure-tinted fingers on her apron, she gave the canvas a critical look.

Filled with euphoria after the wonderful visit to Mr Christie's brokerage, she'd awakened at dawn, eager to get to her studio. It might well be wise to wait for Faith and David to become settled before submitting any work for public display, but rather than slow her efforts, she thought it best to forge ahead so that she might have a body of work from which to choose when the moment arrived.

A 'body of work'. How she loved the sound of that!

In the interim, she might also find a mentor with whom to take lessons. Or, at the least, visit the Royal Academy's collection and study the masterworks. Hal would arrange it.

Hal. Hugging herself, she smiled as a rush of warmth filled her. Now that she'd had time to consider what he'd done for her—this time—she admired him even more.

How horridly embarrassing it must have been for him to force her to face the truth about Sir Gregory. How genteel and forbearing he'd been as she'd railed at him! She felt ashamed all over again, remembering her behaviour.

Through it all, though, he'd remained as he always was: patient, gentle, concerned. Selfless. She didn't think she'd ever met an individual who seemed less preoccupied with achieving his own goals or a gentleman more attuned to the thoughts and wishes of the people around him. Was it the observer's role forced on him by his verbal affliction that made him so perceptive? Whatever forces had shaped him, Hal Waterman was a marvel!

Oh, how she hoped she would see him today! Though she'd have to behave herself. She stifled a giggle. She might not be able to keep herself from at least stroking his hand. She knew it affected him to be touched by her, had watched his face redden, his breathing accelerate.

Did she affect him as powerfully as he affected her?

Probably not, she concluded with a sigh. After all, when she'd leaned toward him in the carriage yesterday, practically begging for a kiss, he'd refrained. Which was for the best, of course. She couldn't imagine what had come over her! Heat flushed through her as she recalled that brazen gesture.

Though he'd pretended not to notice her momentary lapse, he was doubtless an experienced man. Just how experienced? she wondered. What else could he do with the big hands that had brushed her cheek so gently? Was every part of him equally big and capable? Sensation swirled in the pit of her stomach, shuddered through her body.

She was still tingling when the door flew open and David ran in. 'Are you finished, Mama? Nurse said I could come tell you I read my whole book. Can I read to you?'

She'd done enough for this morning. Seizing her son, she swung him around in a whirl of shrieking protest. 'Very well, young man,' she said as she set him back down. 'Let's see how much you will impress your tutor.'

After he'd completed a whole section, for which she praised

him sincerely, he asked, 'Is Uncle Hal coming today? I want to show him, too!'

'Perhaps after nuncheon. Shall we eat now?'

'Oh, yes! I'm very hungry. When we're done, I want to teach Max a new trick.'

'As long as it doesn't involve linen on a laundry line,' she cautioned with a smile.

Some of her excitement dissipated as they walked out. She'd not been too disappointed that Hal had not come by this morning. After all, he'd told her yesterday that he would be leaving London soon and doubtless had many details to settle before his departure. Still, he'd said he would visit again. Oh, she did hope it'd be today!

But as the hours passed after nuncheon with no sign of him, she drifted upstairs to visit with Miss Lowery, taking great pleasure in carrying away the now-drooping flowers Sir Gregory had brought Amelia—an attempt to curry the elderly woman's favour, she thought darkly. Restless and unable to settle to needlework or household chores, when David bounded in begging her to come and see Max's new trick, she willingly followed him.

David had succeeded in getting the puppy to leap up at his command, although since he teased him with his favourite rope to do it, Elizabeth wasn't sure this truly qualified as a trick. But her own spirits lifted by her son's delight in his dog, she found herself smiling at their antics. Impatient to pull the rope from David, the puppy launched himself at the boy, missing her son, who jumped aside at the last minute, but grazing her. Caught off balance, she fell in a crumple of skirts to the stable floor, laughing as heartily as her son while the puppy frolicked in her lap and licked her face.

Oh, that she might jump into Hal's lap, her hair mussed, her gown awry! Part his jacket, loose the buttons of his waistcoat, run her tongue across the contours of his chin… Her sensitised body hummed to life, her breasts, her body heating. She felt aroused, giddy, light-headed, as if she'd imbibed too much champagne.

There was still time for him to visit this afternoon, she thought hopefully, dislodging the puppy and standing to brush the dirt from her gown. She must go and tidy up, in case he dropped by for tea.

Until yesterday, she reflected as she walked up to her chamber, all their conversations had focused around her own and David's needs. She'd found the few details he'd given her about new investment opportunities fascinating.

She wanted to know more about them—and Hal. His interests. His background. What, besides managing complex financial schemes, he liked to do. She wanted to know *everything*!

While Gibbons clucked over her soiled dress and helped her wash and change, Elizabeth sat dreamily, a half-smile on her face, contemplating all the kind and wonderful things Hal Waterman had done for them.

Taking over their tangle of finances, eliminating the frightening Mr Smith, she ticked off mentally. Realigning the estate's income and investments to remove her financial worries for good. Showering attention on her grieving son, making him laugh again, bringing a puppy to befriend him. Urging her to simply love David and reassuring her that she need not send him away. Perceiving the danger posed by Sir Gregory, then girding himself to warn her and enduring her abuse. And, last of the wonders, appreciating her painting and understanding its importance to her.

Truly, she had never before met so amazing a gentleman! Sands had better never frown at him again.

Recalling Sands, she suddenly remembered that with the distressing events of the last several days, she'd forgotten to reassure Gibbons that her position was secure. She was about to do so when a knock came at the door.

James the footman handed Gibbons in a note. Elizabeth's pulse leapt—until she recognised the writer's hand.

Her first impulse was to tear up Sir Gregory's letter unread. But acknowledging that part of her anger was disappointment that the communication had not been penned by a different author, she supposed she ought to allow Everitt's best friend to apologise.

Though she had no intention of accepting his apology.

Her aggravation intensified as she read his pretty missive. In flowery phrases he implored her pardon for their 'misunderstanding' and begged leave to call upon her later, when 'she was less distraught'.

With a sniff of disdain, she walked over and dropped the letter into the fire. 'Gibbons, you may discard any future notes from Sir Gregory. And regarding the unpleasantness with Sands, let me assure you that I trust your honesty and appreciate your service. I would never dismiss you on so slender a grounds as someone else's suspicion. But…' she paused, the memory coming to her suddenly '…was there something more you wished to say?'

'Thank you, ma'am, there surely was!' Gibbons cried. 'I'm so glad you're not gonna see that Sir Gregory. 'Twas his interference got me into trouble. I overhead him asking Sands to report to him on all your doings, especially regarding Mr Waterman. Gave Sands a guinea.'

'Sir Gregory engaged Sands to—to spy on me?' she asked incredulously.

Gibbons nodded. 'I thought if I could find where Sands had hid the coin, I could prove what was going on. I never liked the way Sir Gregory looked at you, not even while the old master was still with us, God rest his soul! But after Sands caught me, 'tweren't no use to speak to you about it in front of him, since he'd only deny it and…and I was afraid, relying on him as you do, you might believe him and dismiss me. But all I ever wanted was to protect you and your sweet little boy!'

After listening with a growing anger, Elizabeth thanked the maid again for her loyalty and dismissed her.

No wonder Sir Gregory had always known where she'd been and what she'd been doing! And to think, after conniving with the baronet behind her back, Sands had tried to induce her to discharge Gibbons! All the while, she thought bitterly, setting her up to fall like a ripe plum into Sir Gregory's hands.

She could hardly believe that the butler who had stood beside her to confront the unsavoury Mr Smith, would do such a thing. It also pricked her deeply that poor Gibbons had thought her too likely to meekly acquiesce to Sands's masculine judgement to dare to tell her the truth.

Shameful as it was to admit, in the past the maid's assessment would probably have been correct. But this was her household to run now, her responsibility. She wanted a staff like Gibbons, who were loyal to her alone.

Perhaps it was Sands who should be dismissed.

A righteous sense of purpose filling her, she walked downstairs and told James to fetch Sands. Firmly she dismissed the niggles of doubt that warned she didn't know anything about hiring a new butler. If she wanted to become a serious artist, to defy society's expectations of a woman of her station, she must learn to exceed her own.

A moment later Sands appeared. 'You called, ma'am?'

As the thought of him with Sir Gregory, their heads together as they talked about her, Elizabeth's anger rekindled. 'I should like you to explain to me why I should not turn you off without a character.'

Shock registered on Sands's face. 'Mrs Lowery, I cannot imagine what you mean!'

'Do you deny that you accepted money from Sir Gregory to spy on me? To report back to him what I was doing, who I received?'

'Spy on you? Oh, no! He merely asked me to…to watch you and let him know how you got on. He was concerned about you. And the money—'twas a vail, merely.'

'A whole guinea? A rather generous tip! Do you deny he wished most particularly to know about Mr Waterman?'

Sands drew himself up. 'It's not fitting that you…consort with another, with the master not yet three months dead!'

'It's not your place to judge my behaviour,' she said, feeling only a twinge of conscience, considering her erotic daydreams about Hal, at borrowing Sir Gregory's argument. 'That gentleman is not seeking to make a…a kept woman of me. Oh, yes, that was indeed Sir Gregory's intention! If you do not believe me, ask among your friends at the other great houses. There was even a wager at White's over it!'

Sands stared at her. 'I cannot believe it!'

'Believe it,' she said bitterly. Her anger, outrage and sense of betrayal combined in the glare she fixed on him. 'Did you not also try to induce me to discharge Gibbons in order to conceal what you were doing? I cannot tolerate having in my employ a man who would spy on and endanger me.'

This time, he made no attempt to deny her accusation. 'But, ma'am!' he protested, fear and uncertainty on his face. 'What would you have me do? I worked for Mr Lowery for more than thirty years!'

'I suggest you apply to Sir Gregory. Perhaps he will write you a character, since you've served him so well. You have not served me. I'll give you until week's end to leave this house. In that time, I do not wish to see your face again.' She gave him a curt nod. 'That is all.'

As she watched her chastened soon-to-be-former butler walk away, a huge sense of relief lightened her. Strolling into the library, she threw back her head and laughed. If anyone had told her six months ago, cocooned in her studio at Green Street, that she'd be gambolling with puppies, thinking of showing her paintings and dismissing butlers, she would have been astounded!

How she wanted to tell Hal all about it. But already afternoon was waning into evening. Perhaps she could write a note, informing him of what had happened with Sands and begging him to come and advise her on the hiring of a new butler.

She felt her face flush at the idea of resorting to so desperate a ploy. Still, so great was her desire to see him, she decided to do it.

When it came to Hal, apparently she had no shame.

She'd dragged out paper and was reaching for a quill when a knock sounded at the door. James entered, bearing yet another note. A second plea from Sir Gregory? she thought disdainfully. Then she recognised the writer's hand and excitement made her dizzy.

She ripped open the seal and read eagerly, then sat back with a huff of frustration. After begging her pardon for the short notice, Hal informed her he'd discovered he must leave London immediately for the north. He hoped to return within a fortnight and claim the privilege of calling upon her as soon as possible after his return.

An enormous sense of disappointment filled her. She'd not see him again, perhaps for more than a week. 'Twas almost a lifetime!

At least, she thought with a secret smile, he'd expressed his desire to see her again as soon as possible. He was welcome to call as early as he desired. Or as late.

Oh, that it might be late. That she might anticipate evening's fall, draw Hal into her arms, undress him slowly garment by garment…

Catching the direction of her thoughts, she felt her cheeks heat again. Oh, this was terrible! She'd never felt like this before, excited and giddy one moment, cast nearly into despair the next.

She knew without doubt she had loved Everitt. But never had she pined for him, ached for him, giggled out loud at his memory. He'd been the dearest friend she'd ever had, an occasional lover whose caresses she'd greeted with tenderness. But she'd not been titillated, tempted, on fire with anticipation as she was at the thought of touching Hal. What she felt for Hal was a different sort of love altogether.

Her mind reeled in shock as the word entered her head. She…loved Hal? But how could that be? She was still in mourning! This was absolutely the worst time and place!

But perhaps…perhaps love had an agenda of its own. When she thought of what poets over the ages had written about romantic love, their passionate lines provided an exact description of the turbulent intensity of what she felt for Hal.

She had loved Everitt…but she was *in love*, for the first and only time in her life, with Hal Waterman. A sense of peace and joy settled over her as she recognised that fact. The time might not be right now to openly express that love. But it would be some day.

Until then, she would honour Everitt's memory—and wait. Treasure the friendship he offered her while trying to inspire Hal Waterman, who had successfully eluded love and matrimony for years, to cherish her in return.

By late afternoon of the next day, despite knowing there was nothing she could do to summon Hal sooner, Elizabeth's restless impatience had intensified. She'd worked feverishly in her studio, taken David to the park and trotted him around until they were both breathless. She'd come back to pour herself a glass of wine, but the sherry was no more successful in calming her distraction.

She had almost decided to go to Hatchard's and ask the clerk for books about canal building when James interrupted, bearing yet another note. Though logically she knew it could not have come from Hal, still a rush of disappointment stung her to discover it was another missive from Sir Gregory.

Only curiosity to discover what mendacious audacity he'd written this time prompted her to read it instead of throwing it directly into the fire.

She'd find the enclosed article from yesterday's newspaper interesting, Sir Gregory wrote, adding he hoped that a certain gentleman had finished settling the Lowery affairs before he'd gone off to pursue his own!

Puzzled, she unfolded an excerpt from the 'Talk of the *Ton*' column. 'How Lord K. must rejoice,' she read, 'that after three Seasons on the Marriage Mart, Lady T. is to wed, however scandalously! Mrs W., too, must rejoice to finally see her son settled. Who guessed 'twould take a flight to Gretna to spur him to the deed? But having seen his carriage bearing Lady T. out of London last night on the Great North Road, 'tis certain he's taken that step at last.'

As the inferences in the column grew clear, she dropped the clipping with trembling fingers.

Her memory flashed to Hal's note. Called away immediately. Business in the north. Gone a fortnight.

Could he have rushed off to Gretna…to marry Lady Tryphena? But he didn't even like the girl!

Fury such as she'd never before experienced filled her. Ripping the article to shreds, she rushed over and threw it into the fire. That action insufficient to blunt her wrath, she seized the wineglass and threw that in too, exulting as the glass shattered and the alcohol blazed.

By the time the flames settled, her sudden burst of emotion was spent. She went back to pacing the room.

It didn't make sense. Hal would hardly write that he wished to call immediately upon his return…unless he wanted to present his new bride? But if Lady Tryphena were willing to wed and his mama was pressing him, why flee to the border? There was no reason the banns could not be called right in London, followed by a great society wedding the bride and his mother would probably adore. Or, if Hal wished to avoid such a spectacle, he could easily obtain a special licence to enable them to wed quietly elsewhere. No, it didn't make sense.

Whatever Hal was doing in the north, whatever the reason

Lady Tryphena had been travelling out of London at great haste in Hal's carriage, he was not carrying her off to Scotland for a runaway marriage.

Elizabeth was sure of it. Almost.

Dismay at her uncertainty succeeded by fury at that dismay, she had to *do* something. A smile curved her lips as she strode back to the desk to seize paper and quill.

After thanking Sir Gregory for his information, she added how amazing it was that a blockish man of little address had won one of the most highly titled prizes on the Marriage Mart. But then, anything was possible for an honourable gentleman of pure intentions.

Chapter Twenty-Three

In the evening some ten days later, Hal sat at his desk in his rented rooms near Newcastle. The business of the elopement had delayed him less than he'd initially feared. Charles Hilliard, amazingly, had turned out to be a responsible young man of good sense who, though lacking experience, affirmed his willingness to learn about estate management. More important, to Hal's great relief, he seemed deeply grateful for Hal's assistance in getting him married to Lady Tryphena, whom he apparently did love as devotedly as she'd claimed.

Hal wished him joy of her. Too flighty and managing by far for his taste, but he had to admire her ruthless resourcefulness. She might mature into a worthy wife.

Now, after having settled the newlyweds on his property at Hempstead Hall, he had nearly finished dispatching his own business. After an absence of almost two weeks, he was frantic to finish the meetings with the engineers and investors and return to London.

Return to Elizabeth. Doubtless rumours had abounded after Lady Tryphena's late-evening flight. He'd insisted she send her parents a letter explaining the whole at their first stop. He hoped Elizabeth would now know the truth.

He'd debated writing to her as well. But though he could express himself much better on paper than in person, he wanted to be with her when he explained, able to see her face, read the language of her stance and gestures to ascertain whether she was angry and disapproving or understanding of his actions.

Would the scandal of it bother her? With her undeterred by the social risk inherent in becoming an acknowledged artist, he didn't think so. If she was angry, surely after he detailed what had happened, she would forgive him.

Still, worry over her reaction was a stubborn burr pricking at the back of his mind, a distraction that made it impossible for him to fully concentrate during his meetings with investors and consultations with the workmen.

Nights were more difficult still. Sometimes he'd wake with a start to the image of Sands slamming the town house door in his face after telling him Mrs Lowery no longer wished to see him. Other nights he'd awake bathed in sweat, tantalising images still behind his eyelids of Elizabeth naked, astride him, her blonde hair flowing over him, her slick skin sliding against his as she moved over him, the taste of her mouth, her nipples on his tongue.

He wasn't sure which dream was worse. After waking, he'd pace, too agitated to recapture sleep. Neither wine nor strong brandy helped relax him. Finally, in desperation, he'd taken up quill and paper and channelled his worry, devotion, desire and pain into sonnets. They now numbered more than a dozen, paeans to her beauty, her sweetness, her talent and his longing for her.

Already he ached for her again. 'Twas probably no use to attempt to go to bed. With a sigh, he drew more paper out of the desk and began to write.

As it turned out, nearly three weeks had elapsed by the time Hal finally sighted the church spires of London in the distance.

Night was nearly falling; driven by the urgent need to see her, he'd pressed on well past dark on every night of the journey.

Only one good thing had come from his extended sojourn in the north. Several of the new investors he'd contacted, middle-class gentlemen who'd made their fortunes in the mills and factories, had expressed great interest after viewing Elizabeth's sketches in having their own offspring immortalised. If she were interested when these gentlemen brought their families to London, he could probably secure her several lucrative commissions.

Would she still wish to pursue an artist's career, or would she, as Sir Gregory had predicted, after considering the ramifications of such a choice by a lady of quality, have decided against a public use of her talents?

Would she even receive him to discuss the matter?

Then there was Sir Gregory. Though Elizabeth had seemed irate after Hal warned of his probable intentions, Sir Gregory was a man accustomed to getting what he wanted. Could he have managed somehow to appease her and weasel his way back into his favoured position in the household? Might he even now be at Green Street wooing Elizabeth, escorting her to dinner or the theatre?

Hal wasn't sure he could tolerate it if Sir Gregory had recovered his stature with her. He might have to find some pretext to call the man out and pummel him senseless.

Entering the city, Hal pulled up his weary mount. He'd ride home, pen Elizabeth a quick note and have Jeffers deliver it immediately, asking for an appointment in the morning. Or perhaps he'd stop by Green Street tonight and leave his card, letting her know he'd returned.

The evening was probably too far advanced to call. And what if Sir Gregory were there?

That decided it, he thought, fury burning within him at the image of the baronet bending his sly lecherous grin upon Elizabeth. He'd go first to Green Street.

Besides, if he went directly to his rooms, he might find awaiting him a summons from his mother. By visiting the Lowerys first, it would be too late by the time he arrived home to wash, dress and go to attend his mother at whatever function to which she commanded him.

Joy and nervous excitement tightening his chest, he kicked his mount into motion.

On the other side of Mayfair, Elizabeth put up her brushes and stored her paint for the night. With the natural light almost gone from the studio, there was no reason to linger here any longer.

And with the coming of night, there was no possibility that finally, today, Hal might arrive back and come to see her. What could be taking him so long? she thought despairingly for the hundredth time.

Though news had trickled back that he had indeed left London with Lady Tryphena—in order to assist her in wedding some penniless younger son—sometimes Elizabeth wondered if the report was true. Yesterday afternoon, desperate for information, she'd even walked with Gibbons in the park while her knowledgeable maid identified the society personages passing in their carriages. She'd stared at Hal's mother, assessing the connection between them and finding one only in the hue of hair and eyes.

As she'd expected from Hal's descriptions of Mrs Waterman, her carriage frequently halted to allow her to exchange greetings with other society matrons or to permit some dandy to climb up and speak with her. There had been no young protégée seated beside her, so Lady Tryphena was definitely gone from London. But not, Elizabeth devoutly hoped, wedded to Hal.

Indeed, her only satisfaction in the whole excursion was the pleasure, when he drove past her, of giving Sir Gregory the cut direct.

Perhaps Hal had already returned to London and simply

hadn't called on her. She had no claim on him. He'd only filled in for Nicky to assist in getting Everitt's estate papers in order. He might feel for her nothing more than a tepid friendship.

But it was more than that, she told herself fiercely. He might not feel the intensity of love she felt or experience the same sharp physical desire, but he did appreciate her work. He'd encouraged her, promised to investigate possible commissions and report back to her. She looked around her studio, assessing again all that she'd accomplished in the last few weeks.

He would call when he returned, she knew he would!

After pacing restlessly, she halted before her current work, the picture that had captured her concentration since she completed the Turneresque landscape of London rooftops.

She told herself she'd begun it as a figure study to prepare for the possibility of accepting commissions. But instead of sketches of children or a sober portrayal of some captain of industry, she'd decided, inspired by the classical sculpture at the Royal Academy, to paint the toga-clad figure of a virile young man. Tall, broad of shoulder, with the muscular physique of an athlete, his proud head crowed with golden curls like Apollo.

Red-gold curls over deep blue eyes with green centres.

Having completed the preliminary work, she'd been at a standstill. She needed to paint with a live model to progress further. *The* model, her inspiration. Hal.

She sighed, envisioning his splendid chest and shoulders bare beneath a draping of toga… Desire and longing throbbed within her again.

With a frustrated groan, she whirled around and marched to the door. She'd drive herself mad if she stayed here, looking at her image of him, pining for him.

Not in the mood even to dine with David, she instructed James to have supper sent to her son in the schoolroom, adding that she might take a tray later in the library. Perhaps she could distract herself by reading.

Entering the library, intent on selecting a book, she paused instead by the desk. She leaned down to rub her cheek against the chair's tall back, inhaling deeply. But among the odours of leather and polish, she was unable to distinguish even a trace of *his* scent, soap and male and a hint of something spicy.

Realising what she was doing, she straightened, muttering an oath she'd overhead in the stable yard. What was the matter with her? She was ridiculous, mooning over Hal like a silly heroine out of a Minerva Press novel.

Irritated, she nearly snapped at Bowers when the new butler—whom she'd hired herself last week from among candidates sent out from an agency, she thought with a glow of pride—bowed himself in. She was only half-listening until the words '…gentleman waiting below' penetrated her abstraction.

The name engraved on the card he held out sent a bolt of excitement and desire through her. Cutting off Bowers's half-uttered question about whether or not he should admit a gentleman so late, she cried, 'Send him up at once!'

As soon as the door closed, however, shyness attacked her. Nervously she smoothed the wrinkled skirt of her old work gown while her heart commenced to flutter in her chest like a bird trying to escape its cage.

She wished she'd changed after painting, put on something that fitted her figure more closely, with a bodice cut a bit lower. She rushed to the mirror, trying to stuff stray wisps of hair back into her coiffure and biting her lips to give them more colour.

Then, before she'd barely finished primping, the library door opened again and he was there.

The bird in her chest beat his wings in earnest now while her dazzled ears couldn't take in whatever greeting he made her. She simply watched him walk in, lithe motion and easy confidence, his big body filling her room. So overcome with sheer joy was she at the sight of him, tears filled her eyes. It was all she could do not to throw herself into his arms.

Her hungry eyes devoured every detail, from his face, which looked weary, to his clothes, which were a bit muddy and travel-stained.

'Sorry so late,' she heard him say at last. 'Should have sent note. Hope not interrupt dinner.'

'No, 'tis not late at all!' she replied, as if the household hadn't already settled in for the night. 'I'm delighted you called. Please, come sit…' she patted a place on the couch '…and tell me all your news.' Which, she devoutly hoped as she seated herself beside him, wouldn't include the acquiring of a wife.

'Shouldn't stay,' he replied, hesitating. 'Still in all my dirt. But…wanted you to know I'm back.'

'I'm so very grateful you did. Nor am I troubled over a bit of dirt, so unless you must depart immediately, I'd very much like you to stay.' She had this silly, panicked feeling that if he walked out, she might lose him again for another interminable three weeks.

To her relief, he took the seat she indicated. Unable to help herself, Elizabeth laid her hand on his arm. She felt his muscles tense as a bolt of sensation rushed from her fingers up her arm.

Closing her eyes, she savoured the shock. And wanted more. Wanted everything. She opened her eyes to find Hal staring at her.

Stop behaving like an idiot, she chided herself. Pulling herself together—but letting her fingers rest where they were—she asked, ' Did the project go well? It took longer than I'd expected. Your note indicated you'd not be gone above a fortnight.'

Flushing slightly, his eyes studying hers, he said, 'Had…complications. Probably heard of them. Hope won't think badly of me. Helped Lady Tryphena elope. Mama's protégée, you'll remember. In love with younger son, not permitted to marry. Scandalous to run to Gretna, but couple determined.'

She wanted to shout with relief and assure him she wouldn't care if Lady Tryphena had married a baboon in Africa, as long as the male she entangled into matrimony wasn't Hal.

As if echoing her thoughts, Hal smiled. 'Preferred she marry him than me. Funded flight to Scotland, found position for husband. Seems nice chap. Hope they happy. Ruined reputation. Mine too, probably. You…don't mind?'

'You learned of the lovers' plight and assisted them, risking your own reputation in the process. I think your intervention was selfless and very kind.'

He shook his head. 'Not selfless. Self-preserving. After that, met investors. Did turn up prospects for commissions. Discuss them tomorrow, if still interested.'

While he spoke, unable to deny herself, she began stroking his arm. Fierce delight filled her as his face coloured, his breathing accelerated.

'Better,' he said raggedly, 'talk tomorrow.' But he made no attempt to move from under her caressing fingers.

Her breathing had accelerated too. More than anything, she wanted to keep him here…but how?

A flash of inspiration striking, she said, 'I've been working steadily while you were gone—on one painting in particular. May I show it to you before you leave?'

Absently he nodded, his eyes focused as if mesmerised at her hand stroking his arm. Rising with him, she retained her hold on his arm. 'Twas a miracle she didn't fall on the stairs, so intently focused was she on his tall body beside hers, the faint warm brush of his breath against her cheek.

Carrying a branch of candles from the hallway into the darkened studio, she led him over to the painting on her easel. 'I thought to do a classical study—perhaps a Roman senator, like the sculpted busts in the hallway at the Royal Academy. But I must confess that as I painted it, I envisioned…you. So much so that to make further progress, I need you to serve as my model. Will you pose for me?'

Chapter Twenty-Four

Looking faintly astonished, Hal blinked at her. 'Me? Pose?'

''Tis not difficult,' Elizabeth assured him. 'You merely need to stand and remain very still. It would be so helpful. I do want to improve my work, make it worthy of showing to a patron. Please, say you will!'

Looking at the flowing classical drapery over the figure's bare shoulder, Hal swallowed hard. 'If…if it pleases you.'

If he only knew how much she wanted him to please her! Concentrate on the painting, she reprimanded. 'Could we work just a bit tonight? With the angle of the posing. So that when I begin tomorrow, I can progress more rapidly.'

'Now?' he asked doubtfully

'Oh, yes. If you would?'

For a moment she feared he would enumerate all the very valid reasons why it would be most improper for him to serve as her model, especially alone in her studio with darkness beyond the circle of candlelight. But before she could implore him again, he nodded.

'What must do?'

Elation filled her. 'Just remain absolutely still. First you must remove your jacket, waistcoat and shirt.' She didn't name the garments without a blush heating her cheeks, but at least managed not to stumble over the words.

He stared at her. 'Remove…' The word died out and he tapped his cravat, as if speech were now beyond him.

A fever of excitement driving her, she nodded. 'Yes. And the coat, waistcoat and shirt.'

She was being restrained, she told herself. She made herself simply watch while he began unwinding the cravat, slowly and carefully as if savouring the gaze she'd locked on him. She had not attacked him with impatient fingers, tugging at his clothing, letting the buttons fly.

As she looked on, mesmerised, he unbuttoned his jacket. After he shrugged it off and laid it on a chair, he looked back, smiling. 'Might mix paints,' he suggested.

'Paints,' she repeated, the word for an instant holding no meaning whatsoever. 'Ah, yes, paint.'

Quickly she walked to her workbench, grabbing her palette and beginning to prepare the pigment, trying to make short work of the process. When she looked back up, he had just finished removing his shirt.

The palette knife fell unnoticed from her nerveless fingers. She stood transfixed, mouth dropping open in awe as her gaze roved over the muscled contours of his arms and shoulders. Down to his hard, flat chest, where the taut nipples stood out in a soft matt of gold hair.

Her husband had been a tall man of sturdy stature—but at the time they married, he was no longer a young man in his prime. Hal was even more magnificent than she'd imagined, she marvelled as she walked over to him. If what lay beneath his breeches was as impressive as what he'd already uncovered, she might faint.

Dangerous as that knowledge might be to her consciousness, she couldn't wait to find out. In that moment, she admitted to herself that the notion of painting him had been just a sham. Seeing him, touching him, tasting him was what she'd wanted, craved, since he walked through the library door. What she'd intended when she lured him to her studio, though she'd not fully realised it at the time.

His face colouring under her rapt gaze, he fumbled for his shirt. 'Sorry. Big lout.'

Her hand flashed out to halt his. 'No, not at all. You're perfect. Large, commanding. A perfect Apollo.'

Nearly sighing with the joy of it, Elizabeth reached out to run her hands over his shoulders, measuring shape and contour down the muscled length of his arms, then slowly back up to his chest. He shuddered when she traced his collarbone, gasped as she trailed her fingertips over nipples that puckered under her touch, down the smooth flat plane of his abdomen toward the waistband of his breeches.

Before she could reach that goal, with a groan, he seized her hands.

'Don't. Can't. Want you…too much.'

'Don't you know I want you just as much?' she breathed, confessing it to herself as much as to him.

Her bravado nearly failed her when, simply staring at her, he did not reply. But having gone this brazenly far, she'd not lose her courage now. 'Well, Hal Waterman,' she said boldly, 'are you going to make me beg?'

He gave his head a little shake, as if he wasn't sure he'd heard her correctly. 'You…want me?'

'Oh, yes. Please. Now.'

Swallowing hard, he brought his big hands up to gently cradle her face. 'Sure? Want you…so much.'

Brazen again, she stood on tiptoe and pulled his head down. Every sense exulted as she captured his lips.

He bent to give her better access, opened his mouth to her

probing tongue. Then somehow she was sitting on his lap while he sat back, crushing his garments on the chair. He cradled her against his chest, pursuing her tongue with his own, exploring every soft depth and lush contour of her mouth, sending rivers of fire to every extremity.

She wanted the kiss never to end. She wanted to break it and move her greedy mouth over the stubble of his chin, nibbling and biting down to the hollow of his neck. Rub her cheek against the golden hair of his chest while she teased the tight, erect nipples with her tongue. Slide her fingers down under the waistband of his breeches and grasp the hard pulsing smoothness of his erection.

But first she wanted to feel her naked breasts against his chest, the soft broad expanse of a bed beneath her while he touched her and she sampled him and then took him into herself, moulded and melded until passion fused them, the two becoming one.

Finally he pulled away, his heartbeat thundering under her fingertips. 'Madness,' he gasped. 'Must…stop now.'

'No!' She clutched his shoulders to prevent his disengaging from her and shook her head frantically. 'Don't stop. Come with me. Please!'

There could be no doubt what she wanted of him. 'Sure?' he asked again, his gaze riveted to her face.

She might have a hundred regrets tomorrow, but at this moment, the demon of need and longing drove every one from her head. 'I'm sure.'

She almost sobbed with relief when, at last, he nodded. Easing her off his lap, haphazardly he threw on shirt, waistcoat, jacket, looped his neckcloth over them and took her hand. She led him to the door, opened it silently and peered down the hallway.

All the servants should be below stairs, relaxing after their evening meal. But with a guest still in the house, one footman lingered in the front entryway.

'Wait,' she whispered to Hal.

Rapidly she strode down the hall. 'James, would you fetch more candles for my studio? The ones there have burned low and I shall need new ones to work tomorrow morning. Then you may retire. I'll show our guest out.'

As the footman headed to the service stairs, Elizabeth ran back to take Hal's hand. Quickly she led him through the entry, up the stairs and into her chamber.

Before he could question her again, before any doubts could assail her at the wisdom of what she was doing, she locked the door behind them, then reached up to pull him to her in another kiss.

As if accepting her decision, there was no longer any tentativeness in his touch. Hunted became hunter as he nipped and sucked her lips before delving into her mouth, teasing her tongue, withdrawing and recapturing it again.

Whimpering, she tugged at his dishevelled clothes. Without breaking the kiss, he shed them until he once again stood only in breeches and boots. But before she could urge him to the bed and reach for his trouser buttons, he caught her hands. After scouring her tongue once more, sending a shower of sparks to her nipples, her core, he turned her and began undoing the small buttons of her bodice.

The garment freed of fastenings and pins, she would have tossed it aside and attacked her stays, impatient to be free of every impediment, but he once again stilled her hands and shushed her protesting murmurs. Drawing the bodice off her slowly, he palmed her through the fabric of her stays and chemise, his stroking fingers burning against her sensitised body. With equal tantalising slowness he loosed and removed the stays, then traced the outline of her ribs and breasts through the fine linen of her chemise, only that thin layer left between his hands and bare skin.

By the time he finally loosed her skirt, petticoat and slid down her stockings, she was nearly frantic for the feel of those warm hands upon her nakedness. But instead of stripping off her chemise, he knelt before her.

With agonising slowness, he raised the garment's hem. She shivered at the cool air on her skin, then trembled violently as he licked and kissed her toes, her ankles, the arches of her feet, leaving in the wake of his tongue a wetness that both chilled and inflamed her.

It was fortunate he then picked her up, for delirious from the incredible sensations induced by his nibbling lips and spiralling tongue, her legs went suddenly boneless. Catching her before she collapsed, he kissed her as he carried her to the bed, his tongue stroking deep, possessing her utterly.

Breaking the kiss, he settled her against the pillows and resumed his slow ascent of her body, tugging the chemise up as he went. Trembling with anticipation, shuddering as he explored and mapped each new inch of her with tongue and fingertip, she arched her back while he moved closer, closer, closer to the throbbing centre of her desire.

She cried out when he parted the glistening folds, sobbed as his tongue glided gently over and around that tender nub. Then she was gasping, frantic, as he deepened the pressure, stroking harder, faster. Tension spiralled tighter and tighter, propelling her upwards until she reached the peak and shattered.

Colours spun and whirled before dissolving into black as wave after wave of sensation shuddered through her. She must have fainted in truth, for when she grew conscious again, she was cradled in Hal's arms, her head tucked in the hollow of his shoulder.

Once her brain resumed functioning, awe and wonder expanded in her chest. She'd been seven years a wife, had slowly come to appreciate the tenderness and pleasure possible between a man and a woman. But though her coupling with Everitt had been gentle and joyous, he had never touched her, tantalised her and brought her to the pinnacle of ecstasy as Hal just had.

With one limp hand, she touched his cheek. 'Wonderful,' she murmured, still too replete to move.

He smiled down at her, such an immense tenderness in his expression that her heart swelled and soared with joy. Surely he felt for her the love she felt for him!

'You wonderful,' he whispered back.

For a few more languid moments he held her, then shifted on the bed. 'Better go now.'

'No!' she cried, clutching his shoulder. Her repertoire of love-making skills might be scant, but she knew that though he'd pleasured her, he had not reached fulfilment himself. How she wished to make for him the same journey he had taken for her! A journey that would be as unprecedented in her experience as the one through which she'd just been guided.

'Not yet,' she repeated, pushing him back against the pillows. Conscious of—yet for once, unembarrassed by—her nudity, she straddled him. A little thrill streaked through her when the solidness of his erection rubbed against her. With a little gasp, she pressed down harder and felt him leap under her, sparking a stronger bolt of sensation.

Perhaps she was not yet fully satisfied after all, she thought with wonder as she pulled the rest of the pins from her ruined coiffure and let the tangled blonde mass cascade down over them.

Then, beginning at his chin, she brought to glorious life the countless dreams in which she had licked and stroked, nuzzled and nipped, descending the ridge of jaw to the plane of his shoulder, the hollow of his collarbone. He cried out when she kneaded the pebbled nipple between her teeth, tasted the salty tang of perspiration on his skin while she licked down his chest to his waistband. With trembling fingers, she finally unfastened the buttons and let his erection spring free.

Marvelling at its perfection, she drew awed fingers down its length, her inner passage quivering at the realisation that, soon, this silken hardness would fill her completely. But first, she simply must taste him.

He cried out again at the first touch of her tongue, then seized her and dragged her up on to his chest.

'Can't…last,' he gasped, his face strained.

Tenderly she leaned down and kissed him before sliding back down to straddle him, guiding him into the passage that ached to receive him.

She felt stretched and gloriously full as she took in more and more of his length. Then, impelled by instinct as old as mankind, she began to move on top of him.

The sensation was familiar—and yet different, more intense, more exciting than anything she'd previously experienced. Joined with him from above, without the weight of his body binding her in place, she was free to move as swift and deep, shallow and slow as she desired.

Hal strained upwards and pulled her to him, capturing one nipple between his teeth. The throbbing between her legs intensified as he suckled her hard and fast.

The sensations built quickly this time, so powerful and intense that she was helpless to slow them. Within minutes she once again reached the peak, plummeting into the abyss as she shattered into a million shards of bliss, exulting as Hal's cry of completion blended with her own.

Damp, replete, she collapsed on his chest. Never had she felt such closeness with another being, nor journeyed with him to such a place of wonder. Snuggling against him, Hal's heart pounding a lullaby beneath her ear, she drifted to sleep.

Some time later, deep in the night, she awoke to feel Hal's mouth at her breast, his hand stroking between her legs. Shamelessly she let them fall open, giving him access, her murmurs urging him on. After bringing her back to the peak of arousal, he moved over her, supporting his weight on his arms as he guided himself into her and stroked deeply. She wrapped her arms and legs around him, arching upwards to take him deeper still as the force of his passion drove her into the bed until they shattered together, his hoarse voice crying her name.

The sky outside her chamber window had lightened to the blue-black of approaching dawn when she next awoke. She looked back to find Hal propped on one elbow, smiling at her in the moonlight.

'Dawn soon. Leave now before servants stirring.'

'Not yet!' she protested, pulling his head down for a kiss. Obligingly he opened his mouth to her, tangled his tongue with hers. She reached down, amazed to find him already fully erect. Kissing him deeply, she stroked from thick base to silky tip, until, groaning, he rolled her on to her back and entered her in one smooth move.

Now he teased her, gliding his full length in, then slowly withdrawing completely before sliding in again. One, twice, a third time he brought her to the edge and held her there until, sobbing, she shattered. The last time, with a few powerful strokes, he drove deep and cried out with his own completion.

This time she did not doze off as he kissed the dampness from her eyes and face, then rolled her over to lay her on top of him while he stroked gentle fingers over her back, her arms, her thighs, her bottom.

She could have lain there for ever, utterly content. But all too soon, he rolled her over and withdrew. He placed a finger on her lips to still her whispered protest and rose from the bed.

Lying back against the pillows, she admired his magnificent nakedness. 'You should never wear clothes.'

Laughing, he pulled on his breeches and walked back to the bed. Sitting on the edge, he caressed her breast with one hand while the other rubbed her belly, then delved down to stroke between the damp curls beneath. 'Nor you,' he said, leaning over to give her a kiss.

Though she did her best to distract him again, he broke the kiss and walked back to pick up his shirt. 'Must go now. Servants up soon.'

He was right, of course. Though Gibbons, who most likely had come to her chamber some time last evening to help her disrobe, probably already knew of their rendezvous. Doubtless the news would be all through the servants' quarters by breakfast.

Good thing she'd already discharged Sands!

Accepting the inevitable, she climbed out of bed and threw on a dressing gown. 'I'll see you out.'

Hand in hand, they tiptoed through the silent house, down the service stairs to the back door. On the threshold, he turned back to give her a lingering kiss. 'Elizabeth,' he murmured in a voice of wonder.

'Dearest Hal,' she whispered back. Then watched the shadow of him, dark against the faint pink of the coming dawn, as he walked toward the mews and disappeared into the night.

Chapter Twenty-Five

Hours later, gloriously tender in places, Elizabeth came fully awake to see bright sunlight streaming through the windows. Goodness, the household must have been up for hours! She sat up with a start, astonished that Gibbons—or David, who always rose early—had not been in to rouse her.

As she rang for her maid, she felt a blush rise. She was still wondering what and whether to explain when the maid walked in.

'A lovely morning, isn't it, madam? I told Miss Lowery and Master David you'd not slept well and needed a bit more rest. I trust now you are well rested!' she added, giving Elizabeth a shy smile.

Elizabeth's blush deepened. 'Yes, thank you. And thank you for explaining my…late rising to the household.'

Gibbons nodded. 'He's a wonderful gentleman, ma'am. After you been so cast down, 'tis a pure pleasure to see you looking happy. I wish you both well!'

'Oh, but he hasn't said…'

'He will,' Gibbons assured her. 'The gentleman adores you. It's in his eyes when he looks at you. It's not just lust, like that other one.'

'You think so?'

'I know so,' the maid said firmly.

Oh, that the maid's assessment of Hal's intent was as accurate as the one she'd made of Sir Gregory's! Elizabeth thought as Gibbons helped her dress.

But after the maid left, Elizabeth's excitement began to subside and the doubts she'd suppressed last night bullied their way into consciousness.

By succumbing to her overwhelming physical need for Hal, she had learned nothing more that what she already knew—he desired her. But did he love her? She had only Gibbons's intuition to support that view.

If he didn't love her, what had she just done?

As she realised the full extent of her indiscretion, a gasp of dismay escaped her. By seducing Hal, she had forced him into a position in which, whether he wished to or not, he might well feel obligated to propose to her. Honourable through and through, unable to support telling the smallest mistruth, he might not be able to reconcile with his conscience having bedded a lady barely three months widowed without offering to make an honest woman of her.

She wanted nothing more than to marry him—but not because he felt forced to ask for her hand. How could she determine his true feelings? If she put aside modesty and bluntly asked him after he'd already decided they must wed, he would doubtless return the expected answer.

Since there was no question that she had deliberately driven him beyond the power of resistance, it might even appear that she'd set out to entrap him. He might think her no better than his mama, who'd spent years trying to manipulate him into wedlock.

The thought sickened her.

But if she dismissed or made light of what they'd done to forestall a forced proposal, it might seem she was a lightskirt who could casually seduce a man mere months after her husband's death. Feeling used and dishonoured, Hal might despise her.

How was she to face him?

Anxious, irresolute—and already aching for Hal—Elizabeth sank down on the sofa in her sitting room and put her face in her hands. She couldn't begin to express the wonder, the joy of intimacy with him. Yet by claiming that one night of bliss, she might at the same time have ruined their friendship and any chance of a future together.

In a fog of bemusement, Hal had ambled home. Blissfully sated after long weeks of frustration, he fell into bed and slept deeply.

Awaking at noon, exhilarated, he marvelled again when he realised that the night he'd spent with Elizabeth had been real, not just a vivid repetition of his recurrent dream. He wanted to throw on some clothes and race back to her, shouting his love to the rooftops.

But in the lucid light of day, his initial euphoria faded. When he went to see her today, how would she receive him?

He'd tried, really tried, to resist her. But with her hands caressing his arms, his chest, all thoughts of protest had stuttered and died…even though the last functioning bit of his brain warned that succumbing to her was a very bad idea.

That caution had been as effective as a puny rivulet meeting an onrushing ocean tide. Overwhelmed in a flood of desire, he'd thought only that if she truly wanted him, instead of the words he dared not speak, he would show her with hands, mouth, body how much he cherished her.

Now he worried that the intimacy had come too soon. She'd not been widowed long enough to fully recover from the emotional blow of losing a man she'd truly loved. Lonely, grieving, she'd been longing for the closeness and comfort she'd lost.

Would she regret having found that in his arms? Would she feel he'd taken advantage of her vulnerability and now despise him for it?

Perhaps he should go down on his knee today, make real the scene he'd imagined any number of times and beg her to become his wife. If he did, would she think he offered for her only because she'd compromised them both? If she accepted, would it be solely to restore her sense of honour?

He loved her so desperately, he was almost ready to take her on any terms. Almost. But if she didn't really love him, if she accepted him out of a sense of duty or obligation, how long would it be before he saw on her face the same scornful, pitying look so often visible on his mother's countenance when she gazed at him?

It would be like having acid eat away at him from the inside to live with her disdain. Better that he say nothing and have her think him a cad than propel her into a marriage with a man she didn't want and couldn't respect.

Did she love and respect him? If he asked for her hand and she accepted, she would certainly affirm that she did. How could he know for sure?

Some time before he called on her this afternoon, he had to figure out what to do. After ringing for Jeffers to bring him some ale, he went to his desk, took out another sheet of paper and sharpened his quill. For the next hour, he poured his anguished longing into yet another sonnet.

Several hours later, Hal drove to Green Street. In his pocket, the lines crossed and recrossed, was the current draft of his poem. Perhaps, since he was much more eloquent in writing than he was in speech, he ought to give it to her, though he didn't think he'd yet captured his feelings and desires clearly enough. Perhaps after he saw her, he'd return home and work on it some more.

Neither was he yet sure whether or not to declare himself. He'd finally decided to see how Elizabeth behaved when she received him and take his cue from that.

Then he was at the entry to her parlour, some stranger announcing him. He walked into her presence and as always, for the first few moments simply let the beauty and wonder of her wash over him, his heart nearly bursting with love. It took all he could do to prevent himself from falling to his knees before her right that moment.

Then she saw him, blushed—and turned away. Hal's hopes and heart sank.

Searching for some innocuous greeting to mask the intensity of his feelings, he said, 'New butler?'

'Oh, yes.' She finally looked back at him and smiled nervously. 'Sands…decided to retire. I engaged another one—all on my own,' she added proudly. 'I am becoming quite decisive, am I not? Speaking of which, would you tell me more about the potential patrons you discovered? You mentioned you would last night, before we…' Her voice trailed off and her blush deepened. 'Anyway, I'm eager to hear what you learned.'

This was his opening. 'About last night—'

'No!' She held up a hand, cutting him off. 'Let's…let's not discuss that just yet. It wouldn't be wise to say things we think we ought to, things that cannot easily be unsaid, until we've both had time to reflect.'

'Wouldn't make you what Sir Gregory wanted,' Hal replied, compelled to assure her at least of that.

Her smile turned genuine. 'I know. You are everything that is honourable. Last night…last night was wonderful. Ill timed, perhaps, but I regret nothing.'

Enormous relief filled Hal. It wasn't the avowal of love he craved—but at least it appeared she wasn't going to send him away. 'Sure?' he asked, desperate to make that point clear.

'I'm sure. I should never regret it—unless it ruined our friendship.' Her expression turned suddenly tentative, vulnerable. 'It…it has not, has it?'

Friendship. Happy as he'd been a moment ago to know he'd

not sabotaged their relationship, a deep ache pierced him that she apparently considered what they shared to be nothing more. But, he told himself doggedly, friendship was at least a start. 'Nothing ever ruin that.'

'Good,' she replied and gave him a businesslike nod. 'Then I should like to hear about the patrons.'

For the next few moments he told her about the successful merchants and financiers he'd consulted who'd expressed an interest in seeing more of her work when they next visited London with their families, with a view to perhaps commissioning portraits.

'Told them not begin yet. Still think should consult Nicky, Sarah first. But work exceptional, should be shared.'

'I deeply appreciate the interest you've taken in it.'

He shrugged. 'Anyone recognise amazing talent.'

'Only you have encouraged me to use it,' she noted.

He gave her a deprecating smile. 'Some think that a mistake. Could compromise position in society.'

She shook her head. 'During your weeks away I've had time to consider that. I've also been painting at a faster pace than ever in my life—and I love it. I would paint even if no one but myself ever appreciated my work. But I've decided I'm not willing to sacrifice the possibility of working at my craft in order to retain a place in a society in which I've never participated anyway. Yes, I shall talk with Nicky and Sarah about the best means to protect the family from scandal, but I'm determined to move forward. In fact, I should like to begin sketching at the Royal Academy immediately, if you can arrange it.'

Hal nodded. 'Do whatever you want. In art—and everything. Whatever makes you most…comfortable.

'And what would make you…comfortable?' she asked.

'What you want,' he repeated. There, he'd come as close to a declaration as he dared. If she wanted him, she had only to say so.

In the long silence that followed, he waited, breathless, for her response.

Looking away, she said, 'I'm comfortable as we are. I treasure your…friendship. I hope you know that.'

Friendship again. Hal's hopes, which had risen once more as she passionately expressed her thanks for his encouragement, plummeted. Friendship is better than a coerced marriage, he tried to assure himself. There was still the possibility of it becoming more.

Or, having tasted him, was she ready to use his services to launch her career and move on? The memory of Sir Gregory's taunt filled his head.

Surely he was more than a convenience to her. Hell and damnation, he didn't know what to believe. He only knew he ached for her in every pore of his being.

He wanted nothing more than to scoop her into his arms, carry her back to her bedchamber, make love to her for weeks, imprint her cries of ecstasy into his head until the joy of her passion convinced his lonely, battered heart that she truly wanted him. Not out of obligation or convenience or because propriety said she ought to accept him, but because she loved him—awkwardly speaking, unfashionable, overlarge Hal Waterman.

'Should you like some tea?' she asked, breaking the silence that had once again stretched between them.

The sharpness of the pain in his chest convinced him that, for now, 'twas better to take himself off than to linger. Restlessly he ran his hands down his waistcoat, straightening the already perfectly arranged garment. 'No. Thanks. If speak to warden at Royal Academy, must go now.'

She nodded rapidly. 'Yes, of course. Thank you for calling. Please come again soon.' She held out her hand.

He gave her fingertips a lingering kiss, then, heart aching, made himself stride out of the room.

* * *

Trying not to weep, Elizabeth watched Hal walk out. For a moment, he seemed to hover near a declaration, but when she gave him the opportunity to speak out, he'd merely affirmed he would do what she wanted.

'Twas hardly the avowal of love for which she'd hoped. Friends. Could she be content with just that?

Maybe he still didn't want a wife. Maybe didn't want as his wife a widow so shameless that she'd casually seduce another man mere months after her husband's death.

But she hadn't read disdain in his eyes. His gaze still held a respectful, almost cherishing look.

Should she have let him speak about last night when he'd broached the matter? But if he did make her an offer because of it, she'd be forced either to refuse him, which she didn't want to do, or accept him without really knowing whether he was proposing out of desire or a sense of duty.

So she'd have to wait, and behave with propriety while she waited—when all she wished to do was lead him back to her chamber and experience the joy of last night over and over again. Restlessly she jumped to her feet and paced the room, pausing at the chair where he'd sat. She was trying to recall and analyse his expressions when a scrap of something beneath the chair caught her eye.

Embarrassed that Hal might have seen her parlour untidy, she bent to retrieve it, vowing to chastise the housekeeper. As she picked it up, however, she discovered the object was a crumpled note. From the slope of the letters, she could tell it was in Hal's hand.

'Twas his, something personal. She ought not to read it. But a compulsion stronger than propriety compelled her to smooth out the paper.

'Twas a verse, she realised, noting the even lines. She began to read—and gasped in shock. 'Twas a verse indeed—written about *her*.

Elizabeth, thy very name creates
Within my heart a melody of longing,
Goodness as much as beauty resonates
Within a form as fair as new day's dawning.
Mute, dumb I stand when I would shout thy praise,
Declare my love with eloquent exclaiming
Persuade, cajole, sweet paeans to thee raise
Devotion in each syllable proclaiming…

He'd penned several more lines, then crossed them out, indicating he was not yet either finished or satisfied with his creation. Incomplete though the verse was, however, from every still-unpolished couplet, Hal's longing, love, anguish and desire leapt out.

She read and reread the draft several times, tears in her eyes and exultation in her heart. Setting it carefully on a table, she hugged herself and danced around the room.

Hal loved her! There was no longer any need to refrain from vowing her own love in return.

She should wait like a proper lady for him to call again. But having already proved how very improper she could be, she didn't want to waste another moment. Seizing the precious crumpled verse, she hurried to the library, took up pen and paper, and swiftly penned a missive begging Hal to call upon her as soon as he received her note.

Meanwhile, having successfully persuaded the staff at the Royal Academy to allow Elizabeth to sketch there, Hal sat in a hackney on his way to White's.

Longingly he considered returning to Green Street to tell

Elizabeth what he'd arranged. But evening was already falling. The mere thought of meeting her again in the glow of candlelight swamped him in images of their night together.

With difficulty he put those thoughts aside and considered instead their meeting this afternoon. Had there been hurt in her eyes when he'd refrained from a proposal? Should he have proceeded despite his doubts?

Friendship was such a pale imitation of all that he wanted for them. But after the bliss of last night, he didn't want to wait weeks or months to learn for certain whether there would ever be the possibility of more.

Suddenly, in the rhythmic clop of hoofs and jingle of harness, the resolution came to him. If Elizabeth was deserving of his love— and she certainly was—she was equally deserving of his honesty.

He ought to tell her how he truly felt. He knew enough of the excellence of her character to believe he could trust her not to marry him for money or convenience or even because of the improper, ill-timed but extraordinary passion they'd shared. She would wed him only if she felt she could love him as completely as he loved her.

But how could he express his convictions convincingly enough?

He thought of the sonnets he'd written, so much more reflective of his love and desire than his halting speech, and the idea came to him. Though he had great difficulty getting out the words to express thoughts as they occurred, he had no trouble writing. If he knew what he wanted to say, he could write it down beforehand and simply recite it. He could reveal his love and propose to her in verse.

Doubt immediately assailed his resolve. He'd never attempted to articulate a speech that lengthy. What if he forgot or stumbled over the words?

This would not be a bit of irrelevant Shakespeare plucked at random by some schoolmaster that he had attempted to memorise, he countered, but verses that mirrored the thoughts that occupied his days, the desires that haunted his nights.

To win Elizabeth, he would enunciate every word and not stumble. And, for once in his life, be eloquent.

Excitement seizing him, he reached in his waistcoat pocket—only to find it empty. Blast, the draft he'd stuffed in there must have fallen out somewhere in his travels this afternoon. He could do without it; he had other drafts at home; besides, he meant to write another poem, a better one, that not only extolled Elizabeth's beauty of face and character and proclaimed his love, but asked for her hand.

He'd dine at White's, turn down any invitations to sit over cards or brandy, then return to his rooms to compose and memorise the most important verse of his life.

Chapter Twenty-Six

After dispatching her missive, Elizabeth dined with David, then read him a story and tucked him in bed. Her ear straining for the sound of an arriving carriage, the cadence of Hal's footsteps approaching in the hall, she wandered up to the library and tried to occupy herself in a book. She felt sure he would respond to her note, so as the hours went by without his return, she concluded with frustration that he must have gone out for the evening before receiving it.

Difficult as it was going to be, it appeared she'd have to wait until tomorrow to confess her love. However, she vowed, if Hal did not appear at Green Street by mid-day, she would demonstrate her brazen new sense of independence again by searching him out at his rooms.

Tired as she was, after the bliss of the previous night, her solitary bed seemed cold and uninviting. Consumed with thoughts and imaginings of what she would say and do when she saw him, she went to bed late and slept poorly, then woke early and went to her studio.

Even her beloved painting couldn't calm her agitation. Nearly frantic with the need to see Hal, she had almost decided she would, in fact, go and seek him out when Gibbons ran in. 'He's here, madam. Quick, now, give me your apron and let me tidy your hair!'

She'd barely smoothed her gown and had Gibbons tuck up her errant locks when the door opened and Bowers announced him. As she saw his beloved face smiling at her, her heart filled with such a rush of joy, she felt sure she must float a foot above the floor.

The thought of delivering the speech she'd nervously rehearsed brought her back to earth. 'Thank you for returning so promptly,' she began.

'Sorry not come by last night. Didn't get note until late. Arranged for sketching yesterday.'

She took a deep breath. 'There's something I must tell you—'

But before she could continue, Hal took her hand and dropped to one knee before her. 'Not polite to contradict lady, but me first.'

Still holding her hand, he began,

Possessed of every virtue, every grace,
Elizabeth, thy beauty has enraptured
My heart, for more than loveliness of face
'Tis purity of soul that has mine captured…

The beautiful, sonorous phrases fell from his lips with just the barest of hesitations. Awed and humbled by the depth of his love and his courage in exposing himself in his greatest vulnerability—difficulty with speech—tears welled up in her eyes as she listened, spellbound, until the final couplet:

Into thy tender grasp I place my soul.
Accept it, marry me and make me whole.

When he fell silent, she said tremulously, 'You spoke in complete sentences!'

'For you, I can brave anything. Some time later, after mourning over, will you marry me? Never eloquent, fashionable enough for you, but—'

'No, 'tis I who will never be respectable or fashionable enough for you!' she contended, reaching out a finger to still his lips. 'A widow who seduces a proper gentleman before her mourning period is even over! Who prefers to spend the afternoon sketching at the Royal Academy rather than riding with the *ton* at Hyde Park. Shall we be unfashionable together? Me with paint on my fingers, dogs running through the house, David at home until he's old enough for Oxford. I don't need society. I don't even need commissions. I need only you, my darling. Yes, Hal Waterman, I will marry you.'

'You will?' he echoed, as if not sure he'd heard her correctly. 'I will indeed.'

He kissed her hand fervently. 'Make me the happiest of men!'

She smiled. 'Which is only fitting, since marrying you will make me the happiest, most content, most satisfied of women.'

'Ah—women.' The fervent light in his eyes dimmed a trifle. 'Must warn, probably can't prevent Mother coming to inspect you. Won't be happy didn't marry her choice.'

'Have I not discharged a butler and sent Sir Gregory packing? I think I can deal with your mother's scrutiny.'

Hal shook his head. 'My brave darling.'

She clasped his hand in hers. 'I am now—thanks to you. What an exciting new life you've opened to me! I shall learn all about investments, canals and railroads. Sketch and paint the children of your business colleagues—and some day, I hope, our own.'

He smiled. 'Happy to provide *that* opportunity.' Gently he caressed her cheek with his fingers, then tipped up her chin and kissed her.

She was just deepening his kiss, the spiral of desire he ignited so readily and powerfully tightening within her, when the door flew open and David burst in.

'Uncle Hal!' he exclaimed before stopping short in surprise. 'Why are you kissing Mama?'

Hal faced her son squarely. 'Love her. Love you. If you like idea, want to marry mama.'

David looked at them thoughtfully. 'Then you'd be my bestest friend for ever? And live here with us?'

When Hal nodded, David gave a whoop of glee. 'Can I get that pony now?'

Laughing as Elizabeth scolded, Hal said. 'Anything.'

David raced over to give Hal a hug. 'I'm glad you love us, Uncle Hal. I love you, too. I better go tell Max!' he exclaimed and ran out.

Hal drew Elizabeth back into his arms, gazing at her with an intensity that made her feel light-headed. 'Must be dreaming,' he murmured.

'No, 'tis better than the most wonderful of dreams,' she whispered and drew his face down for another kiss.

Long, luscious moments later, he broke away. 'Marry me in nine months, three days?'

The end of her year of mourning, she realised. But having found her life's love, she had no intention of waiting that long. 'I'll marry you tomorrow. As soon as you can get a special licence.'

He smiled tenderly and kissed her forehead. 'Not fitting. Eight months, at least.'

She tipped his face down and claimed his mouth again, her tongue probing, teasing before releasing him. 'Two weeks,' she murmured.

His blue eyes looked both aroused—and troubled. 'Not fitting. Disrespectful to husband. Six months.'

Elizabeth shook her head. 'Society sets the time for mourning. If I'm to scandalise the *ton* by working as an artist, why bother about their rules now? This I know: Everitt loved me. He would want me to be happy, not wait an eternity to earn the approval of a society he himself disdained.' She traced the outline of his lips with her tongue. 'Two weeks.'

Hal groaned. 'Call banns, at least.'

She shifted in his arms, rubbing herself against his hardness. 'Only if your honour insists. But you must stay with me every night. Or, hussy that I am, I shall come to your rooms.'

He shifted, fitting her more closely against him. 'My hussy,' he murmured, nuzzling her neck.

Disentangling herself from Hal's arms, Elizabeth sprang up, went over to lock the parlour door and returned to lift her skirts and settle herself on his lap. 'Your hussy,' she agreed, greedy hands reaching for the buttons on his trousers. 'Here, now, always, my love.

Epilogue

A week after the final calling of the banns, Hal stood before the parish priest, humbled, honoured and nearly incoherent with joy, as he and Elizabeth Wellington Lowery exchanged the sacred vows promising to love, honour and cherish. After escorting her in to sign the parish register, with pride and delight he helped his new wife and her exuberant son into a carriage to drive to the reception in Grosvenor Square his mother had insisted on preparing.

Hal had cautioned that, since their wedding before Elizabeth emerged from mourning would be thought scandalous by many, Mrs Waterman should make this a small family affair. Though he placed no reliance on her promise not to turn it into a gala event, Hal only hoped that the *ton*'s dowagers would be more affronted by their refusal to observe mourning customs than curious to see the woman who had finally lured Mrs Waterman's son into marriage.

He was pleasantly surprised to find, as they entered the drawing room to the cheers of those assembled within, that the group comprised only Mrs Waterman's current cicisbeo, Lord Kendall, the two matrons who were her closest bosom bows, several of his schoolmates and Ned Greaves, lured out of his country estate for the event. Spying another of his Uncle Nicky's best friends, David headed for Ned with a shout of delight.

The reception room was splendid, having been transformed into a bower of early spring flowers. The sideboard and small tables dotting the room were covered with platters of lobster patties, sweetmeats and candied fruits while a footman hovered with a tray of champagne.

Ned came over to pound Hal on the back and give Elizabeth a hug. 'Congratulations to you both! May two of my favourite people enjoy a lifetime of happiness together. I'm just sorry Nicky, Sarah and the rest of the family couldn't be here to celebrate with us.'

Hal looked at Elizabeth, Ned's comment echoing his own concern. 'Sure not disappointed to wed without family?'

Elizabeth wrinkled her nose at him. 'As you well know, had the choice been entirely mine, I wouldn't have waited to call the banns. Nicky and Sarah can host a lavish party for us when they return.'

Then his mama walked over. 'Mrs Waterman, we do so appreciate your going to the trouble…under the circumstances,' Elizabeth said. 'The reception is lovely.'

'Beautiful, Mama,' Hal echoed. Though his mother was never happier than when presiding over an elegant party, she'd protested vigorously when she learned that the young couple refused to wait another nine months so she might turn their wedding reception into the *ton* event of the year. Instinctively Hal braced for her response.

She didn't disappoint him. 'Seeing what a lovely creature you are,' she said, inspecting Elizabeth's new gown critically, 'I don't suppose I can blame my son for not delaying the proper interval to make you his wife. But who would have guessed such a slowtop could win a beauty like you, all on his own!'

Elizabeth drew herself up. 'I'm sure 'tis only joy at this happy event that makes you misspeak so, Mrs Waterman,' she replied, icy reproof in her voice. 'Everyone knows my husband is the most intelligent, well spoken and handsome of men.'

At Elizabeth's rebuke, the room fell silent, Lord Kendall breaking off his sentence with a gasp. Everyone's attention riveted on Elizabeth and Hal's mother.

Anticipating one of his mother's famous set-downs, Hal stepped forward to place a protective arm about his wife.

Mrs Waterman blinked rapidly, as if she couldn't quite believe what she'd just heard. Then, to Hal's amazement, tears welled up in her eyes.

'I suppose you see him differently,' she allowed, dabbing at her eyes with a scrap of lace. 'Perhaps I've sometimes been…hard on him. But all I ever desired was his happiness!'

Elizabeth nodded graciously. 'As a mother myself, I'm sure that is true. Come, Hal, shall we get David a sample of your mama's delicious cake?'

'My ferocious champion,' he murmured in her ear as they walked away.

'If you could take on that horrid Mr Smith for me, I suppose I can confront your mama,' she said, wrapping herself in the circle of his arm.

Happiness filling him, warm and sweet as honey, he kissed her golden head. 'Together, we can face anything!'

* * * * *

Harlequin® Historical
Historical Romantic Adventure!

From *USA TODAY*
bestselling author

Margaret Moore

A LOVER'S KISS

A Frenchwoman in London,
Juliette Bergerine is unexpectedly
thrown together in hiding with
Sir Douglas Drury. As lust and
desire give way to deeper emotions,
how will Juliette react on discovering
that her brother was murdered—
by Drury!

Available September
wherever you buy books.

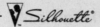

SPECIAL EDITION

Kate's Boys

A late-night walk on the beach resulted
in Trevor Marlowe's heroic rescue of a
drowning woman. He took the amnesia
victim in and dubbed her Venus, for the
goddess who'd emerged from the sea.
It looked as if she might be his goddess of
love, too...until her former fiancé showed
up on Trevor's doorstep.

Don't miss

THE BRIDE WITH
NO NAME

by *USA TODAY* bestselling author
MARIE FERRARELLA

Available August
wherever you buy books.